BLOOD

OF THE

PANTHER

Richard A Labram

Richard A Labram has asserted his right under the Copyright, Designs and Patents Act 1988 to be identified as the author of this work.

Copyright 2011 Richard A Labram

ISBN: 978-0-9520658-4-5

All characters and dwellings in this publication are fictitious and any apparent resemblance to real persons living or dead, or such dwellings are coincidental.

Acknowledgements

To my wife, Jacqueline, who has patiently read and re-read each chapter to find my undiscovered errors.

OTHER PUBLICATIONS

POETRY COLLECTIONS

Breaking Waves (2006)
In the Songs of Icicles (2007)
Remembering Love (2011)
Just for a While (2011) Kindle

FICTION

Summer Shorts (Collection 2011) Kindle

SHORT STORIES

Numerous (2001 – 2011)

RADIO PLAYS

Early Retirement (2002)
The Eighteenth Birthday (2002)
The Big Four O (2002)
The Naming (2002)
The Wake (2002)

TELEVISION PLAYS

Desperate (2003)

CHAPTER ONE

John Henderson checked the mirror. The silver Mercedes was still tailgating; matching every change of speed and direction. The sight of the magnified bonnet had become intimidating. He tried to encourage the other driver to overtake by reducing speed and hugging the kerb. He signalled with his Ford's left indicator, but the driver made no attempt to overtake.

The narrow country road conspired against him, but whenever the road broadened for a short distance the Mercedes dropped back. He was tempted to scythe up onto the verge and stop. That would force the issue; but somewhere deep inside him alarm bells were ringing. He had dismissed his initial nervousness as paranoia and the provocation as unreasonable impatience. But now he realised this was more than just a simple piece of road rage and he began to panic.

John pressed the accelerator pedal to the floor easing back only when he found his car careering round corners on the wrong side. The tyres squealed in protest as he maintained his high speed getaway. Irrational decisions produced wildly erratic driving.

Henderson was hoping to discover some slow moving traffic ahead. It might provide a chance of putting a vehicle between them, but there was a busy stream of oncoming cars. The rain speckled headlights flashing star burst patterns.

He had to change the game; improve his chances. Without signalling, Henderson took a sudden left onto the wider Ringwood road. The rear of the Ford started to break away forcing him to use the steering and the brakes to correct an alarming lurch onto the grass margin. Turf and gravel scattered into the air. There was no time for reflection on his stupidity, or any room for considered thought; he just had to get away.

John Henderson felt the accelerator pedal bottom as he thrust it down in blind terror. He checked the mirror. The Mercedes' driver had been taken by surprise, but was still there, accelerating rapidly in his more powerful car. On this road the approaching traffic seemed heavier. Overtaking was going to remain difficult, but half a mile ahead he could see a slow moving domestic fuel tanker. Recklessly, he held the pedal to the floor as his car continued to accelerate until at the last second he wrenched his estate to the right in an attempt to overtake. He braced himself against the accelerator pedal and could feel the metal floor buckle under the force.

The approaching traffic was narrowing the gap too quickly! His brain went into overdrive and the scene became a slow motion mirage in which nothing seemed real. He watched as the gap continued to close. He was going to die! This was his fault! He considered doing the decent thing and steering deliberately into the ditch opposite, but all action had frozen. He was now just a spectator and in his transient world he did not see the bright braking lights of the lorry, nor the smoke curling from its melting tyres. He only saw the driver of the approaching car force it into the raised bank on its near side; its driver's eyes fixed in a ghostly stare. The gap between the car and the tanker hovered between life and death. Would there be sufficient room? He focussed his attention dead centre of the gap as if the car would understand his intention. His Ford estate scraped the tanker's wing; ricocheted onto the offside of the approaching car; and lurched back into real time to a chorus of blaring car horns.

Once he had stabilised his vehicle John Henderson checked the inside mirror. Behind he could see a line of stopped traffic and the drivers embroiled in the mayhem he had caused. He could not believe what he had done. He was a civilised, polite person who had never committed a traffic violation in his life. He dare not stop now! He would have to face up to what he had done later. He did not doubt that the police would want to interview him and probably charge him.

He checked the mirror again. The Mercedes had not followed. He began to think that with his pursuer temporarily unable to overtake, he might be able to loose him once he had overtaken a few more cars ahead. His heart rate began to return to normal. John Henderson attempted to relax using slow deep breathing; He turned off the windscreen wipers. The heavy rain of the English autumn had become a light intermittent drizzle.

This couldn't be happening to him! There was no rational justification. He reflected on the day's events. The main item on his itinerary had been a visit to Peter Langdon, a dealer in antiques, in London. The man owed him some money in settlement of recent trades between them. At first, there had been a heated disagreement based on Langdon's inability to reconcile the account and an acute lack of funds. Eventually, John left with a large carved Black

Panther. Langdon had claimed it to be equivalent to the debt. John Henderson had reluctantly had to accept the offered prize in the absence of any satisfactory alternative.

His second call of the day had been to his friend's house and workshop in Winchester. Michael Morley was an antique restorer and valuer. The two friends had worked together for many years and John Henderson trusted Mike's judgement on antiques without question. When he had called, Michael Morley was out on business, so he had left the Panther with Mike's partner, Jane. She had promised to get Michael to phone John as soon as he returned.

John recalled how it was only after he had left Winchester that he had noticed his persistent motoring companion. Was there a possible connection with the visit to London? He imagined the following day's headlines: Local antique dealer, 60, killed in mysterious road rage incident. An involuntary shiver rippled down his spine.

The sudden frisson snapped him back to consciousness. He glanced up at the mirror. He was once more staring at the image of a silver bonnet filling his interior mirror. Would he never escape? John Henderson reduced speed as he caught up with the slower moving traffic ahead. The driver behind matched him. Was this to continue until he reached home?

His suspicions intensified when the two vehicles joined a short section of dual carriage-way and the driver of the other car made no attempt to overtake. Surely, anyone charged up with road rage would take the opportunity to draw alongside and discharge a tirade of abuse? Wouldn't someone desperate to pass have got on with it? It confirmed that the driver behind intended something quite different. John's arms began to shake.

The normal turn-off to Lymington took both cars across the New Forest; through its tree bowered avenues and empty winding roads. The alarm bells in Henderson's head were now deafening. Is this what his pursuer wanted? An empty road and no witnesses! His fit of shaking worsened. Beads of sweat formed streams down his forehead and ran into his eyes, stinging them. He dragged the back of a hand across his forehead. The road ahead was straight for half a mile; there was plenty of room to overtake. Once more the game had to change. Henderson was now compelled to deny the Mercedes' driver any chance of overtaking. He had to return to the high speed option.

At the end of the straight section there was an approaching car. John delayed slowing until the last moment, but failed to judge the timing correctly and caught the offside of the other car with a metallic scraping that sent his car careering round the bend in a series of corrective zigzags. All the cards were on the table now: the pursuit had to continue until a winner emerged; perhaps until one of them was dead!

At the end of the next straight section the superior power of the Mercedes brought it alongside Henderson's Ford Estate. Immediately ahead was a tight s-bend. Henderson shot a quick glance at the opaque side window of the car. He could determine nothing from the cold sinister black glass, but its vehicle's movement betrayed a driver preparing to ram him.

The final die was rolling. It was going to be all or nothing. In an attempt to minimise severity, Henderson swerved his car onto a gravel path that formed a tangent at the first bend. Unable to stop on the scattering gravel, the car smashed through a five bar gate. The Ford rolled up over the debris flipped onto its side and bounced across a ditch. The hard impact bounced him off the driver's air-bag twisting him against the seat belt hammering his head and right shoulder into the door. His brain drove him down a dark tunnel. Thinking stopped.

At first, John Henderson had no recollection of unconsciousness; or for that matter, any previous period of consciousness. As his disorientation began to resolve he became aware of people rummaging in the back of his estate; dragging out its contents; casting them onto the gravel path. He heard the sound of breaking glass. Someone in dark clothing, wearing dark glasses, peered down at him through the broken passenger side window and declared, in what he thought sounded like a South African or Dutch accent, "he's as good as dead, but we might still get him to talk before he dies." Henderson clearly heard the sound of a fist of one hand being smacked into the open palm of another in frustration. The man bent low into the car and stretch out an arm that pulled at John's clothing. The man failed to elevate his target as John was securely trapped between the seat and the driver's door. The man had just switched his attention to ripping open the passenger door when he was interrupted by the sound of voices and people running on the gravel. John Henderson heard car doors slamming and the roar of a car being driven away at high speed. Helping hands tore open the passenger door and began tugging him free. His right arm and shoulder hurt like hell. Pain intensified as willing hands yanked him out by his left arm and laid him on the coarse ground. Somewhere in his head a road drill was pounding mercilessly. He fancied he could see flashing sirens and hear blue lights whining in the distance. Strange, he thought as everything faded to grey. The day had ended as it had begun. Badly!

CHAPTER TWO

Monday had not started well; it had been raining in torrents. John Henderson hated motorway driving at the best of times. In these conditions it had been with marked reluctance he'd driven the eighty miles to London.

By the time he arrived at the premises of Peter Langdon he was in a particularly bad mood.

John had been forced by the pressure of declining business to visit the London antique dealer. The two men had a long standing commercial relationship. He and Langdon had undocumented agreements about the conduct of trade between them. The essential element of the business centred on the exchange of goods and services rather than cash. The arrangement was convenient when the equivalent price agreed could not be realised in a particular market place. They would then establish a new value for it, or exchange it for sale in another market. In this way items that were not popular in the north could be shipped south, or a re-evaluation agreed that made it attractive where it was. Each dealer kept a note of what had been exchanged and periodically settled any accumulative difference in cash. This arrangement had many advantages - although John Henderson felt that occasionally some of them crossed the line into questionable legality.

In his early years, Henderson had been a bit of a wheeler dealer in a broad spectrum of antiques. He had won hard bargains against his fellow traders and bent the truth if a vague moral code seemed to justify it; but he'd never deceived his customers. Now a tall smartly dressed man of sixty, often exhibiting a colourful bow tie, he had mellowed into a knowledgeable character with a firm reputation for honest dealing.

Business was tough in the current recessionary times and Langdon had managed to accumulate the largest ever known difference between them. John Henderson was experiencing his own problems and needed to realise some of that capital. He suspected that the growing difference was driven by the London dealer's own lack of cash. Several phones messages to Langdon had gone unanswered; increasing John Henderson's concern. The only solution had been to go to London and confront Peter Langdon at his business premises. He did not go with any sense of optimism. On the contrary, he anticipated insurmountable difficulties.

The shop bell danced on its coiled spring as he entered the dimly lit premises. John Henderson hesitated at the open door. He was surprised by the chaotic shambles. Langdon may have been a bit disorganised at times, but never like this. Items of furniture were so tightly crammed together that they left little space for potential customers. A continuous thin layer of dust covered everything. Along the rear wall was a row of long case clocks - sentinels of time standing to attention: grand-fathers nestled with grand-mothers and grand-daughters. Elsewhere, glass fronted cabinets exhibited porcelain; flatware, watches and what could only be described as a poor collection of bric-a-brac. In the centre of the room where there was normally ample space for customers to browse stood several tables and cabinets; some stacked one upon another.

He closed the door. Almost shut, it stuck for a second then covered the final two inches with a jerk. The loud bang brought a man running from a side door. He was short, in his early fifties, wearing brown corduroys and a coarse check shirt wrapped in a sleeveless multicoloured pullover. He extended a hand towards his visitor. "Henderson! John! Good to see y'." The apparent exuberance failed to disguise a note of surprise and concern in his voice. He nodded towards the door, "D'y' like the intruder alarm?"

Henderson was puzzled; "the what? Oh...I see; it must get a lot worse in this wet weather." He shook the extended hand.

"Wha' brings y' to the smoke so early on this evil Monday mornin'?"

"You do." Henderson replied flatly. "You and our problems, I suppose."

"You, too?" Langdon desperately tried inscrutability.

"Come on, Langdon, you must realise the situation." Henderson's irritation rose quickly. "You've built up a credibility gap of tens of thousands. In fact, the largest we have ever had."

"These are desperate times, John; you must know that, as well as I do." He affected a Gallic shrug. "Everyone does." He waved his hand towards the stacked items; "but we cover that with trade for trade – goods in kind."

"Goods aren't so useful if they won't sell. You know the agreement! We settle any difference in value with cash once it becomes too large."

"But I've sold all the agreed stock!" Langdon protested.

"Good, then you will be able to settle the difference with cash."

"I ain't got no cash." Peter Landon showed his empty palms. "Y' knows what it's like; tons of bloody stock an' no sodd'n customers." He gestured around the shop and repeated his mantra in crisp east end accent, "I ain't got no cash."

It was what John Henderson had feared. He had problems himself. It was the very reason he wanted to collect outstanding cash debts. He could not restrain a loud sigh. "Peter, this won't do. I've got my own debts to sort out. I must have half of what's owed at the very least." His reasoned soft southern accent sounded almost like abuse. Langdon grabbed the speaker's arm and pushed him towards the piled up dust covered stock. "John – you ain't listn'n to me; I ain't got no bloody money – jus' this load of bloody tat." He began to rummage through the stock. "There's this – or y' can 'av that." Langdon pulled item after item out into the gangway forcing John Henderson to scramble over the obstacles in order to reach the owner to stop the madness. "Langdon, that's far enough! None of this will do. I need cash and I need it now."

"Well, as I keeps a tellin' y' – I ain't got no cash!" He thought for a moment. "But I could auction some of this lot!"

"Auction? I need you to settle this today."

Peter Langdon opened his mouth to repeat his protest then stopped. He looked furtively around the shop before moving to a new location and checking from there. Henderson raised his eyebrows expectantly; "Well?"

"I might 'av somefin' y'd take." He exhibited great reluctance before he finally squeezed between some tables and over others before disappearing through a door. John Henderson wondered if that was the last he was going to see of Peter Langdon. He was frustrated that he had ever thought this approach to business was going to work. He idly cast his eye over the stock in front of him. It was rubbish. Peter Langdon had always been the sort of person to whom one listened despite his rough exterior and voice. He had good ideas, knowledge and leads, was shrewd and knew exactly where to find the right quality. John Henderson realised that what he was now looking at was not the work of the Peter Langdon he knew.

John Henderson decided he was wasting his time and was just about to leave when the owner reappeared, but through a different door. Henderson stared in disbelief as Langdon scrambled over his stock; pushing a carved Black Panther in front of him. Langdon puffed with the struggle. "Now this is...something...worth 'aving – something of...great...value." He thrust the animal towards Henderson. "This is like pure gold and should be worth a lot more than I owes y'." Henderson cautiously stroked the surface of the animal and then tapped it with a knuckle. Although made of wood the Panther sounded very solid. The surface had been roughly carved and poorly painted. Much of the colouring was flaking. About two feet head to rear; it balanced well on its four feet and had its head turned to look at the observer. Each pupil sparkled like a cut and polished jewel. There were a number of areas where the body had been knocked. Most of the damage was superficial, but the underside was worse with splinters of wood missing.

"What am I supposed to do with this?" Henderson sighed. His spectacles slipped down his nose. He repositioned them with one hand whilst placing the other under the Panther's belly. He began bouncing the animal to gauge its weight. It was unstable and heavy enough to need the immediate support of both hands. John ran his hand over the rough back, then turned it palm up to reveal flakes of paint. "You consider this valuable?"

Peter Langdon drew nearer, placed a hesitant hand on John's shoulder and spoke in a low conspiratorial voice. "John; John mate. You don't realise how desperate I am. If the people who sort of own it knew that I had it, I'd be dead meat."

"Sort of own it?"

"The people who owned it before they suddenly discovered they didn't; if y' knows what I mean?"

Henderson had often come across individuals who inflated importance, value or threat and decided to dismiss what he had heard as gross exaggeration. "I know little of this sort of object; I really can't imagine its current market value." He handed the Panther back to Langdon. The dealer tugged at his arm and leaned forward once more. "It has a long history..." hesitating before adding almost inaudibly, "...and a secret."

"A secret?" Henderson managed a smile before pressing Langdon to elaborate. The man blushed in response and fidgeted, rubbing his palms together roughly.

"I can't tell you. I'm taking a terrible risk."

"But you have told me. You might as well finish your story."

"I can't. Both of us could end up dead."

"But if they, who ever they might be, don't know you have this animal how can it be a threat?"

Peter Langdon was thrown by this simple piece of logic. "But they might find out." He blurted.

"They might do that anyway. Telling me is not going to change much and if there is the danger you suggest, it would be in my interests to remain silent." Henderson felt he could indulge Langdon's romancing since it was highly unlikely to be true.

"I'm not sure."

"Look, you were quite prepared to offer me this animal in exchange for what you owed me. That suggests you were prepared to pass the risk on to me?"

"It was made around the end of the 19th century." Langdon relented.

"And that's the secret and source of its great value?"

"No, let me finish." Langdon coughed and seemed to struggle for breath. "It was made in South Africa." He emphasised the country.

"South Africa at the end of the Boer War?" Alarm bells began to sound in Henderson's mind. "So, we are talking Kimberley and, these days; Zimbabwe?" Henderson retrieved the Panther from Langdon and examined the eyes more closely. Its glazed slit pupils were studded with glass beads or, possibly diamonds. If the origin was Kimberley it would be consistent that the bright shiny pupils were small gems. He was not certain, but he realised that if they were of top quality they were too small to go any way towards the value he needed.

Kimberley had been the centre of diamond mining operations at the time of the Boer War. Was it possible that there was a larger intrinsic value than he imagined? Could he trust Langdon, or was this a Trojan horse? "This has little value as far as I can tell." John Henderson mused aloud.

"But think of the secret!"

"What secret? I don't believe there can be a secret large enough to satisfy your debt to me." His voice revealed his increasing annoyance and frustration at his inability to get the dealer to take him seriously.

"Wait, John, hear me out!"

"Convince me then – quickly!" He shouted.

"I'm in real trouble, John. If I let you have this it could spell the end of me."

"Then stop messing about and give me an alternative."

"I can't, John, and that's the problem."

"Then it's the Panther or nothing!"

The colour drained from Langdon's face. "I was given this to look after by someone – he said it was just as security against his debt to me, but the debt was too small to justify it. I think I was being given it to look after. It might have been to keep it away from police eyes or from someone else in the criminal world."

"How long have you had it?"

"That's the point: a couple of months; too long. I think he may no longer be able to collect it."

"In prison?"

"Or dead."

"And you want to pass this on to me?"

"I'm the only one at risk here; no-one will know where it went."

"You will; and is this the secret?"

"No. The Panther was made to hide a stash of crude uncut, unpolished, diamonds stolen before one of the tunnels was flooded."

"Flooded?"

"It's not easy to smuggle diamonds from a diamond mine. Security is so tight no-body can even fart without it being detected."

"So how did anyone manage to do so?" The intrigue was beginning to draw Henderson.

"They didn't know if they could. They thought they were safe as long as the diamonds they acquired stayed within the mine."

"I can't see how that's a plan for success."

"They were waiting for the day when something went wrong, some disaster when there would be a major diversion and they could take advantage of it."

"That's a pretty far fetched plan. They could have waited for ever."

"I don't know, maybe they had a plan to start a riot, or a fire, or something like that. But the flood saved them the trouble."

"This was an accident?"

"No; it was deliberate. The Boers had the town of Kimberley surrounded and the inhabitants could have died of thirst if they hadn't allowed one of the shafts to flood. They simply switched off the pumps that kept the mine dry."

"How did that help?"

"Well, apparently in all the confusion as workers had to evacuate tools and drums of oil or chemicals that would poison the water. It was the perfect opportunity to get the diamonds out, smuggled in a harmless looking Panther."

"It sounds too easy; even in war time."

"Well, apparently it wasn't."

"So, inside this special container there are a lot of raw diamonds; how many and how much?"

"I don't know; maybe none at all"

"So this Panther you're offering me is not going to solve my problem?" Henderson's frustration had now become raw anger. He had travelled all that way in foul weather to argue with someone who owed him a fortune and was simply being messed about. Although a gentleman at heart, this was now too great a burden. He grabbed Langdon by the collar dragging him over a table into the passageway just inside the door. "Langdon, if you don't give me my f*****g money right now I'm going to kill you. I'm going to grind you up and feed you to my bloody pigs. No-one will ever find you!"

Langdon was alarmed by this sudden aggression. In the testosterone fury neither man had heard the door bell clang. Now Langdon's expression changed from alarm to one of forced pleasure as he looked towards the door. Henderson caught the mood change and turned to look. A short middle aged man in a blue anorak carrying an orange supermarket shopping bag had entered the shop. Shocked by the violence and seeing John turn towards him the man dropped his bag and ran from the shop.

The two men stood panting with exhaustion watching the man as he hurried across the street without looking back and disappeared down the road opposite.

"Hear me out!" Langdon pushed Henderson away with both hands. "Hear me out!"

"Okay, you have one minute." John needed to get his breath back.

"That was over one hundred years ago."

"So what are you telling me?"

"It established a smuggling route into Europe. It lasted through both world wars; changes of government; and everythin'"

"You're telling me that they still smuggle diamonds from a mine in South Africa by flooding it regularly?"

"No! Blood diamonds!" Langdon panted. "They realised they had a route that worked for them to smuggle anything they wanted. But the diamond guys wanted to keep it purely for their business – they had important backers in governments – drugs would increase the risk of discovery."

"How is this going to help me?"

"The Panther contained a coded list of who was next in the chain. Before each man passed it on he would take his share as agreed and mark it on the list."

"What stopped the first man taking the diamonds and doing a runner?"

"Guaranteed death!"

Henderson reflected for a moment. He could understand how such a system might work, but still doubted Langdon's veracity. "So how did you come by it?"

"I was offered it to settle a debt. But I was too scared to cut it open. The next thing I know; the guy turns up dead in the Thames."

"Okay. You have told me all I need to know. I can't take something that will lead to me being dragged dead from the Thames."

"I think the eyes are diamonds; real ones; polished; not like those carried inside. They should be worth something."

"It's illegal."

"Take it anyhow; think about it; I don't want to see it again. You can throw it away if you like."

John Henderson turned to leave, but then thought of Michael Morley his restorer friend. He could get him to give an opinion on the value and the legal position. If all else failed he could simply hand it in to the police.

"Okay, I will take it but you must not tell anyone what happened to it. Do you understand?" Even as he uttered the words he had a feeling of great foreboding.

Soon after his failed attempt to recover the debt, John Henderson found himself driving his Ford estate full of low grade items including a carved wooden Black Panther. He turned onto the M3 and headed for Winchester.

CHAPTER THREE

"Mr. Henderson?" The nurse moved a little closer. "Mr. Henderson; you have some visitors."

John Henderson tried to raise himself, but the effort sent pain coursing through his body and he slumped back in agony.

"Who is it?" He peered towards the end of the bed. He could just make out two yellow blurs.

"It's the Police, Mr. Henderson." The nurse picked up the controller and began to raise the head.

"No; please; no more." The patient protested as the pain increased.

"Mr. Henderson, I'm p.c. Hockford and this is my colleague, w.p.c. Brand." The officer moved so that he could be seen. He studied Henderson's face and tried to assess his comprehension. "You've had an accident, Mr. Henderson; my colleague and I need to ask you some questions. Do you feel able to answer?"

The patient exhaled a long breathy sigh. "Hmmm."

The w.p.c. turned to the nurse. "You did say he was fit to interview?"

The woman flipped over a page of the file she was carrying, running a finger down the sheet. "The doctor has written that Mr. Henderson may be questioned using discretion."

"When was that note written?" The male officer looked at his watch.

"During this morning's rounds; at about nine."

"That was two hours ago." He mused.

"Mr. Henderson comes and goes; he's very weak."

"We spoke to his wife earlier and she was happy that we interviewed him." W.p.c. Brand stroked the screen of her e-pad.

The officer moved closer and bent to address the patient. "Mr. Henderson, do you know why you are here?"

There was a long pause as waves of uncertainty and pain rippled across his face. "No; I hurt everywhere. Where is Mary?"

W.p.c. Brand stood and shook her head. "He's definitely not fit to interview."

"I'm afraid not." Her colleague agreed. "We'll make enquiries elsewhere first and check with you later."

"Yes, that seems best," The nurse acknowledged John Henderson's cognitive relapse. "Perhaps you could return when his friends do."

"Yes;" agreed p.c. Hockford turning to leave.

"Wait! Just a moment;" the w.p.c. restrained her male colleague. "Friends? You said he had friends who visited?"

"Yes, just after his wife had left. They said they were very worried about their friend and wanted to talk to him, but he had gone to sleep by then."

"Did they leave a message, or say who they were?"

"No, they were a bit oppressive; frightening even."

"In what way?"

"They expected me to wake him up – even after gentle rocking failed to rouse him."

"And you refused?"

"I had to. He is my responsibility and seriously injured."

"How did they respond?"

"Really badly; one of them pushed past me and I was forced to threaten him with the doctor if he didn't calm down. He became quite abusive."

"But they did leave after that?"

"Yes. The big man pulled the other one away and said something I didn't catch. Then they left."

"What sort of age, build etc.?"

"One was of average height and weight, about thirty – he was a bit muscular around the biceps; the other man was larger, over six feet; I would say around 16 stones and guess forty something." She illustrated each statement with movements of her arms.

"That was all?"

"No. The smaller of the two spoke with a Dutch accent."

"When did all of this happen?"

"About half an hour ago."

"And you didn't get a name; address; or telephone number for them?"

"No, nothing."

"Is that because you didn't ask, or they didn't volunteer?"

The nurse became defensive. "I didn't think…have time to ask…it's not my job."

"It's alright;" the w.p.c. touched the nurse lightly on the arm; "I have to ask these questions in case you can provide some information that will help us understand what happened." W.p.c. Brand steered the nurse away from the bed. "They've not been back since?"

"No."

"Did they say how they knew he was here, in hospital... that they'd witnessed the accident?"

"No. They were not the sort of people you would engage in casual conversation, if you know what I mean."

"I've got something." P.c. Hockford had been scrolling through the witness notes he had made after the accident. He turned the device so that his colleague could see the screen. "You see this comment?" He pointed to a particular note; "that remark there."

"South African?" The w.p.c. looked puzzled; "but the nurse said..."

"...Dutch, I know; but there are similar and easily mistaken."

"It was Dutch." The nurse affirmed.

"You're sure?" P.c. Hockford furrowed his brow

"Yes, my sister is married to a Dutchman."

"What about other witnesses?" The female strained to see the screen.

"No. Just that one reference; we may have to re-interview some of the witnesses."

"What are we going to do now?"

"Has Mrs. Henderson left the hospital, or did she say when she might return?" P.c. Hockford asked the nurse.

"She has gone to get something to eat. She could return at any time, but she didn't say."

"Is she eating here, in the hospital?"

The nurse was interrupted in her reply by the approach of Mrs. Henderson who upon seeing the two police officers hurried forward. "What has happened? Has John got worse? She fretted.

"No; he's fine Mrs. Henderson." P.c. Hockford reassured without justification. "We wanted to question him, that's all."

"And you were unable?" Henderson's wife looked pale. She turned to the nurse, "How is he?"

The nurse reassured her that the police presence had no bearing on her husband's condition. Not satisfied by the response, Mrs Henderson rushed to her husband's side and shook him firmly until she had roused him.

"Mary? Mary, is that you?" He groaned as he tried to turn. "What's wrong, Mary?"

"Nothing, John. It's alright now." Temporarily reassured, she turned to address those around her. "So, has my husband been able to help you?"

"Not yet, Mrs. Henderson." The w.p.c. clasped her hand, "but I'm sure he will in time."

"I'm so worried. He was always such a careful driver."

"We suspect it may not have been your husband's fault." P.c. Hockford opined against all training directives. Immediately his colleague shot him a warning glance before softening it to an understanding smile as she realised he was responding to the overriding need of a vulnerable spouse. She then dwelt for a moment on her colleague's unexpected sensitivity.

Quickly regaining her objectivity, w.p.c. Brand explained that it would be helpful if Mrs. Henderson could remember anything about her husband's movements for that day.

"I'm not sure I know anything that would be helpful. You say it might not have been John's fault?"

"We need anything that will help us establish that."

"I don't know anything; anything that makes sense, anyhow."

"What do you mean? Let us decide what makes sense."

"When I first arrived, he was fearful of a black eyed silver monster. He repeated it several times."

"Were you able to ask him what he meant?"

"Not at all; I thought he was delirious. When he became cogent, he couldn't remember."

"Do you know where he went yesterday?"

"He went to London to see a dealer."

"A dealer in antiques?"

"Yes."

"Do you know the address of that dealer?"

"I can probably find it at home for you."

"That would be helpful. Do you know if he went anywhere else?"

"Not until early yesterday evening. Michael Morley phoned to say John had left something for him when he'd been out."

"Did he say what it was?"

"No, and I didn't ask."

"He didn't enquire about the accident?

"Even I didn't know about it at that time."

"Who is this Michael Morley?" The w.p.c. began to make notes of the meeting.

"He is a dear friend; both he and his partner, Jane."
"Where does he live?"
"In Winchester; I expect John called in on the way home from London."
"We will need an address for Mr. Morley and a telephone number if you have one."
"I will write it down for you when I collect the other address."
"It's quite important, Mrs. Henderson. Can we give you a lift home now?"

She hesitated and looked at her husband who had fallen asleep. "I don't think I am of much help to John at present, so I suppose it would be better to do it now, thank you."

"How did you get here? Only we won't be able to bring you back. We have other duties." The w.p.c. smiled sympathetically.

"I came by taxi. It was too urgent to mess about with buses and I don't like driving in the heavy rain. It will be all right; I will return this evening. I might be able to talk to John then."

Police Constable Hockford led the way towards the hospital entrance and began re-examining notes he had made earlier. Janet Brand took Mrs. Henderson's arm and followed. "You said that your husband's friend, Michael, had a partner?" She enquired.

"Yes, Jane; she's a lovely girl." Mary Henderson understood she was being unofficially interviewed, but feared no consequence from complying.

"Is that as in business partner, or...?"

"...yes and no." Mary had anticipated the question.

"A romantic partner who helps out, then?" The policewoman smiled, trying to maintain a casual conversation.

"Don't worry, dear; I understand you have a job to do. Jane used to work as a receptionist and secretary for my husband when he had the workshop in Winchester. When he partially retired last year and we moved to Lymington he sold the workshop and showroom to Michael. Jane continued to work part time for Michael until....well, until they fell in love, I suppose. She now works all the hours possible – just like Michael."

"Your husband knew Michael Morley before he bought the business?"

"Yes. They've been friends for as long as I can remember, but Michael only bought the premises, not the business."

"Your husband still runs that?"

"Yes."

"Here we are." Constable Hockford held open the door for Mary. He closed the door after she was seated and drew Janet Brand away from the vehicle. "Can we have a few words?"

"What's up?"

"I've just received an update. It appears that John Henderson may have been driving dangerously for miles before his car crashed. Serial damage to other vehicles has been reported and witnesses have used words like maniac."

"That doesn't seem to fit, somehow." Janet Brand seemed mystified. "It isn't consistent with Mary Henderson's view of her husband's driving and doesn't reconcile with the people found rummaging through the contents of his car?"

"Do you ever know what others will do? The rubbishing of his contents could just have been opportunism." Her male colleague lamented.

"What if he had been running away?"

"From what or who?"

"Those thugs who turned up at the hospital."

P.c. Hockford reflected for a moment. "We mustn't read too much into that. Nurses often suffer abuse from the public."

"Maybe, but all of these things happening together?"

The constable placed a reassuring hand on her shoulder. "Not our problem at the moment. The suspect is in hospital and not likely to be going anywhere. We can question him whenever we are ready."

"I bet you're regretting your premature comment to Mrs. Henderson about it not being her husband's fault."

"Get in the car, harridan."

CHAPTER FOUR

"Mary?" It was the familiar voice of Michael Morley. Mary Henderson held the receiver closer to her right ear.

"Michael, how are you? How's Jane?"

"We're both fine, thank you Mary. I hope John's cough has cleared up. Is he there? I was hoping to talk to him about the Panther he gave Jane today. He left a message asking if I would call him as soon as I got in."

"A Panther? That sounds different; not a live one, I hope?"

"Don't worry; it's quite dead. I just need to know how far he wants me to go with it."

"Was it for valuation?" Mary prompted.

"He didn't say, but Jane said he looked a bit flustered. She thought he might have had some sort of trouble." Immediately he spoke Michael realised his error.

"He's in trouble? What sort of trouble?" Mary's voice rose by half an octave.

"I don't think it's that sort of trouble." Michael tried to reassure her. "I expect he had to drive a hard bargain with someone and needed me to give him an opinion as to its value."

"I do hope so. He's not normally this late. Not these days. It's quite worrying."

"I expect he has all his calls nicely lined up to bring him nearer home with each one."

"I don't think he had that many. He had to go to London and you know how much he hates that."

"Well, he certainly got there and back safely, Mary. He told Jane he had acquired the Panther in London; but that was all. He didn't say if I should repair it – there is some damage, or simply give a general valuation."

"I don't know - all I can do, Michael, is make sure he contacts you as soon as he arrives. It's a bit worrying though, because now I think about it he was planning to be home early to move some things out of the loft this afternoon. I only remember him mentioning the London visit."

"It's more likely that he had problems with the dealer and that's made him late."

"What time did he reach Jane?"

"I've only just missed him apparently, so he should be with you in less than an hour." Michael lied. He knew it had been nearer to lunch time when John had called.

"Did I hear you tell a fib?" Jane slipped her hands under John's arms from behind and locked them across his chest. She leaned over the back of the hall chair and snuggled her head close to his.

Michael rubbed his head against hers. "Hmmm; I'm sorry, but I had to. I think John may have a problem."

"What sort of problem?"

"The sort that would cause you to tell me that you thought he had."

"Oh, I was probably imagining something that wasn't there."

Michael Morley took hold of one of Jane's arms and pulled her round to one side. He smiled before adopting a more sombre expression. "Why exactly did you tell me you thought he had a problem?"

Jane slid her legs to sit across Michael's lap and adopted a similar expression. "He still had the impatience of a man who had recently been angry." She pecked him on the lips.

"What did he say?"

"Nothing more than wanting to talk to you, but his breath was short and his voice had that tell tale quaver in it."

"Did he mention anyone's name, or an incident?"

"No, but his clothing was rucked as if he had been in a skirmish, if not a fight."

"And this all has some connection with a tatty carved Black Panther?" He slipped Jane off his lap and returned to the lounge. "We'd better have a good look at this Panther."

When Jane got to the lounge door Michael had already retrieved the creature from the coffee table and was holding it whilst hiding behind the door. "Roarrrr!" he cried and thrust the animal towards her as she entered. She squeaked and jumped back in mock horror. "Idiot! Are you sure that roar is the appropriate sound for a Panther?"

"I haven't the slightest idea." He laughed; "but we'd better have a look and find where he keeps it."

Michael Morley repeated what John Henderson had done. He bounced the specimen lightly in his hands to judge the weight. "Very heavy," he declared, passing it to Jane whilst he went to fetch his magnifying glass. When he returned he examined the animal by eye and with the glass alternately; moving systematically from its head to its tail. He removed some of the flaking paint to examine the wood beneath before turning it over to pay particular attention to the splintered section below. Finally, he placed the carved animal on the coffee table and rocked it to test its stability.

"Well?" Jane was keen to hear the verdict.

"It was made late 19th century, but not with love and attention. It's a pretty rough example of its kind."

"What in particular makes you think that?" Jane was more than Michael's romantic partner; she had developed a professional interest in the restoration business and took every opportunity to learn more.

"The whole piece has been constructed of more sections than desirable. The best examples are made from very few pieces; producing fewer joints to smooth afterwards. No attempt has been made to eliminate the multiple joints that comprise this beast."

"Meaning?"

"Someone put this together in a hurry. A craftsman would never let a piece like this see the light of day."

"Could it have been made for the tourist trade; a quick sell and nobody around to complain later?"

"I don't think so. Even the least well informed tourist would smell a rat with this one."

Michael Morley ran his hand across the painted surface revealing the flakes to Jane. She took a close look at the particles. "It is old though. Wouldn't you expect the paint to come off after all this time?"

"Not like this. The Panther has been painted whilst the wood was wet; far too careless for a craftsman. The mock teak that has been used is still an oily wood and the carving's maker should have known that it would be better to polish the oiled surface and present it in the natural state. Then there's this." He turned the carving so that Jane could study the underside.

Jane flicked at the splinters of wood protruding from the lower joints. "What has happened here, Mike?"

"Don't know for sure, but I would guess that it had, or was certainly thought to have had an opening."

"A secret hiding place?"

"Not necessarily, but it is possible that it was used to conceal or simply contain something."

"A piggy bank?"

"Could be anything, or for any reason; I will need to have a closer look at it."

Jane picked up Michael's magnifying glass and began examining the sparkling eyes. "These are real diamonds!" she smiled at Michael.

"Brilliant!" he declared.

She looked puzzled for a moment then laughed at his joke. "Fifty five facet; brilliant cut."

"Quite, but not the originals; if there were any diamonds originally."

"You think they were added later?"

"All most certainly."

"Why?"

"I will tell you in a moment, but first I will have a better idea if I can get a look inside."

Michael Morley took the Panther through to his workshop at the rear of the house and selected a narrow bladed tool. He proceeded to test each seam until he found one that allowed the instrument to enter. "That's what I thought."

"What did you think?" Jane had caught up with him.

"I think there is a door like a Chinese puzzle in the stomach of this carving. The last person who tried to open it had no idea and that's why we see all these splinters."

"Why didn't they simply cut it open?"

"Maybe they were going to, but were interrupted; or needed to keep it intact."

"You mean not let anyone know they had tried to get in?"

"I have no idea, but it's a thought. Perhaps they were going to affect a crude repair in the hope no one would notice."

"No one would notice?" Jane held up the Panther so that the splinters were plainly visible.

"Well, it was only an idea. It makes the whole thing more intriguing."

Michael retrieved the animal and this time managed to find places where two tools could be inserted. He slid one along to the end of a slot and a corner sprung up a centimetre. "Blue handled blade, please." Michael nodded towards a toolbox. Jane complied with the request and was impressed to observe the progress.

"If I can get this one in at right angles, we shall have it, I think." He struggled roughly at times with the partially open section until suddenly almost without effort it fell open, dropping heavily onto the bench.

"Voila!" he cried in triumph.

Jane bent down to peer inside the cavity; "can't see a thing, Mike." Michael Morley swivelled the carving to expose the underside and held it under a lamp. "Empty, I'm afraid; no hidden treasure after all." He passed it in front of Jane so that see could see.

"Yes there is!" Jane exclaimed and tried to reach in with her fingers. "Damn! My hand is too big."

"Use the tweezers."

A second attempt was successful and Jane withdrew a small piece of folded paper. Michael briefly turned to observe the discovery before continuing to inspect the nature of the cavity for clues. Jane spread the folded paper flat on the worktop and smoothed it.

"Did I say no intrigue?" Michael stood back and carried out a few exercises with his hips. "That is a very heavy object."

"What have you found that's so special?"

"You should see it, Jane. It has been configured with some specially shaped materials. The whole of the inside wall is plastered with them."

"With what?" Jane looked once again inside. "I can't see anything unusual. What am I supposed to be looking at?"

"I'm not positive, but I think we will find those pieces are made of different materials and different shapes to appear innocent if x-rayed."

"Why would anyone go to that trouble; customs?"

"Exactly. If anyone tried to disguise what they were hiding by blocking the x-rays with a solid mass, a piece of lead for example, it would be too obvious. There would just be a large black hole where nothing could be seen. That would guarantee that customs would cut it open."

"So what do these shapes do?"

"By having different densities; giving shades of grey; and appropriate shapes, the appearance of any object could be created."

"Wouldn't the shape of what was hidden still show through?"

"Possibly, but might not be noticed if it sort of blended with, or became part of the pattern."

"That's amazing! Are you sure about all of this?"

"I haven't the faintest idea, my sweet one, but you come up with a better suggestion."

Michael turned his attention to the flattened paper. "What have we here?"

"It could be a strange shopping list. However, I believe it's a message sent by Martians to their spies on Earth telling them an invasion is imminent." Jane raised two hands above her head and wiggled her fingers.

"Very funny, my little pudding;" Michael laughed loudly at Jane's inventive retaliation.

Any further jesting was interrupted by the business phone ringing. Michael wiped the black flecks from his hands and picked up the phone. He was still laughing as he picked up the phone. "Hello?"

The line was open; he could hear the background hum, but no one answered. "Hello?" The silence remained until he was about to replace the receiver.

"Mr. Morley?" A deep voice enquired. "Mr. Michael Morley?" This time Michael just caught its South African intonation.

"Yes, I'm Michael Morley; how can I help you?"

"You are an antique restorer?" The voice ignored the previous question.

"I am. What can I do for you?"

"You have something of mine, Mr. Morley." The voice remained level, emotionless.

"I don't understand. Who are you? I don't recollect having anything of anybody's for which…"

"I want it back, Mr. Morley." The voice interrupted with dark intimidation.

"Who are you? I'm sure I have nothing of yours and…"

"My Black Panther, Mr. Morley; You have my Black Panther. I want it back and I shall be calling for it soon. Take very good care of it."

"I really do not like your tone of voice…hello?...hello?"

CHAPTER FIVE

Detective Inspector Kevin James hesitated at the open door. The room that had once stored buckets and brooms had recently been converted to an interview room. The sickly smell of its fresh cream paint lingered.

Newly appointed, Kevin James had been given the room as a temporary office until his formal one was ready. The paint smell was so bad that he had remained a nomad unless forced by circumstances to use it.

Two constables perched on the room's major item of furniture; a faux wooden topped table, chatting. Detective Sergeant Derek Forest leaned back, scanning his notes, in one of five plastic chairs.

"Right everyone; let's have some order then." The D.I. squeezed past two chairs grabbing the second placing it at the long side of the table. He waited whilst the others had aligned chairs facing and gestured that they should sit. He removed his baseball cap and placed it and a few papers he had been carrying on the polished table. His new colleagues stared in amusement at the faded red and white striped cap.

"Thank you for being prompt at such short notice, Sergeant, and you two for hanging back. I'll clear any duty problems that may arise."

He spread his documents on the table and toyed with them; placing a finger first on one then another. He shuffled them lightly before placing them together once more, carefully aligning their edges.

"Clearly, this is no longer a traffic accident." He vigorously tousled his hair with his finger tips. "What's the latest, Derek?"

The D.S. held up an A2 sheet of paper and nodded towards the wall behind the Inspector. Kevin James turned and saw the quick release paper holder mounted on the wall. "I'm pleased to see I've been given the latest technology." He smiled and stepped away from the table to permit the Sergeant access to the track.

Derek Forest smoothed the sheet and tapped his knuckles against the name written at the top in bold and underlined. "We have John Henderson, 60, a semi-retired dealer in antiques living at this address in Lymington."

"Anything known?" The D.I. leaned against the wall.

"Nothing at all; not even parking violations."

"There's no business suspicions; dodgy dealing; known associates; something a bit near the margin?" The D.I. frowned.

"There's nothing at all and that's almost suspicious in its self."

The D.I. returned to the table and scanned the top sheet of his notes.

"So why, if I am reading the reports correctly, do we have so many witness reporting him as driving dangerously and causing hundreds of pounds worth of damage during a period of about an hour?"

The Sergeant nodded towards the two constables. "These were first on the scene and took witness statements and also saw what had happened before anything was moved."

The D.I. extended a hand towards Constable James Hockford. "What solid evidence do we have about what happened?" He tapped the pile in front of him. "This is very scrambled."

"There were no witnesses to the event at the scene, so there can be no certainty about what happened until Mr. Henderson is well enough to be interviewed. All the witnesses are motorists who have reported acts of dangerous driving relating to Mr. Henderson's vehicle before the incident."

"I understand you visited Mr. Henderson in hospital. Were you able to get any idea at all about what happened?"

"Not from Mr. Henderson," replied w.p.c. Janet Brand, "but we did obtain something from the nurse." She looked at her colleague who nodded.

"Yes, that was good thinking." He agreed.

"Oh, why was that?" The D.I. puzzled, "Janet picked up on the fact that the nurse had said two men claiming to be friends of John Henderson had visited."

"And what was their contribution to our knowledge of what happened?"

"Not the sort you might expect, but it looks as if they may have been involved in some way."

"Your evidence for this would be?" Kevin James seated himself.

"The nurse said they were aggressive; not nice people." W.p.c. Brand responded quickly.

"That is a subjective view; a lot of innocent people appear not to be nice at times." The D.I. was keen to observe the principles of evidence at all times.

"I think these two probably had been pursuing Mr. Henderson causing him to drive dangerously." The sergeant leapt to his junior officer's defence.

"Speculation, Sergeant. We need facts." The D.I. spun his cap on the polished surface. "You realise that on the basis of the witness statements alone we have reason to arrest Mr. Henderson?"

"He was nearly killed!" Janet Brand reminded the D.I.

"Yes, but it might be argued in court that he always had the option to stop."

"That would not be easy if the person pursuing him had been shooting at him, or going to if they could catch him."

"Again, speculations for which we have no evidence Constable Brand; however, if that situation were to be true it would be a question of mitigation for the court."

James Hockford felt aggrieved at the instant dismissal of his colleague's suggestion. "Sir, I think we have sufficient evidence to pursue the two men who appeared at the hospital. The witness statements we took at the scene described two similar characters ransacking the contents of the car and who drove off at high speed in a silver Mercedes."

The D.I. flicked through two sheets before briefly reading a third. "Yes, Constable, I agree, we may have sufficient prima facia to warrant interviewing these two men." He turned to his Sergeant. "Can we retrieve the close circuit camera evidence from the hospital? We know what time they were there. It should be quite an easy matter. Also let's check for any cameras that might have picked up the car in the Lymington area."

The two constables smiled at the decision. The D.I. spun his cap once more before placing squarely on his head tugging at the peak.

"Let's get together again as soon as we have the camera evidence, Sergeant. And can you two check this morning on the condition of Mr. Henderson, please?"

"If he is well enough to speak, should we caution him about the dangerous driving?" Janet Brand was still concerned for patient

"That remains a matter for the normal protocols. Be careful. If he is in danger of incriminating himself it might prove useful for a defence council later. Stick to the rules; they have been well tested."

The D.I. called a final instruction as they reached the passage. "Re-interview your witnesses and concentrate on whether or not they saw the Mercedes following Mr. Henderson's car. If they did; get statements about speed attitude etc."

CHAPTER SIX

"Should I pick it up?" Jane's hand hovered over the phone. "It might be him again."

"No. Wait a moment!" Michael Morley grasped his nose between the finger and thumb of his left hand. "We must think this through."

"You have to pick it up sometime."

After a short pause, her partner decided. "You're right." He gestured towards the phone, "answer in your most professional receptionist's voice; apologise and say that Mr. Morley is out on business."

"What if that's not acceptable to him?"

"You can deal with that when the need arises."

"This is crazy, Mike. You must deal with it." She stepped away from the hall table.

"Why not phone the police and tell them that you've been threatened."

"And say what? That someone has threatened to come round and collect something that belongs to him?"

Jane emitted a heavy sigh, returned to the table and snatched up the phone. "Hello?" She snapped in a coarse voice. There was no response. "Hello? She repeated in the same tone. Jane held the phone at arms length so that Michael might hear the hum and shrugged. She was about to replace the receiver when she heard a voice.

"Jane? Is that you, Jane, dear?" Mary Henderson sounded nervous.

"I'm sorry, Mary. I thought you were somebody else." Jane hastened to apologise.

"Are you alright? Did you think I was a nuisance caller?"

"Something like that, Mary. Mike and I are fine; how are you two?"

"John's been in a motoring accident; that's why I'm calling."

"How is he? Where is he?" Jane turned to Michael, "John's been in an accident." She offered him the phone, but he declined with a wave of his hand and a shake his head.

"He's in the General. He was unconscious for some time; bruised all over, but not in any danger." Mary elaborated. "He's discharging himself, the stupid man. The doctors are advising against it, but he's insisting."

"Why doesn't he stay until he is rested at least?"
"That's what I said. I think he's delirious from the medication or shock."
"What do the doctors think?"
"They agree and say he ought to remain under observation for a few days."
"Would you like us to come to the hospital and help persuade him otherwise?"
"No, Jane, dear, he says that we are in danger and he must get home. Could you or Michael meet us at the house; I might need some assistance getting John inside?"
"We'll be there. What time?"
"About five, I think."
Michael Morley took the phone from Jane's hand. "Hello, Mary, we could come and pick you both up from the hospital now."
"No, Michael, I have the car; it will be easier that way."
"I'm sorry if I gave you false hope when we last spoke. I really did think he would be back safely…"
"…and you didn't want me to worry. Don't fret, Michael; I understand."
"How is he reacting to the accident? Was it serious? Were others involved?"
"He seems to have developed a fixation in which he is being chased by a silver car. He says they came to the hospital for him."
"They?"
"I know; it's crazy, but he might improve when we get him home; back to his familiar surroundings."
"Yes, you are probably right. We'll meet you at your house."

John Henderson steadied himself on his wife's arm. He moved slowly with calculated steps towards the hospital entrance. He and his wife debated the benefit of using one the wheelchairs parked nearby. Conscious of his muscular weakness and realising that he would have to cover the one hundred yards to the car park, John Henderson never-the-less decided it was better to soldier on and force his body back to work. His wife protested against her husband's stubbornness, but yielded to the inevitable.

Mary struggled to keep the passenger door open in the narrow access between adjacent vehicles. She wished she had thought of driving the car out first. If she had blocked others it might have proved a stimulus for assistance. However, after much manoeuvring, her husband was finally settled and she concentrated on belting herself into the driving seat. Once comfortable she turned to check John was prepared to leave. Mary was shocked to see that his face was drained of colour. He was staring ahead in a fixed focus looking petrified.

"Am I that bad a driver?" she joked. He failed to respond and she realised she'd trivialised some deeply felt emotional trauma.

"Memories, John?" She asked with deep sympathy.

He remained looking stiffly ahead for a moment. "Hmmm," he nodded slowly before forcing a weak smile and adding; "just for a second, dear; gone now. Let's get home."

Mary thought it better to approach Lymington from a different direction in order to avoid making her husband revisit the scene of his recent accident. She still had in mind the police officer's reassurance that it was not her husband's fault and wondered if not, whose was it and what had really happened?

"I'd like a couple of plants for the garden, John, shall I go via Beaulieu?"

Realising his wife's discretion immediately, John Henderson thought it churlish to be less tactful. "Yes, that would be nice, dear."

Plants safely stored in the boot of Mary's old Ford, it seemed only minutes before the car was climbing Church Hill. The vehicle had to stop at the pedestrian crossing lights. As it was pulling away John let out a startled gasp and twisted his head to watch a car that was passing in the opposite direction.

"What's the matter, John?" Mary pulled over to the kerb. "You look absolutely terrible, what ever happened? Are you ill? Should I take you back to the hospital?"

He waved his wife's suggestions away. "No, I'm okay. It was the sight of that car; it reminded me of something."

Mary looked in the mirror. "Which car was it? There's a large silver car I can see; don't ask me what make it is."

"A Mercedes;" John observed in an even tone. "I think I may have seen it before; I'm not certain. Seeing it frightened me, but I don't know why." The colour began slowly returning to his face. "We're nearly home, keep going."

Mary turned left into their close. The house was at the end of a short private road lined with mixed deciduous trees. The house was set back from the road on the left hand side.

The trees nearest the house were flashing with the reflected blue light of two police cars. A small crowd had gathered on the drive of their home.

As they drew nearer the Hendersons could see one police car parked askew on their driveway and the other parked just before the entrance. Mary slowed and pulled up across the driveway. As she did so Michael and Jane's car overtook and stopped just in front. Mary saw the flashing blue light of their intruder alarm and heard its high pitched warble. A few neighbours approached the Henderson's car window and began pointing and speaking, but Mary was unable to make out what they were saying. She opened the door and stood beside the car. As she alighted, a policeman came forward and after checking she was the owner, warned her that the house had been burgled. He advised her to remain outside until the officers had checked the property and made sure the intruders had left.

Mary was instantly distraught. After all the worries about John and his accident this latest event proved an emotional wrecker. Michael and Jane comforted her advising her to wait until the police had checked the house and promising to accompany her when it was time to inspect what damage had been caused.

The police officer hurried to join his colleagues. Michael decided to follow and made his way to the house, leaving Jane to console John and Mary.

The front path that bordered a well tended lawn curved away from the driveway and led directly to an arched front porch. By the time Michael arrived, the front door had been closed. He looked around hoping to see the officer or one of the officer's colleagues, but they'd all disappeared. He knew the property well and decided to check the rear.

Michael followed the right hand path leading to the conservatory. As he rounded the corner he expected to see the policeman, but there was no-one. He headed for the tall wooden panelled side gate. As he reached for the twisted ring handle he paused. Something had moved in the shrubs.

An evergreen border separated the garden from a private gravel service road running parallel to the house. He patted his coat pocket intending to use his mobile phone's torch light. Damn! In his hurry to get to the Henderson's house, he'd left it on the hall table. His listened for a moment; it was difficult to hear sensitively above the distant, but clearly audible chattering of the spectators at the front. Michael Morley began moving slowly towards the hedge. In a sudden rush a dark shape leapt at him. Michael fell backwards and sprawled on the damp grass. He sat up quickly, his heart pounding in his chest. Something darted off to his right. He twisted his head to look towards the road and saw the disappearing shape of a black cat merging with the flashing blue lights.

His heart still hammering, Michael struggled to his feet and braced himself to continue; a task to which he returned with increased circumspection.

Having recovered, he opened the gate slowly and entered the rear garden. "Hello?" He called softly in case the officer was nearby. There was no response. He ventured further. All assistance from the blue rotating lights of the distant police cars had ceased. He was now in total darkness until his eyes could acclimatise. Michael thought he could make out the roof line of John's workshop and headed towards it. As he moved he sensed he was not alone. There had been a change in the background sound; someone's presence was changing the local resonance. He stopped and immediately sensed somebody was very close. He thought he heard a footstep. He listened intently. He could just make out the sound of feet stepping slowly; deliberately. He called again. "Hello?" Again there was no response. His sight was improving. He moved to one side so that he could make out the sky between the house and workshop. He could now see a dark outline moving towards him. "Hello?" He called for a third time; "is that you officer?" The figure suddenly dashed at him and he felt a hard blow to the side of his head. He slumped onto the ground. Fearing a repeated blow Michael sprang to his feet. The figure was trying to force his or her way through the shrubs and out onto the road. A self righteous anger arose in his temple and Michael rushed at the fugitive catching and grasping at its clothing. Too late! His attacker tore free and escaped onto the road. He heard the sound of running feet followed by the slam of a car door. The road had only one access and that was across the front of the Henderson's property. Michael Morley turned to race the vehicle and intercept it. He'd only taken two strides when he was brought sharply to the ground by a flying rugby tackle. As his face crashed into the soft damp turf somebody shouted at him. "Stay down! Stay down!" He heard the metallic crack of a policeman's night stick being extended. The officer in his excitement fumbled the radio protocol and resorted to straight dialogue, "Tess? Tess? I got one of them, officer needs assistance."

"Where are you, Frank?"

"Right side of the house just beyond a side gate."

"I'm not one of them; I'm a friend of the family." Michael protested.

"We'll soon see about that, sir. Don't struggle!."

"As you will observe, officer, Frank," Michael puffed. "I'm laying here quite quietly and possibly badly injured. I'm not going anywhere."

"You are certainly right there, sir."

"What did you think you were doing, Frank?" The officer's female colleague accompanied by another officer had located him. "Officer needs assistance! He doesn't appear to be putting up much resistance." She bent down beside Michael, "if you could just bring your arms together, then it won't hurt as I apply the 'cuffs." She slipped the handcuffs over Michael's passive wrists; secured them; and stood back. "Why didn't you use your own cuffs, Frank?"

The constable looked embarrassed. "They twisted round as I dived at his legs and the top end turned and went into my pocket. I couldn't free them and hold on to him at the same time."

"He doesn't appear to be resisting, Frank, and he looks injured."

"Not my fault!" He protested.

"He could claim otherwise."

"But he won't officer." Michael Morley wanted to clear up any misunderstanding quickly. "I'm not about to claim anything except that the man you want has just jumped into a car in the lane and at this moment is heading round to the front."

"What were you doing in this garden? You don't live here." The female officer challenged.

"I'm a friend of the family and my wife and I came to help."

"How did you know there had been intruders?" She persisted.

"I didn't. My wife and I came to help John when he arrived home from hospital. You can ask his wife."

"If you follow me, sir, I will do that right now."

"What you need to do right now, officer, is get to the front of the house and stop the intruder escaping." As he shouted, the sound of spraying gravel from accelerating tyres came from the track alongside the house.

"Go! You need to stop him now!"

"Yes, you would like that wouldn't you?" We all rush around like the proverbial whilst you slip away."

"Where am I going with these?" He twisted he back to display the handcuffs.

The fleeing intruder drove across the front of the Henderson's house with tyres squealing. The small group of neighbours scattered in all directions. One pair of officers jumped into their car and after other vehicles had been moved raced after the suspects.

"I'm sorry, everyone, but I need to collect names and addresses as you are all potential witnesses." Police officers Frank Morgan and Tess Kent moved among the gathered shivering witnesses making provisional notes. Michael Morley rubbed his chaffed wrists after the handcuffs had been removed. His head was examined by the officers and declared as superficial. They apologised and recommended a formal medical inspection. He acknowledged the police apologies and declined any encouragement to file a formal complaint.

Michael and Jane wanted to take the Hendersons home with them, but they preferred to stay at the local hotel over night so that they could help the police the next day with the forensic task of identifying what had been taken or damaged. Their house had become a crime scene and further contamination had to be avoided.

Michael and Jane remained with their two friends until they had settled in at the hotel. Despite the added trauma he had suffered, John seemed to be taking things in his stride. Both Jane and Mary worried that it was an expression of something more serious going on beneath the surface. Michael remained sanguine. He thought that John would see his accident in a broader context now and would be trying to put the chain of events into perspective.

John then remembered taking the Panther to Winchester for valuation. "What did you discover about the Panther, Michael?" John declined an alcoholic drink.

"It seems it had two lives; maybe more, but certainly two." Michael smiled.

"What a strange and unexpected thing to say. You'd better explain."

"It was made around the end of the 19th century; most likely in South Africa."

"South Africa?"

"It might help if you could tell me what the London dealer as its origin."

"He wasn't very helpful. He practically forced the animal upon me claiming it was worth a great deal…he said something…" John Henderson paused; so long that Mary began to worry he'd had a stroke.

"John?" She rocked him by the shoulders.

"Hummpf." He recovered. "It's coming back to me. He said there was a problem with it. Somebody else owned it, but had lost it…or something like that."

"Lost it?" Michael suspected a deeper meaning.

"Who ever it was seems to have been unscrupulous. They tended to kill those who upset them."

"Oh, no!" Mary was horrified. She covered her face with her hands. "We must get rid of this accursed animal straight away!" She grasped Jane's hand. "This is absolutely terrible."

"Maybe not; they don't know that you have it;" Jane tried to reassure, but knew she was stretching credibility to the limit.

"Then why have these people invaded our house?"

"Perhaps they were making sure you didn't have it and are now satisfied." Jane clung to optimism.

"Why, oh why, did you have to bring this thing back to us, John?" Mary was in complete despair.

John looked crest fallen, but turned in hope to Michael. "I believe Michael will solve the mystery of this animal and remove any threat." His eyes appealed to Michael for a positive response.

Michael hesitated before answering. "There is a lot we can tell from the animal and we maybe able to use it to solve its origin and purpose."

"What was its use?" John remained focused. "You implied there were at least two options."

"Mike; I think John needs to rest for the moment. You can discuss it tomorrow." Jane touched her partner's arm, "and you ought to have your head examined."

Michael smiled at Jane's faux pas and felt the side of his head.

"Please don't be concerned about me, Jane; I need to know what kind of Trojan horse I've been given." John was earnest.

Michael frowned. "Are you sure you want to?"

John Henderson nodded and gestured that he should continue.

"Did your man say anything about diamonds?" Michael reflected.

"Diamonds? Yes, he did. He said he had been told it had been used to smuggle diamonds from a mine when it flooded."

"Who told him that?"

"The man who had given it to him in settlement for a debt."

"The same way you acquired it; did he say when it was in use?"

"He thought it was last used a couple of months ago; but he wasn't absolutely sure."

"Did he mention the Boer war at any time?"

"He'd been told it had first been used when diamond smugglers had been surrounded by Boer fighters."

"Yes, but in South Africa at the end of the 19th century everyone must have been surrounded by Boers." Mary noted the over simplicity of the statement.

"I think something similar happened in Kimberley." Michael was a keen historian.

"What, diamonds being smuggled? That would hardly constitute a surprise." Mary remained cynical about the whole concept of this mystery Panther and just wanted it gone.

"No; flooding a mine in order to provide adequate drinking water." Michael Morley clarified.

"So, did this continue until the present day? It doesn't seem practical to have to keep arranging to flood a mine."

"No, John neither do I. It's possible that what was intended as a one off event in extremis expanded into a principle. The Panther provided a transport vehicle."

"Customs aren't stupid; they would have suspected it right from the beginning."

"You're right, John, but I have examined the inside lining and it appears to me to have been designed to fool or frustrate x-ray examination. However, to me it seems more likely to have been used more as a carrier amongst dealers."

"I can't understand the benefit of that."

"It might have been an inventive way of fencing stolen diamonds. Jane managed to retrieve a small piece of paper from inside that has written on it what looks like a list of coded names."

"That's what I call intriguing. Can you decode the names?"

"I'm sorry John, but you've pushed me into the realms of fantasy. I am only making what might prove to be the wildest guesses imaginable. You'll have to let me have more time to consider it."

"This seems like a good point at which to leave." Jane stood and held out her hand to Michael.

Mary yawned. "I agree." John you must get some sleep, wait until I've seen them out and I'll help you get to bed."

As John Henderson stood he offered one final caution to Michael Morley. "Mind how you go, Michael; take care. Those men may be out there and they'll still be after their Panther."

CHAPTER SEVEN

It had begun to drizzle. The October shower sparkled in the headlights as the wipers thrashed across the windscreen. Michael Morley and Jane Fisher stared silently through the gloom, deep in thought. Today's events had left them stunned. In all the years that he and John had been in the antiques business Morley had never known such a determined display of violence. The Panther had to be at the root of it. Offering it in settlement of a debt was bizarre, although not entirely inconsistent with the way in which John Henderson and his associates conducted business. Michael felt the story about its South African origins and his own speculations about it were tenuous. He needed more time to investigate.

Jane worried if the association with the Panther would place Mike in danger. Would it place them both at risk? She shuddered at the thought of the damage caused by the intruders at the Henderson's house. She loathed the thought that somebody might trash her own home.

"How's your head?" Jane broke the silence before it became sealed by elapsed time.

"Not too bad, thanks; though I might change my mind when try to get to sleep."

"We must return first thing in the morning and see what we can do to help."

"I agree. Poor old John; I suppose it does all stem from his visit to London?"

"Why would you doubt it?"

"Because I'm not sure that even John is able to recount accurately what happened yesterday."

"You think he's lying, or…?"

"No, not at all; I think it's all blurred by experience and injury. He may remember better in a few days."

"Do you think we'd better hide the Panther – just in case?"

"Maybe; but first I'd like to give it another examination."

"What I'm really suggesting is that we get rid of it before it's too late." Jane's voice trembled.

"That could bring us even more danger. If we have it and are confronted, we always have the option to hand it over."
Jane remained unconvinced.

Michael Morley reduced speed after leaving the motorway and kept to the back roads until he steered the vehicle smoothly onto his drive and parked. Settling deeper into the driving seat he released a long sigh.
"Tired?" Jane hoped it was that simple.
"Just weary, my little pet;" he patted her leg, "driving through the rain and dark after a traumatic evening is not my favourite pastime."
"Nor mine. Let's get inside and have a drink." She twisted in the passenger seat and opened the door.
Before she could step out Michael grabbed her arm: "Did you see that?"
"See what?" Jane followed his gaze.
"I thought I saw a movement."
"I'm surprised you saw anything in this weather."
"Something caught my attention – as if I hadn't seen it, but my subconscious mind had."
"Unconscious mind more like," Jane smiled sympathetically.

The warm welcome of the central heating swept over Jane as she tapped in the alarm code. She waited until the system emitted its confirmation before slipping off her coat and hanging it up. When she turned to close the door Michael had disappeared. She opened the door again and called him. There was no reply. The garden intruder detectors had gone manic; their red lights flashing and sirens squawking. It must be Mike! She put on her damp coat; retrieved her front door keys; and ventured once again into the dark blitz. "Mike!" No response. She called again, louder, "Mike!" Jane checked he was not in the car before hesitantly following the path to the back garden.
She hesitated where a large shrub disguised the end of the wall. Things had been going horribly wrong today; was this to be the continuation of the nightmare? Tentatively peering around the corner she was suddenly confronted by a dark shape. She screamed loudly before realising that it was Mike. "What the hell were you playing at?" She shouted; and for a moment she wanted to punch her fear into him.
"Sorry, Jane; I just had to check the back of the house."
"In this weather; why the hell didn't you come in and look out of the window?" She gesticulated wildly.

"It's not the same; much better to check from the outside." He turned for a final look behind.

"What are you expecting to see for heavens sake?" She began corralling him towards the door.

"There's something not right, but I can't put my finger on it."

"You need more than a finger putting on you, Michael Morley." She gave him a relieved hug and closed the door. "You're becoming paranoid because of what happened to John!"

"If I am, it's because of what happened to me not three hours ago!" He pointed to the side of his head.

"Go in the lounge and I'll bring some wine through." Jane disappeared towards the kitchen.

Mike needed no encouragement. He slumped his six feet into the settee and operated the footrest. This was not his accustomed posture. Although not overweight, Michael Morley had a well developed upper body that he liked to top up once a week at the local gym.

He cleared the small coffee table in preparation for the drink. But when, after a few minutes, she had still not re-appeared he reluctantly struggled back to his feet and headed for the kitchen. Paranoia heightened, he listened at the door before slowly opening it with wild imaginings coursing through his mind.

"You haven't been out through the back door since we got in have you, Mike?" Jane raised her eyebrows at the sight of Michael creeping into the kitchen.

"Don't be silly. You know I haven't; I've only just come home with you, why?"

"There's a wet muddy footprint on the door mat..." She pointed down near her feet.

Michael joined her to stare at a faint outline on the fabric. "I can't see it."

Jane drew her finger slowly around what she saw as an inward pointing muddy footprint.

"You've got a good imagination, that's all I can say." Michael stared at the floor.

"...and there!" Jane indicated a clearer wet print on the floor tiling.

"That's an old mark!" He bent down and wiped a finger across the print and held it up for Jane's to see. He checked where his finger had wiped. A wet stain was more obvious now that he had smeared it and his finger was moist. Michael grasped the back door handle and tested it. The door was secure. Taking down a key he unlocked it and inspected outside. There were no signs of tampering and the rain had washed away any prints. He relocked the door. "Hmm, it wasn't raining when we went out, so we couldn't have made those prints." His concern increased.

"It was drizzling last night – I emptied the rubbish this morning. It must have been me." Jane's worrying abated. Michael was not entirely convinced, but was unable to think of a less convincing explanation.

Jane brought in two glasses of wine and settled down to watch the 24 hour news. Michael turned his attention to an unfinished sudoku in an attempt to blur the day's events. Within minutes, the combination of wine and exhaustion took hold. Michael began to catch his brain micro napping. He sat up and rubbed his eyes. "Time for bed, I think, twinkle."

"Yes, I'll join you." Jane reached for the controller.

"What was that?" Michael looked towards the light switch.

"What?" Jane retrieved the handset.

"The light flickered."

Jane pointed at the television. "The picture jumped as well. It's just one of those minor glitches we get from time to time." Jane thought Michael was entering the realms of fantasy and sleep might be the best thing for him.

"No, something's wrong." He sat up sharply, now wide awake.

Jane tried to look attentive, but failed. She was just about to cajole him, but as she opened her mouth to speak, he put a warning finger to his lips and motioned towards the door. Jane picked up the hand control and automatically pressed the mute button. He crossed to the door, switched off the light and listened. He opened the door sufficiently to observe the passage then closed it again. "Did you put the outside alarms on silent? He hissed softly.

"Don't be silly, of course I didn't." She dropped the controller onto the settee, "I bet the rain has got in somewhere and that's why the lights flickered." Jane tried to remain positive.

"Well the alarm lights are flashing; we must have visitors."

"Mike!" She grabbed his arm. Her husband's concern was unsettling and the colour drained from her face.

"I must check the house…shit!" The lights went out and the television died.

"Mike!" What should we do?" Jane squeezed his arm tightly.

"Stay calm!" He ordered.

"Sit on the settee so that I know where you are." He slid Jane's arm from his and lowered her into the seat. He felt his way to the sideboard. "Is there still a torch in the drawer?"

"I think so." Jane's voice quavered.

"I'm going to check every room; just stay where you are." He located the torch and gave the handle a few winds before testing it.

Mike eased himself through the door crouching low. The alarm panel lights, now on backup batteries, were flashing and illuminating the passage. The door to the dining room opposite was half open. Keeping low he entered the room. He remained still and listened. Only the ticking clock marked out the silence. Once confident he was alone he flicked on the torch and panned it around the room. There was no-one there and nothing appeared to have been disturbed. He relaxed for a moment.

Perhaps Jane was right and he was over reacting. Perhaps water had got into the system somewhere. The rain was wind driven now.

He left the room and headed along the passage towards the study. Its door was wide open! That door was never left open! The room had an open fireplace and its downdraught could chill the whole house within minutes. Michael hesitated at the open door. He now understood what had made him suspicious earlier; he had felt the cold draught. He breathed deeply to counteract the paralysing cold of fear. He had few options: he could rush in by torch light and confront whoever was in the room; retreat to the lounge and call the police; or he and Jane could flee the house and go to the neighbours. It would prove embarrassing if he raised a false alarm. He would be dogged by a reputation he'd not cherish, but he had his wife's safety to consider.

Any need for a decision was eliminated as a swift movement and unseen hand pushed him back. The bright light of a powerful torch blinded him. He felt something hard against his chest as he was thrust, stumbling, down the passage and into the lounge. Jane uttered a brief scream of alarm as she saw the darkly clad figure pointing a handgun at Mike's chest. The assailant, dressed in dark navy blue trousers and bomber jacket wore a baseball cap and a full-face plastic mask. "Get back!" His voice snapped. Mike complied until the back of his legs contacted the settee. Before Michael Morley had time to think a second darkly clad figure appeared and remained blocking the doorway. Two torch lights flashed around the room and a confused silence followed. It seemed it was an unplanned event for intruders and intruded alike.

"Lie down!" The first man spoke again, stepping away and jabbing towards the floor with his pistol. Michael remained standing and turned to his wife. "Move away from me." His wife obeyed and began to shuffle along the settee.

"Wait!" The man yelled, "I said get down on the floor!" He jabbed his gun again and moved towards Jane.

"Don't shoot; please don't shoot!" Jane screamed. Mike quickly moved in front of her, blocking the gunman. The weapon was now within Mike's long reach. The man saw the adrenaline light up in Mike's eyes and hastily retreated two steps. "'Cuff him!" He ordered his colleague. The second man unzipped his bomber jacket retrieving a set of auto cuffs from his belt.

"I'm not going to let you put those things on me." Mike was defiant. "I'd be helpless and you could do what ever you wanted."

"If I put a bullet in you you'll be pretty helpless!" The reply was terse. Mike noted the trace of an Eastern European accent.

He stood squarely facing the gunman. "Who are you and what do you want?"

"Shut up!" The man waved his accomplice forward with his weapon: "Cuff him, I said!"

Mike persisted: "You can't break into people's houses and expect to receive co-operation. What do you want?"

"You know what I want! I want the Panther!"

"Panther? You'll need a zoo or menagerie for Panthers."

"Don't try to be clever with me, Morley. You know exactly what I mean."

"How would I have come by such an animal?"

"You got it from Henderson. He hasn't got it anymore, so you must have it!"

"Henderson?"

"Cut all this crap, Morley, I'm in the mood to kill you right now."

"That's not going to help you."

"It will make me feel a whole lot better." He jabbed his gun at his companion, "Get on with it and 'cuff him, I said."

"Don't even think about!" Mike threatened the second man.

"Just hand it over and that will be an end to it." The second man said weakly.

"Or us more likely."

"For Christ's sake; bloody 'cuff him!" The gunman roared at the second man.

The man moved cautiously towards Mike intending to pass behind him and apply the handcuffs. Michael turned his back towards him as if being helpful. The nearer the man came the more Michael Morley turned until he'd forced the second man to pass between him and the gun. Just as the gunman realised the mistake, Mike spun round clamping the second man's arms to his body. Using years of gym induced upper muscle he lifted the man off the ground and thrust him into the gunman.

The gunman staggered, but remained standing. The gun arm was briefly deflected. Mike seized the extended wrist and twisted his own body under it thrusting the arm up behind the gunman's back pushing him face downwards towards the floor. Locked together they fell, landing heavily. The shock discharged the gun sending a bullet into the gunman's neck and skull, blowing off the back of his head.

Michael was conscious of a hot sticky substance on his face. Thinking he had been injured, Jane screamed and ran to her partner. The gunman's torch now lay on the floor illuminating the second man who was struggling to his feet. The man reached his right hand across to his left hip. He was going for a gun!

Everything ground to slow motion. Mike released the dead man's grip on his firearm; pushed Jane away; and after what seemed an endless turn; instinctively fired three rounds at the second man. Fear and adrenaline drove him, there had been no time for right or wrong – the threat had to be eliminated.

The first round hit the man in the hip. He spun dropping his gun as the other two bullets smashed into the wall. Despite his injury the man managed to roll back up to a standing position. He turned and rushed limping from the room. "I'll be back for you Morley! You'll pay for this!"

Michael Morley allowed the gun to fall and stood motionless. Jane screamed: "What have you done? What have you done? You've killed him, for Christ's sake!" She began a cycle of hysterics: beating her fists on the wall; flapping away imaginary flying objects, shouting abuse: "This isn't happening! Tell me this isn't real!" Mike caught Jane mid flight and embraced her tightly in his arms: "Stop! Stop! It will be all right. They made some sort of mistake."

"They made a mistake?" She struggled to free herself, "they made a mistake! What the hell did you make, then? You said that if we had the Panther and were threatened we would be able to hand it over." Jane went limp in his arms. He guided her to the settee where she slumped, eyes closed.

Michael Morley's army medical training kicked in. He quickly examined the wound to the man's head. He had often seen that type of injury in Iraq. They were usually caused by a sniper's high velocity round passing right through the skull and the air filling its vacuum blowing out the brains. Such wounds proved fatal. He looked down at the gunman. The man's body exhibited a few twitches. Michael felt the side of the man's neck. There was a faint pulse. He rushed to the under stairs cupboard and retrieved his medical bag. He knelt down beside the man. What was he going to do? Part of the man's skull had been blown with hair and flesh still attached against the adjacent wall. The rear of the brain had disintegrated. He had to phone for assistance and face the consequences. It was the only moral option, even though this man had been prepared to kill him. He checked again for vital signs. The body was no longer twitching; there was no sign of breathing and no longer a detectable pulse. He had never known anyone with such an injury to survive. He now had to balance the risks and morals. This man was dead. It could be argued that with full medical assistance it might be remotely possible to save him. Was it for him to make that judgement? He reflected on his experience in war and how such evaluations under fire had different criteria. What standard should he apply to a man that was so clearly in his judgement beyond revival? The man was dead; he had to think about his and Jane's continued safety.

A sense of urgency grew. "What had he done? How could he explain away something like this?"

Jane recovered and began to cry, her body trembling: "Why did they come to us – these monsters - bastards?" Michael moved to comfort his partner. "They wanted their Panther back. They must be desperate to have it." He held her hands between his. "Whatever happens now, I know that I'm in big trouble; others will come."

"Who?" Jane feared more attacks.

"The police; they will be here soon."

"What can we do? We are innocent!" She began to become hysterical again. Michael's attempts to reassure and comfort Jane had more of a cathartic affect on himself and he began to clarify a strategy: He needed time: more than he could expect right now. Michael headed for the kitchen. He used cold water to wash away the warm residues of the gunman. Returning to the study, he retrieved their passports and the cash they kept for day to day business expenses. "It will be impossible for me to explain what happened. I need time to think – get to a solicitor. I can't defend myself from a prison cell."

His partner panicked. "You can't just run away. You are innocent, we are both innocent. We must explain…"

"They will not believe us and they hold all the cards. They will just call me a terrorist and isolate me from anyone who might be able to help." He grasped Jane by the shoulders: "You heard what the other gunman threatened. This gang will come back for us. Our lives will always be in danger. They could hold you as a hostage. We must get out of here together and find somewhere safe."

Jane was in no state to accept the need to run. She was flustered and confused; things were happening too quickly. Mike sat beside her and put a reassuring arm around her. "Jane, you must realise that we can not stay here. The police will come and that might be the last you see of me for a long time and I would be unable to protect you. These men will return and that might prove worse for both of us."

Jane nodded unconvincingly. "Where will we go?"

"I could go to my aunt's holiday cottage on the Island. She hardly uses it these days."

"So we are going to do that now?"

"No. I will go alone. We need to avoid detection. Two of us will be easier to spot; we must separate."

"Separate? I can't do that." Jane sobbed.

"Only for a while; just long enough for me to sort out what needs to be done."

"Where will I go, then?"

"You must take enough money to stay at the George. Using a credit card would be detected." Set deep in the forest, the George Hotel would provide isolation. He thought about publicity and her name. "You must use your maiden name." He decided.

"What, Brown?" Jane had been divorced from James Fisher the year she started to work for John Henderson.

"Why?"

"...because the name will not be given out on radio or television bulletins."

"Oh, no; I can't do that – it's terrible to even think about it!"

"Listen, Jane, if we are to get through this you must do it. You told me you still have an old building society book in the name of Brown. That would prove useful if the financial sector hasn't got around to reconciling the change."

"So, I must go to the George and register as Miss Brown?" Jane tested the words to see how felt.

"Yes."

"How will I get there?" She was going to prove a very reluctant fugitive.

"That will depend." He went to the window and eased the curtains to peer out. The rain was falling in torrents and the wind was pounding on every exposed surface. He checked windows opposite for signs of life. There were only a few lights. It was possible that no-one had heard the shots or thought anything of them, given the weather. A plan began to finalise.

"You must take your bicycle early tomorrow and ride to Brockenhurst."

"Why?"

"...so that you can take an early train to Sway. You can go the back way on your bike and avoid any cameras. The police will check all the local cctvs, but there aren't any across the forest. It will be some time before they realise and broaden their search."

"That's a lot of trouble to go to. What should I do about the bike?"

"Leave it away from the station; hide it if you can." Michael Morley wanted to make sure that it wasn't possible to link a woman seen leaving Winchester on a bicycle with a train journey to Sway.

"It's so much trouble, Mike." Jane still doubted the point of such deception.

"I know, but it will guarantee that neither the police nor thugs will find you. As soon as you can, buy a pay-as-you-go mobile and ring me on the number I will give you; it's the cottage number."

"They will trace that."

"No they won't, because some time after my father's brother died, my aunt took up with a boat builder on the Isle of Wight. They never married, but kept the house just outside Winchester and used his old cottage on the Island as a holiday retreat. He only died recently and my aunt has left everything as it was. I don't think there has been a reading of any will yet; if there ever was one. He had no immediate family. I'm betting everything is in his name still. Our names will not be linked on databases when anyone carries out a search. When you phone I will give you the number of a pay-as-you-go mobile that I will have bought by then. After that we will be home and dry."

"Mike! I can't believe we are thinking of such things!" Jane remained pale.

"Why can't I come with you? What will you do?"

"I'm going to yomp across country to avoid detection; you wouldn't be able to keep up. Besides, I need you on the mainland in case I need to contact someone. You would have the only secure phone. I'm going to follow a devious route on foot to Beaulieu. I can risk an out-of-county bus to cover the middle part of my journey; any cctv record will not help my pursuers. Then I will take our kayak to Gurnard on the Island; hide it if I can; and walk the coastal path, or the diagonal footpaths towards Ventnor."

"What about money?

"I won't need much; I'll just take a hundred or so. I'm sure there will be tins of something at the cottage and I can buy what else I need in small shops away from the village."

"This is dreadful. Can't we just phone the police?"

"No. I must get help first. Solving the mystery of the Panther would be the best thing I could achieve."

"Are we to leave now?"

"We may have a little time to prepare. I think this bad weather is helping. We must keep a careful watch, but I think we may have until the early morning at least."

"I can't stay in here with that!" Jane had just caught sight of the gunman lying on the floor. She ran to the door and vomited into the passage. Mike guided her into the dining room opposite and brought her water and a clean towel. "You rest here and I will pack the things we need for the morning. We must be away early."

"I will keep watch from this window; I'm not going back in there." She sobbed quietly.

CHAPTER EIGHT

John Henderson sat uneasily on the plastic chair. His face displayed a mixture of concern and anger as he drummed his fingers on the table. He glanced at his solicitor sitting beside him who was busy scribbling on the untidy pages of a thick pad. The diminutive writer had curled himself into a foetal position, bald head down; the wire framed spectacles balancing on the end of his nose completing a Dickensian posture.

Across the room a uniformed police constable stood at a loose attention near a recently painted blue door. The acrid smell of industrial paint was still evident.

The door opened and three plain clothed police officers entered. The first officer, wearing a baseball cap, nodded to the constable who left, closing the door. The officer positioned himself behind the empty plastic chair opposite John Henderson. He rested his hands on the back of the chair. "Good morning, gentlemen, I'm Detective Inspector Kevin James and this is my colleague, Detective Sergeant Derek Forest and this Inspector Groves of the Metropolitan police." He indicated that the Sergeant should be seated opposite the solicitor. Inspector Groves selected a chair at the head of the table

The D.I. removed his baseball cap and spun it onto the table. "I'd like to thank you for your prompt response to my request. I'd like to make it clear that this is just an informal interview for the moment. However, the reason I suggested that Mr. Henderson should invite legal representation was the potential for this to become a serious matter." He pulled the chair away from the table preparing to be seated; "Mr. Henderson I know, but I…"

"…Abram Leitz, solicitor for Bates and Bates, acting for Mr. Henderson." The solicitor partially unfurled himself and shook the Inspector's hand. "May I ask why you believe that this informal interview might develop into something more serious?"

"Not at present, Mr. Leitz; to reveal that now would prejudice the course of the interview. However, I'm sure that all will become evident."

"Is the seriousness of which you spoke associated with the Metropolitan officer?"

"Inspector Groves is at this informal meeting as an observer and is here at my invitation."

The solicitor remained silent and made a few notes on his pad.

The Inspector addressed John Henderson directly. "Thank you for agreeing to this interview, Mr. Henderson. I acknowledge that you've recently been involved in a motoring incident and also have suffered a disturbing burglary. If at any time you feel unable to continue, I am prepared to delay the interview if at all possible."

The solicitor raised his eyebrows at the comment. "May I clarify the basis of this meeting once more?" Abram Leitz turned a page on his pad and appeared to be reading from it. "It is my understanding that Mr. Henderson had not been arrested; that he is providing assistance voluntarily and that he may leave at any time. Do you agree?"

Both officers were puzzled by this approach. D.I. James turned to his Sergeant.

The sergeant answered with a trace of annoyance "Yes, your client is here under the conditions you have just stated."

"And the process will not be taped?"

"You know it will not."

The solicitor glanced briefly at the Met Inspector; "I'm sorry to insist, but I must be clear about the conditions."

Inspector James interjected. "I caution your client again that should I subsequently discover grounds for it, I will not hesitate to arrest him. May we now proceed?"

The solicitor again made notes without comment.

"John Henderson, three days ago, you were involved in a traffic incident. One in which you received injuries that necessitated you being detained in hospital. Would you like to tell me about the circumstances leading to that incident?" The Inspector leaned back expectantly.

"I'm not sure. I remember being followed – they would not overtake..."

The Inspector interrupted. "I'm sorry to stop you, Mr. Henderson, but could you take me back to the beginning of that day? Where had you been?"

"To London." John Henderson looked at his solicitor who glanced once more at the Met Inspector before nodding.

"You were on a business trip?"

"Yes."

"To see whom and for what purpose?"

"I'm not sure it's important for you to know, but I went to do business with Peter Langdon, a dealer in antiques. A man I often see."

"It may become important to me later. Can you tell me the precise nature of the business?"

"No, it's complicated…"

John's solicitor touched his arm and spoke quietly in his ear.

"I'd prefer not to go into details at this time." John Henderson spoke confidently.

"I may bring you back to that later. However, for the moment you were driving back from London when something happened?"

"Yes, after I'd reached Winchester. I noticed the vehicle behind."

"Had you done anything you're aware of to antagonise the driver?"

"No! Nothing, he just appeared and stayed behind following my every move."

"You said earlier that he would not overtake; can you elaborate how it was they would not over take?"

John Henderson was slowly drawn question by question through the events of that day. He described how he had made several turns in a series of futile attempts to either permit the other car to pass or to avoid it altogether by taking an alternative route. The Inspector's patient approach established that his interviewee thought it had been a silver Mercedes that had pursued him that day. After the initial round of questions, the D.I. asked his Sergeant if he would like to clarify anything.

"During all this zigzagging were you aware of other traffic?" Sergeant Forest was more direct than his Inspector.

"Other traffic? In what way?"

"Other road users. Did you notice if there were other road users whilst you were ducking and diving in your car?"

The solicitor sighed and added notes to his sheet.

"There were others on the road, yes."

"And did you feel free to overtake when it might have suited you, but not necessarily been helpful others?"

Abram Leitz raised his hand. "I think this is becoming bullying."

"Mr. Leitz, your client is perfectly entitled to answer no when asked these questions. Sergeant Forest is simply trying to clarify what Mr. Henderson remembers of his journey." The Inspector defended the Sergeant's more robust approach.

"Were you in a hurry?" The Sergeant continued without hesitation.

"No, certainly not."

"Racing, perhaps? You were late getting home and decided to hurry things along a little bit?"

"No, I protest. I was being followed."

"…by a silver Mercedes that's not been seen since?"

"But, surely there were witnesses?" John Henderson was not happy about accusations of bad driving, or fabrication.

Kevin James signalled that he wanted to take up this new area of questioning.

"Witnesses? Yes, Mr. Henderson. What would your reaction be if I said some witnesses say you were driving like a madman?"

"A madman? No! I was being chased by the Mercedes!"

"Did you at any time consider pulling over and stopping?"

"I did briefly, but I could tell from the behaviour of the driver that I could have suffered serious harm as a result."

"How did the driver telegraph this potential harm to you?"

John Henderson was embarrassed as he realised he had embarked on the impossible. "It was the position and the way he followed."

"Interesting; but some might question just how precise such an observation could be."

"I know, but at the time it was the constant harrying."

"Do you remember overtaking and hitting some vehicles?"

John Henderson's memory had recovered to the point where he could recall hitting some cars. He thought it best if he continued to deny its return for a bit longer. "I'm not sure."

"Really? I have to tell you that there was extensive damage to one vehicle, a fuel tanker, which could have had serious consequences. Can you recall that?"

Abram Leitz touched John's arm and shook his head.

"No!" John Henderson replied accepting his solicitor's advice.

Detective Inspector Kevin James turned his attention to Abram Leitz.

"You should be aware that I am not satisfied with your client's answers and that I will require him to return for further interview in the near future. I should warn you that there is a strong possibility he will be charged with serious motoring offences."

The solicitor nodded; made a final note; and began to rise.

"There's something else we need to talk about before your client leaves; a much more serious matter." With one finger the Inspector twirled his cap on the table.

The solicitor glanced quizzically at his client who shrugged in response. The solicitor re-seated himself. "This has the feel of something irregular, Inspector." He looked at the Met Inspector and wondered about any connection with his client's visit to London.

"No! I assure you, Mr. Leitz. It is quite in order." The Inspector brushed imaginary dust from his cap before returning it to the table.

"John, you said it was after you visited Peter Langdon at his premises in London that you ran into trouble on the road?" The D.I. spoke slowly and deliberately.

Abram Leitz had picked up the cunning nuance hiding behind the familiar address. "My client may have said many things, Inspector James, but he did not mention that he met Mr. Langdon on the man's premises that day."

Inspector James looked at his London colleague before continuing. "I'm sorry; did he not? Well, John, perhaps you could clarify that now. Where did you meet Mr. Langdon?"

John Henderson was once again embarrassed. His own solicitor was making it appear that he was being devious. "I saw Peter Langdon at his shop, but I can't understand what difference it makes where I saw him?"

"all the difference in the world." Unable to restrain himself, the Sergeant interrupted his Inspector. The Inspector signalled that the Sergeant should continue.

"How well did you know Langdon?"

"Not that well. We did business occasionally."

"You knew him so well that you had a kind of credit arrangement with him!" The Sergeant revealed the depth of his research.

"Nonsense!" Henderson cried.

The solicitor began whispering to his client.

"Mr. Leitz, you are not helping Mr. Henderson at present." Derek Forest was becoming annoyed.

"I and Mr. Henderson will decide that!" He snapped.

"No, Mr. Leitz. I and the Inspector have to decide at which point this casual conversation ends and an arrest begins. Mr. Henderson should assist us in our enquiry, so that our minds can be put at rest about his involvement in murder."

"Murder?" John Henderson had gone pale. He appealed to the Met officer. "Whose murder? I know nothing of any murder!"

The Metropolitan Police officer remained passive.

Abram Leitz, unfazed by the revelation, spoke without looking up. "My client is an innocent man who has consented to come here and help your enquiry. He is due the respect owing to a man who has devoted part of his very precious time to public service."

The Inspector placed a restraining hand on Derek Forest and substituted the Sergeant's fire with a softly intoned question. "John, do you have any knowledge of the incident in which the antique dealer, Peter Langdon, was murdered on the day you visited him?"

"The day I visited him? I have no knowledge about that at all; none what-so-ever; that is shocking news!" Henderson began shaking.

The Inspector continued in the same level tone. "Do you know of, or suspect, any reason why he might have been killed?"

John Henderson looked towards his solicitor. Leitz gave a reluctant nod.

"None what-so-ever." Henderson repeated.

"Explain to me the nature of this loan arrangement you had with him?"

John Henderson was keen to explain the arrangement by which goods were swapped after an equivalent value calculation had been made. The Sergeant and the Inspector listened and questioned until they had a full understanding of the unusual business method.

"As a result of this trading method he owed you money, didn't he?" The Sergeant rushed back to interrogation.

"Some, yes."

"I think he owed you a lot; that you needed that money; and he could not afford to pay. Isn't that true?"

"Yes." John Henderson was fed up with having to appear devious and ignored his solicitor's impassioned flapping.

"So you argued and during heated exchanges you killed him?" The Sergeant pressed the point.

"He was alive when I left him."

"How could you walk away? He still owed you money."

"No, we….." John hesitated. He was going to mention the Panther, but that might involve Michael and put him and Jane at risk. He decided not to continue.

"No, we what?" The Sergeant persisted.

"No, we agreed that he would pay after he had sold what he had in the shop."

"But you couldn't wait that long; he'd let you down; and so you killed him!"

"No! No! I was annoyed with him, yes, but in the end he agreed to let me take some of his stock so that I could sell it."

"But wasn't that your normal arrangement? That wasn't going to work this time was it? You needed cash in a hurry and so you killed him in anger and took what you could find in the shop. Isn't that true?"

"No! No! No!"

Abram Leitz held up a restraining palm. "My client has given you a clear answer, you must let that rest."

The Inspector sensed his Sergeant rising in his seat to meet the challenge to his authority. He touched Derek Forest's arm and shook his head. The Sergeant paused for some time before yielding to his superior's request and resuming his seat.

Detective Inspector James addressed the solicitor directly. "Mr. Leitz, bearing in mind the nature of this interview, I have permitted you more freedom than I might normally allow. My Sergeant and I must be able to test Mr. Henderson's account of what happened that day. Serious charges could follow." He looked at his Met colleague and raised an expectant eye brow. The Metropolitan officer indicated that he did not want to question the witness.

"Are you charging my client?"

"Not at present; I need to ask more questions to help me be clear about Mr. Henderson's involvement." The D.I. turned to look at John Henderson's face.

"John, you have a lot of damage to your face."

"You must know it resulted from the accident." John realised how incriminating it appeared.

"Yes clearly; but there's also some bruising around your eyes and along one cheek; did Peter Langdon cause those?"

"He may have done. We did scuffle a bit."

"Just before you killed him?" The Sergeant was quick to capitalise on a confession.

"No, I've told you he was alive when I left. He even helped me load the car."

"Witnesses! Were there any witnesses to this?" The Sergeant felt on top of his game.

"No! I don't know. How should I know?" Henderson was confused by the speed of the questions.

The Inspector tried to help him; "John I assume you were at the shop for some time. How long would you estimate?"

"Oh, over an hour, I suppose, maybe as long as two."

"Was the shop open during the time you were there; and, if so, did anyone come into the shop during that period?"

"Yes, it was open, but there was only Peter and I."

"That's incredible! Are you telling…" Sergeant Forest targeted what he saw as a weakness.

"…no, wait!" John Henderson had remembered. "There was a man. He left his plastic bag on the floor!"

"Can you describe him?"

"No, but the bag was yellow."

The D.I. made a note to check that piece of information.

"So, we have to believe that a man you can't describe came into the shop; left a yellow bag; and went away again; is that it?" The Sergeant was developing a marked dislike for John Henderson.

"Yes, that's all I can say."

Inspector James sought clarification. "How long did this man stay and did he buy anything?"

"No."

"No; what?"

"He just came in and ran out dropping his bag."

"Because of what he saw?" The D.I. asked very quietly.

"Yes. He saw us struggling."

Sergeant Forest was keen to press an advantage, but his superior was beginning to understand John Henderson and wanted to expand his knowledge. "John, witnesses arriving after the incident in which you were injured say that there were men rummaging through the things in your car. Presumably, the things you were bringing from Peter Langdon's shop. Can you explain why they might be doing that?" He waved away what he thought was a likely objection from Abram Leitz.

"I don't know. I wasn't aware of what they were doing."

"I know and I wasn't asking if you saw; only if you knew why."

"I have no idea at all." He shook his head.

"Are you keeping something from me; afraid of someone; or protecting somebody?"

"I'm afraid those who attacked me might do it again, or even harm my wife."

"Has anyone you suspect of attacking you contacted or threatened you?"

"No."

"Apart from your wife, are you protecting anyone else; someone who might have been with you on that day or who helped you afterwards?"

"No, no-one." John Henderson replied softly.

The Sergeant turned to his superior expecting him to arrest John Henderson. On the evidence they had heard he felt there was sufficient justification. In stead D.I. Kevin James asked the London Inspector if he was content with the interview. The officer confirmed he had heard all he needed and stood to address the meeting. "Thanks for giving me this opportunity, Kevin, I think I have heard all I need to for the present." He faced John Henderson; "Mr. Henderson I believe you have been involved in something that is linked both to the death of Peter Langdon and to your own motoring incident. At present I'm unsure if you took part willingly or as an innocent man. When I have more evidence it may be necessary to interview you formally in London. However for the moment I am content to leave the investigation to continue here." He turned to Kevin James; "Thank you Inspector James; I think you have it under control here, but we need to keep each other updated daily."

Inspector James thanked Henderson and his solicitor for their co-operation adding that they should note the comments already made adding that John Henderson should inform him if he remembered anything he had not already confirmed.

As they left the interview room Sergeant Forest could not contain his criticism. "We had him bang to rights, sir, why didn't you arrest him?"

"I understand your enthusiasm, Sergeant, but he is simply not guilty of murder."

"I can't believe it. He has as good as admitted it! And that little wizen bastard got up my nose!"

"Sergeant! I will pretend I did not hear you insulting a solicitor who was only doing his duty."

The Inspector held Forest back. "Look, Derek, I appreciate your solid passion for bringing criminals to book, but that man is not guilty of murder."

"I disagree he's not only guilty but pretty much said so himself!"

"Derek. You are wrong…pretty good is not enough to convict a man; we need evidence. I believe he is guilty of something and I mean to find out what, but he is not guilty of murder."

CHAPTER NINE

Michael Morley raced along the riverside path. He'd made better time than anticipated. The wind of the previous night had abated and the sky was clearing for a fine day. Checking no-one else was about; he turned down a short track leading to a shrub cover edge. Michael scrambled down one side of some dense bushes. The kayak was still there, hidden beneath a green cover he'd bought when he first decided to berth his and Jane's tandem craft.

Michael slipped off the cover and checked the orange and red boat's condition. It was dry and undamaged just as it had been when stowed two weeks earlier. Opening the forward hatch, Michael retrieved his buoyancy aid, but ignored his wet suit. He was in too much of a hurry. The craft was a 16 feet tandem sea kayak that he and Jane used for relaxation. They looked forward to time off when they could spend a pleasant day paddling down the Beaulieu River. Once out in the Solent, they would seek a sea shore idyll where they could beach the kayak and picnic, or just laze in the sunshine until tide, time or weather forced them to return.
    Today, the kayak was going to aid his escape to the Isle of Wight. He had considered using the Wight Link ferry from Lymington, but there would be cctv cameras. He did not want to leave any traceable record.

Earlier that morning, Michael ensured that Jane Fisher had everything she needed to get to the George Hotel. She had remained distraught most of the night fearing the return of the gang. She had great reservations about Mike's current plan, but had reluctantly agreed to follow his instructions. Michael was not concerned about the gang; believing they would not come back that day for fear of police activity. He was more concerned about the police, themselves, who would pursue him as a killer.

Equipped with what he needed, including the Panther, Michael had set out for a lengthy stay on the Island. He followed a longer, cautious, route. He had taken two short bus journeys after walking a few miles from

Winchester. In that way, it would take hours of studying any bus cctvs before it would be possible to join all the journeys. He hoped that tracking his route would prove too onerous for the police. Where he was able, he yomped across country, but limited how much he did for fear of attracting attention.

On occasions, he had walked alongside busy roads, but only those where there weren't any shops. They might have their own cameras. Then he had crossed and re-crossed roads so that tracker dogs would not be able to follow him. It was much more effective and drier mixing his smell with traffic fumes than walking through streams.

Once he had reached Beaulieu it had only required a walk of a mile or so along the riverside path towards Bucklers Hard to reach the hiding place where he stored the kayak. He held an annual launching permit and had no need for such subterfuge. It was just a more convenient place than the official slipway.

Today he was lucky. The tide and calm weather would permit a daytime crossing. If conditions had required waiting until evening, his crossing might have drawn attention. The Solent Coastguard radar or infra-red would have focussed on him as a possible craft in distress. During his daytime crossing he would blend in with local inshore yachts and other craft.

Michael strapped on the buoyancy aid; folded his clothing; and placed it in the forward hatch resealing its cover.

He considered the empty front cockpit. Jane's weight normally provided the forward trim. She might not be very heavy, but her absence could change everything. The kayak had a good rocker from stem to stern. This curve under the water made steering it livelier than normal for a long boat.

Michael thought a large rock might provide an adequate substitute, but rocks were not common at that point. It took more than ten minutes to locate and place a large wet rock in front of Jane's seat. He secured it hard against the forward bulkhead to maximise its effect. In uncertain conditions the sea might be more likely to enter the open front cockpit. He quickly applied the elasticated front spray deck and sealed the gap where Jane's body would reside by pulling the draw strings tightly together. It was the best he could achieve. If the boat shipped water it could exacerbate the trim.

He moved the bailing pump into the rear cockpit as a precaution. With any reduction of the forward weight the bow would rise. This would make the kayak a bit skittish and with the rudder sitting deeper in the water, a bit too responsive.

The kayak with its improvised trim was now ready. It would take Michael Morley about an hour to reach the Solent; just in time for the first high tide. He would then have a slack water of around two hours before the Solent's second high tide; a beneficial freak of having the Isle of Wight as a neighbour.

A casual diagonal course towards Gurnard on the Island should prove fine. He was quietly confident. It was a journey he and Jane had made many times and today conditions were at their best. He slid the bow into the water and pushed it out until his cockpit was in line with the waters edge. Michael climbed in and sealed his rear spray deck. As he pushed off he heard what he feared most; the sound of approaching sirens. Was it the Police or an ambulance? How could anyone have found him so easily? He waited. He gauged their direction and possible destination from his knowledge of the local roads and the volume of the sirens. They were heading towards Lymington or Bucklers Hard. The sound seemed to hover for ages before waning. In doubt, but with few alternatives, Michael headed for the open Solent.

The trim was not excellent, but better than he had feared. The first thing he noticed was the lack of power with only one person paddling. His previous calculations would need amendment. Michael settled down to a steady rate and tried to affect a casual relaxed style that would detract from the observation that there was only one person in a tandem kayak.

Jane and he did not use the river more than once or twice a month so the chances of recognition were acceptably low. The main problem for Michael would be passing the Harbour Master's cabin at Bucklers Hard. There were fewer boats on the river at this time of year. It would be easy to spot a kayak for which a permit had not been issued that day and, more suspiciously, one that had not launched from the only permissible slipway nearby.

The kayak turned into the last broad bend before reaching the main moorings. Michael could see the flag above the Harbour Master's cabin hanging limply; a clear sign of fine weather. He plunged the paddle blades in more deeply and lengthened his stroke. He had to get passed this exposed position.

As the kayak hit the deeper water Michael felt the force of the main inward flow of the tide. Although it was almost high water, there was still a little counter energy left in it. Michael steered the boat down the far side of the moored yachts to delay detection. As he emerged into the clear again and started his final run passed the hard he heard the sirens again. He turned to observe the slipway. A few people were running towards the water's edge and he could see a Police car's blue flashing lights approaching down the main gravel road. He bent forward and pressed on. The kayak was soon a hundred yards beyond the slipway and detection. He wondered if they'd seen him. How could they have known he was coming!

A second sound soon joined the sirens. It was the engine of the Harbour Master's boat. It was approaching from behind. They were coming for him!

As the patrol boat pulled level with the kayak. Michael risked a glance. In stead of the multitude of policemen he anticipated, there was only one occupant. He looked again. The man was waving at him to stop. Michael was confused. He thought about the permit. Was this about him not having bought a permit that day? He had his annual permit in the rear hatch. He could show it, but it would destroy his anonymity. What had the police to do with permits anyway? He could not hear what the caller was saying, but he turned the kayak and headed back as directed by the man's extended arm.

As he approached the slipway, policemen came hurrying towards him. He had been caught! How was it possible after such careful planning? The policemen were shouting at him and pointing beyond him to the Harbour Master's boat. He turned and saw its skipper desperately waving him away from the slip. Even at this late stage could he beach the craft and make a run for it? Could he manage it? Running with his spray deck around his ankles would not look at all dignified and he would not be able to outrun so many police officers. He gave up such thoughts and surrendered.

He complied with the shouted directions and steered to one side of the slipway. Another police car and ambulance were racing down the road with lights and sirens operating. Two policemen had got out of the first vehicle and were heading directly for him. All hope of escape was completely lost. The two police officers reached the edge of the water and reached forward. They grabbed the bow of his kayak and began to pull it ashore. They tugged so vigorously that it came clear of the water onto the stony shore before Michael had time to raise the rudder. Michael stood with his hastily disconnected spray deck hanging limply from his waist wondering what would happen next; his arrest, perhaps? Why the ambulance?

The nearest officer spoke. "I'm sorry sir, but could you move to one side please? We don't want anyone to be injured." The police officer indicated the reversing ambulance. At that moment, Michael became aware of the heavy roar of a power boat's fast approach. Within seconds the boat arrived at the slipway and paramedics rushed forward. Almost immediately he saw the casualty of a boating accident being rushed into the back of the ambulance. In minutes all the vehicles had departed and Michael remained where he had been directed with his spray deck still dripping water onto his feet. He felt his knees weaken and he had to crouch down quickly.

CHAPTER TEN

Michael Morley arrived off Gurnard in good time. Turning his kayak parallel to the beach he slowly followed the coast about a hundred metres out. He hoped it would disguise his intended landing place. He passed the normal picnic spot he and Jane often used and thought about the happy days they had spent there. On this occasion, Michael would have to find somewhere with plenty of cover and minimum landward access. Discovery of the kayak might arouse suspicion and lead eventually to his discovery. In any case he would find the stored boat useful for his return.

After the distraction of the rapid planning and determination he had to employ getting away, he now had more time to think. He reflected how a single rash moment had jeopardised both his and Jane's futures. He tried to imagine how he could have reacted differently. Each alternative carried the certain outcome of harm to them both.

He needed to complete his escape and buy himself time to plan what he might do next. His nervous system was in turmoil. He had killed a man. The Police were at this very moment trying to put together his likely escape route. They would be seeking cctv footage; and questioning anyone who knew him. He was glad he had thought quickly enough to get Jane away from the house. He wondered if she had got to the hotel safely. He would buy a pay-as-you-go phone later as planned ready for when she contacted him. He wondered if the cottage still had a working phone.

He forced himself to stop time wasting thoughts. For the moment he had to concentrate on beaching the kayak.

After two passes he had identified an ideal spot. There was a beach that even at low water would only expose a narrow strip of shingle. Beyond, rose a steep gorse and broom covered slope, unbroken by any pathways. It rose fifty or more feet to a minor road far above. He headed for the beach on a long diagonal course to mask his intention.

Around the curve ahead were a couple of young people on the wider beach busy stone skipping pebbles across the water. They noticed his approach and diverted their aim to avoid any accidental contact. Blast! He could not land now. He immediately turned the kayak away from the beach and headed out into the Solent. Not wishing to take this deviation too far, he slowly changed direction until he was once again running parallel to the beach but away from the couple.

Michael idly paddled for a quarter of an hour before turning and heading back towards the site. The late autumn day was beginning to grow dark. He had to get ashore quickly to give himself enough light to get to Carisbrooke. Even as he thought, he realised it was a pious hope. He fixed his gaze on the curve of the coast looking for any sign of the people. On his final approach the beach was clear. He had to get in quickly before others came. Paddling flat out he drove the bow hard up the shingle. Quickly releasing his spray deck and springing out, he grasped the bow handles and pulled furiously until the kayak was halfway into the undergrowth. Taking up the stern handles he pushed the craft deep up into the gorse.

It was whilst opening the forward hatch to reclaim his dry clothes, he heard voices approaching. It was the previous couple. Although far into the undergrowth, the kayak's safety colours of bright orange and red were in evidence. They would spot it straight away! He abandoned his attempt to retrieve his clothes and sprawled himself across the stern with his back to the sea hoping his black buoyancy aid would help to camouflage him.

    The voices grew closer. If he was discovered now it would be too suspicious to pass without it being reported. He wished he could see where they were. It sounded as if they were immediately behind him. He dare not look! The shore was so narrow that he could hear their clothing chafing against the gorse bushes as they squeezed passed. For a moment, he thought he had successfully survived when one of them exclaimed. "Bloody hell, what's that?" Turning to greet the inevitable he found the young couple with their backs towards him staring at something in the water. The male stretched forward and pulled something from the sea. Mike quickly resumed his position. He could not hear what was said. There were some indistinct comments followed by laughter and then the voices faded. They had gone.

It was a race against time. He withdrew his dry clothes and a towel from the forward hatch and changed his shirt and pullover. He did not have time to be tidy and stuffed the buoyancy aid and wet clothes into the empty space.

He then removed kayak's green cover from the stern hatch and spread it; making sure he tucked all the edges under the hull. He added handfuls of gravel until he was confident the strongest of winds would not disturb it.

Michael Morley scrambled up the steep bank receiving cuts and scratches at each move. As he neared the top he paused to gather his bearings and check the area was clear. He could hear the sound of the occasional car as it passed on the road above. He knew there was a minor road that connected with the A3054. He needed to follow that when it was impossible to follow an adjacent footpath. Fortunately, the Isle of Wight was littered with good, well marked footpaths. He should be able to keep away from traffic, although the occasional dog walker might prove a hazard.

He waited at the edge of the road until it was clear then walked smartly across and headed for Carisbrooke. He was familiar with the island. He knew that if the whole journey proved impossible in the remaining time, he could exploit one of the many little narrow tree lined paths and hollows that surrounded the castle. He had brought two picnic packs that had been kept in the fridge at home. Each provided a sensible meal. Before he had reached the A3054 the daylight had deteriorated to the point where he was obliged to use his phone as a torch to read signs. Once he had crossed the main road he knew he would have to rest up near the castle. It was not his lack of fortitude that prevented him travelling further, it was the fear that he would startle somebody in the dark and that they might raise an alarm.

He exercised care as he approached the castle. There were still a few cars about and a few people returning from early evening walks. He tried to look inconspicuous as he lingered. He wanted to be certain that the evening activity had ceased. This proved easier in its planning than its execution. Several times he had to move away.

Eventually, he elected to move down one of the paths towards Blackwater. He forced his way off the path to a small hollow covered in closely growing trees. It seemed ideal, but he had not anticipated the folly of others. He had just set about flattening a small area when a dog walker in hot pursuit came crashing through from another path the other side of the thicket. The man gasped in surprise. Michael had been discovered! In a flash of inspiration on seeing the man's dog break through on to the path he shouted; "Buddy! Is that you! Come on boy!"

The shocked man grabbed his dog and fitted a lead to its collar.

"Oh; sorry!" Michael apologised. "I thought it was mine. Oh! A Border Collie, I can see now. Mine's a Labrador." He patted the man's dog before asking; "You haven't seen my dog by any chance?"

In the dark the man shook his head and muttered a limp "no."

"Mad coming out at night with a black Labrador, isn't it?" Michael laughed and moved passed the man calling; "Buddy! Buddy, com'on, boy!"

After that encounter he knew he had to make it all the way. Michael Morley shouldered his rucksack and set out for Niton.

CHAPTER ELEVEN

Michael Morley had to risk jogging along the road in places. The rucked footpaths in the dark were slowing progress. The larger ones had been impacted by thousands of feet. On these he could maintain a reasonable speed, but the less frequently used had unseen dips. In places the remains of old metal field posts protruded.

The Island suffered constant erosion and walkers needed to keep clear of the cliff edge. In wet weather whole sections could slip away. Blue slipper clay under the top soil was a particular problem. When the paths dried during the summer, great cracks could appear, indicating the possibility of dangerous overhangs. The boundaries of some fields and roads had constantly to be reviewed.

When using the road it was easy to spot an approaching car's headlights, but the traffic had remained light. By the time he reached Niton he'd only had to avoid two vehicles. On each occasion he had stepped behind the roadside bushes and remained undetected.

At Niton Michael Morley hoped to use the cliff paths, but was not able to until further on. When he reached Old Park he could at last complete his journey along the coastal path.

These paths he knew well and was aware of the more dangerous parts for a night time trekker. The cottage lay about half way along the coastal strip and he would arrive before midnight. The thought of a wash; cooked food; and a night's rest lifted his spirits. There was even the chance that he would discover some of his late honorary uncle's clothes. He set out with renewed purpose.

As he neared the cottage Michael Morley was channelled onto a diversionary path. It was taking him in a northerly direction. Determined to avoid being forced out onto the road he pushed his way through the shrubbery seeking a recognizable path; a difficult task in complete darkness. He had to negotiate gullies that had become completely overgrown with brambles and creeper until, suddenly, he emerged onto a familiar path. Even in the dark he knew exactly where he was.

His aunt rarely used the residence and never since the death of her partner. Now much older, she suffered mobility problems. It remained for a local friend to pop in occasionally and tidy or clean as required. Excess foliage was cut back twice a year, but no attempt at improvement was ever made. His aunt had threatened to sell the bungalow, but a lingering reminiscence had somehow intervened. As a result it was to remain a quiet idyll, hidden from the rest of the world. Right now it was exactly what Morley needed.

Morley stood at the gate and gazed up. It was just possible to make out the gable end against the eastern sky. For a moment he was transported to forgotten summers when he came there on holiday from college. He remembered the rocky cliffs and shore below with its quiet peace and the soothing sound of the waves. He began to wish he had brought Jane with him.

Suddenly, his pleasant recollections evaporated as he caught sight of a light flickering across the lawn. With his dark accustomed eyes it appeared as if the cottage was on fire. He prepared to force open the low gate, but stopped with his hand resting on the top rail. Using the remaining power of his mobile phone's battery, he shone the light on the gate. The foliage he expected to block his progress had already been disturbed; torn roughly away and strewn across the ground. He tested the gate. It moved freely. It was strange that his aunt's friend would have freed the gate and failed to tidy up afterwards.

He moved cautiously along the paved terrace that extended across the front of the property. Opposite the house and its terrace an unkempt grass lawn sloped downwards, allowing uninterrupted views of the sea. Behind the building, a tree covered slope rose steeply.

He advanced in a stream of mixed emotions: a guilty feeling that he shouldn't be there competing with growing paranoia.

Before he reached the cottage Michael could see that the flickering was light from one of the rooms rippling shadows across the terrace. This was alarming! He knew from the last conversation he'd had with his aunt a month earlier that she did not want to let it. He'd recommended that she did in order to secure some extra income, but she'd declined, saying it would be more trouble than it was worth.

His paranoia increased. He remembered that he was a man on the run. Had the police worked out his intentions already? How could the criminals know his about his aunt's hideaway? Had they intercepted Jane before she could get to the George? A cold sweat formed on his forehead and he felt a weakness in the knees. Jane had to be safe; or he'd failed her. His brain remained frozen. His planning hadn't allowed for this contingency. He took a few deep, breaths. Michael had to maintain control of his emotions. He had to advance with caution. It was too soon for anyone to know where he was. This was an extra mission.

Michael bent and carefully tilted the earthenware tub that was home to a short leafless bay tree. He slid his hand beneath. No key!

There was a tang of wood smoke in the air. The house was occupied; but by friend or foe? It was reasonable, given what he already knew about the maintenance of the property that local friends would not be inside over night. He knew his aunt's reluctance to let the property. This had to be enemy action.

He crouched and moved beneath the window. He peered in from one corner to minimise his exposure. There was a flickering yellow light coming from the fire place. He had to raise himself before he could see the crudely stacked fire of broken branches and fruit boxes. An arm extended and added more wood; an arm wearing an old brown long sleeved coat frayed at its wrist. How many were in the room? Mike risked discovery by moving to observe the whole room. He could only see one individual: a man of around fifty; scruffily dressed and surrounded on the carpeted floor by crumpled empty beer cans and dirty eating utensils. No animals.

Michael Morley tried the front door. It opened. He checked the garden to make sure the occupant did not have colleagues outside the cottage, before making his way silently along the familiar passage to the living room. He listened at the door. The only sounds he could detect were some strange groans and a noise like pub singing. No radio; no television. He moved smoothly passed the door and made his way to the kitchen. Its door was open and the light was on revealing a complete mess of used pots and pans and empty milk bottles. Michael Morley checked each of the remaining rooms until he was satisfied there was just the single occupant in the cottage.

Returning to the living room he braced himself for action and pushed at the half open door. It moved freely. He thrust the door fully open, rushed into the room and stood hands on hips confronting the man slumped awkwardly in the fireside chair. "Who the hell are you?" He shouted. The man struggled to his feet and mimicked Mike's posture.

"Who the hell are you?" The man mocked and retrieving a long branch from beside the fire swung it wildly. Mike blocked the swing; removed the wood from his grasp; and threw it into the grate.

"There's no need for that, my friend." He pushed the man in the chest sending him drunkenly back into the chair. "What's your name?"

The individual squinted for a moment then rolled his eyes before answering. "William Jonathon Parker." He slurred.

Morley leaned forward supporting himself on the arms the chair. "And how long have you been here, William Jonathon Parker?"

"Two...two... twww."

"Two days? Two weeks?"

"Weee..eeks." Parker hiccupped.

Michael guessed it was futile to ask why and considered the more important questions. "How have you been feeding yourself? Have you been into town, or to the local shop?" He knew the nearest town was Ventnor, but Mr. William Parker might have found the local shop. It was important to know how many people might know this man was a squatter in the cottage. There was a danger that if he threw the man out, he would be a loose canon. The man would almost certainly betray him, inadvertently or otherwise. The old anecdote about enemies, tents and pissing came to mind. Morley would have to keep William Parker right where he could see him pissing.

"Shoooop;" was the late reply.

"Right, you have bought food at the local shop; does anyone know you are here?"

Parker stiffened. He may be the worse for wear, but his life style had forged him quickly into a street wise expert. He understood the immediate risk of phrases like, "does anyone know you are here?"

"I 'ave to go, must be gettin' alooong." He began to struggle to his feet pushing Michael aside.

"Woooah, old son." Michael restrained Parker as the man started to flail the air. "Wait, Bill Parker, you are not in any danger. I am not going to hurt you."

Parker stopped his assault and looked directly at his captor. "Why shooould you be dif...rent?"

"Because not everyone is the same and I might like you to stay and help me."

"You're on the ruuuun, like me! You wanna take over my squat!" Parker was quick thinking in emergencies.

"No, I am not." Morley replied unconvincingly.

"You are to me matey!"

"No, I do not want your squat, because unlike you I have a right to be here." He took Parker by the shoulders and pressed him back into the chair. "I will make a deal with you, Bill Parker."

"William Jonathon Parker, I'm no Bill." Parker corrected him.

"Alright, William Jonathon Parker; if you sober up and help me tidy up this mess, I will let you stay here a bit longer."

Parker in his drunken stupor weighed the odds. "Hoo..oow much longer?"

"I don't know; and can't make any long term promises, but let's say for a few weeks at least."

"Weee..eeks?" he hiccupped again.

"Yes, but only if you help keep the place clean and tidy."

"Will I gee..eet paid?" Parker still harboured a suspicion that all was not what it seemed and that there might be money to be made.

"How do you get paid now - Social Services? What do you tell them?"

"Paid?"

"Okay, let's skip that for now. You must not tell anyone we are here, do you understand?"

"Oooohhh! I understan's 'bout right, matey."

"Never mind that - I will feed you and look after you – clothes, for example."

"Right....that sounds...oooo...ookay." William Jonathon Parker had fallen asleep.

Michael Morley's first task was to hide the Panther where it would be safe. There was still unfinished work to do and it held both the secret of and the solution to his current troubles. He retrieved the carved animal from his rucksack and left the cottage to explore the wood store at the rear.

He found a new addition to the shed. It had a new side bin. He opened it. It was half full of coal. Using a small hand shovel he found inside he made a hole at the rear of the pile. He was about to place the Panther in the cavity when he stopped. If that had been the first thing he'd thought of....? Too obvious! He rummaged around behind the shed and found a better place deep in the shrubbery and its undergrowth. Having stuffed a dustbin bag with the animal he placed the Panther well into the cover, he made his way back to the warmth of the cottage.

As the effect of adrenaline began to wear off, Michael Morley was overcome with weariness. He had been on the go continuously since sunrise. He wondered if he there would be hot water for a bath or shower. He looked his new companion slumped in the fireside chair and noticed for the first time that the man was clean shaven. After two weeks? Morley went straight to the bathroom. There were a few items of clothing piled in one corner, but otherwise the bath was clean and the room tidy. He turned the hot tap. After a short wait there was hot water. He looked at his weathered face in the mirror; could he hold out long enough to have a bath and a shave? As he pondered his attention was drawn to the mirror shelf. There standing in a clean mug stood a razor together with a toothbrush and tube of tooth paste. Who was this strange occupant of the cottage?

CHAPTER TWELVE

Detective Sergeant Derek Forest stifled a yawn as he smoothed the A2 sheet on the wall. "Shall I begin?"

"Yes, the others will have to catch up when they arrive." Detective Inspector James caught his Sergeant's yawn and masked it with a hand.

It was an unexpected early shift; called because there had been a shooting in Winchester during the early hours of that morning. "What have we got?" The Inspector blinked.

"A witness reported hearing gun shots last night."

"Time?"

The Sergeant looked at his watch. "Hours ago. It's seven now and the witness reported hearing shots at about eleven last evening!"

"When did he report it?" The Inspector remained calm.

"Six o'clock this morning. He says he wasn't sure and waited until he got up to go to work."

"When did we get there?"

"At six fifteen – entered the property; found a male victim shot at close range; and had secured the property by six forty."

"No other person found on the property?"

"No."

"Shot at close range? Where?"

"Shot in the back of the head. The guys on site said it looked liked a gangland assassination. Apparently, the gun was held so close it blew off the back of his head."

"Do we have a weapon?"

"Yes, I believe it's a Glock."

"A Glock? Hmmm; I take it we're looking at the weapon and the identification of the victim?"

"…yes sir; and for connections with previous crimes and possible associates."

"Keep on top of it, sergeant; we mustn't let this trail go cold." The D.I. made a few notes against an item on one of his papers before examining another.

"Who lives there? Do we know yet?"

Before the Sergeant could answer the door flew open and two detective constables hurried into the room.

"Good morning; Lucas; Prowting. Please be seated, I'm sorry about the early hour, but we've had a local shooting. We've been asked to involve ourselves, because we are already investigating what is believed to be a connected matter."

"Which?" Detective Constable Lucas asked before he was seated. He was the youngest of the group and like his female colleague, Christine Prowting, had only recently been made a detective.

"I must admit I'm not entirely sure at present. This is a fresh incident, but I think Sergeant Forest will be able to connect the dots for us right now; Sergeant?" The Inspector spun his baseball cap on the table.

"I've put two names at the top." Derek Forest indicated the names of Michael Morley and John Henderson written boldly at the top of the displayed sheet. "John Henderson was involved in a motoring incident as you all know. Subsequently, we have interviewed him on suspicion of murdering a Peter Langdon, a dealer in antiques, in London."

"Wait!" The Inspector stopped him immediately. "Sergeant, we have only interviewed John Henderson informally. There is no prospect of charging him at present and as you know perfectly well it is my opinion that we will not charge him."

"I'm sorry, sir, but as you know I believe strongly that he did it, but as you said earlier we must wait for the evidence."

The Sergeant turned to the board. "…and I think," he tapped the name Morley, "…that this is the connection we need."

"I think you had better explain that possible connection carefully."

"During the informal interview with John Henderson;" the Sergeant emphasised the word informal; "Henderson mentioned that he had called in at Morley's address on his way back from London."

"Yes, but Morley was not at home, was he?" The Inspector wanted to keep the Sergeant to the facts.

"No; but this morning's shooting took place at Morley's combined business and domestic premises." The Sergeant scrawled the two facts under the respective names. He stepped back with notable satisfaction.

"Ahhhh;" the two constables jointly reflected the Sergeant's note of fulfilment.

Detective Inspector James considered for a moment. He recognised Derek Forest's pleasure and did not doubt for a moment that his officer would reinforce his previously expressed bias on the subject of guilt. "You've no need to say it, Sergeant." He held up his hands in mock submission. "It's an interesting development, but we must still bring this together with the evidence."

"I have every confidence that we are now only this far away from it, sir." He held up his pinched thumb and forefinger and smiled. Without waiting for a response he returned to add a note to the board. "...and both killings took place on the same day!"

The Inspector found it hard to disagree with the apparent prima facia evidence. He could imagine any young officer rushing off with it and arresting everyone connected. However, his experience cautioned him. He had interviewed countless criminals, many of whom claimed innocence until otherwise proven. But Henderson's responses had the feel of a man hearing accusations with the full horror of an innocent man. "Clearly we have to stay with this link. You should have your officers turning every stone until we are confident one way or the other, Sergeant."

"I've already got someone on data searching; and as soon as we finish here, I will have these two," he indicated the two constables, "going door to door in the area."

"Let me know if you need more people." Kevin James felt it better to get this phase over quickly. If the Sergeant was right about the connection between the two men it was important to take them off the street straight away. If the opposite was true, he could direct his men quickly to broaden their search.

"Don't we need to find this character Morley, sir?" Christine Prowting was surprised that the logical things to check were in danger of being buried by a contest between the Sergeant and the Inspector.

"Yes, we do, Constable." He added a twirl to his cap. "Sergeant, can you have your people checking all the cctv records. Traffic will have some, but so will shops in the area."

"Already on my list, Sir."

"What do we have on this Morley so far?"

"He owns an antique restorer's workshop and showroom." The Sergeant pointed to a note below Morley's name on his chart.

"Where?" The Inspector noted the street's name.

"It's the nature of Winchester; the old capital developed over centuries. You have to look upon it as being a side street rather than back street, so-to-speak. Space is at a premium and plenty of decent businesses are to be found there as you know."

"Anything known?"

"Nothing at all; not even traffic violations."

"I've asked this of Henderson already, but no business suspicions; dodgy dealing; known associates; something a bit questionable?" The D.I. raised an expectant eyebrow.

"Nothing at all, except that Henderson and Morley are known to each other."

"Hmmm. The D.I. paused to scan his notes. "So why, if I am reading your initial notes and others correctly, does this paragon suddenly blow the head off someone, possibly unknown to him, with a hand gun, in the middle of the night?"

"You're thinking burglary?" The Sergeant feared a distraction.

"Well, we can't rule out the possibility." The Inspector was happy to agree.

"It's possible that Henderson delivered something valuable from London. If so, it's likely that a London connection with Langdon did not agree to its removal and came to Winchester get it back." Derek Forest was convinced he understood the motive.

The Inspector reflected on the information presented. Something was missing. "Does anyone else normally occupy the premises; his wife, for example?"

"Yes sir; his live-in assistant, Jane Fisher, 30..." The sergeant paused to consult his notes; "...well, that's how she is described in tax records and on the electoral roll for that address."

"So, not married, but are the two an item?" The D.I. sought clarification.

The sergeant looked towards the two detective constables, "can one of you check what uniform have so far?"

"Now?" Christine Prowting stood having noted that the Sergeant had been looking at her when he'd said one of you.

"If you can achieve that in the next ten minutes it would be helpful." Derek Forest glanced at the Inspector for approval. Kevin James nodded.

"Right;" the Inspector summarised his notes. "We have two people; Michael Morley and Jane Fisher in some way associated with a suspicious death. Both are missing, but we have no evidence to suggest whether their disappearance from the scene was voluntary, or if one or both were taken hostage. We need to keep open minds and collect more evidence. We must see what the cctv turns up. Don't forget Banks. If they try to withdraw money at an ATM we need to look at the cctv. The images will tell us whether or not they are being held hostage. Forensics will no doubt be able to shed some light on our current darkness; but we will have to wait a day or two for that."

The Inspector looked up at his Sergeant. "What else do we have on the Henderson motoring incident?"

"Not much more, Sir."

"Did they have any more to add about the make of the other car?"

"Uniform guess from witness descriptions that it was probably a Mercedes."

"Anything else, model etc?"

"According to the first witness on the scene, the two men were definitely rummaging through the contents. They were seen to be dragging them out onto the ground."

"...in an attempt to rescue the driver?"

"No. The witness said he thought one was trying to attack the driver. He was aiming punches into the car, but was impeded, because he could only gain access from the passenger side."

"Then what happened?"

"The witness said he thought the man was going to turn on him, but other drivers arrived just in time and both attackers ran off."

D.I. James thanked the Sergeant and asked him to add the details to the wall sheet. He stood and considered the information. "I think we have the makings of a very interesting connection: they were searching the contents of Henderson's estate; but what were they looking for?" He continued to stare at the data.

"Well, you know my opinion," Derek Forest was not one to let go of a bone easily; "they were after something Henderson brought back from London. Something so valuable he had been prepared to kill for it."

"Yes...." Kevin James let the familiar mantra flow over him, "...I take it the contents were antiques?"

"Yes sir mostly antiques; but uniform at the scene thought they were a bit tacky."

"I had no idea we had so much collective expertise, Sergeant. So, antiques: two men possibly attacking Henderson; Morley's connection with both antiques and Henderson; and Morley's involvement with the death of an unknown man in Winchester." He returned to his seat and tousled his hair with his finger tips. "We have to develop these connections. The thing that concerns me is the lack of previous for the two main suspects. These are older men; their guilt now goes against all existing statistics. They've not even been cautioned for riding a bike on the pavement! We could be looking at a series of innocent co-incidences."

The Sergeant was about to deliver his profound thoughts in response when he was interrupted as Christine Prowting reappeared carrying a thin plastic document folder. She paused beside her chair and waited for an invitation to speak.

"Let's hear the latest, Constable." The Inspector twirled his cap on the polished table expectantly.

Christine Prowting tilted the open file to reveal it contained only a single sheet of paper. "Not much at present, I'm afraid." She laid the folder open on the table and quoted from its few entries. "According to one of the uniformed officers who interviewed some neighbours earlier today, the two occupants of the premises acted like a couple. One said they thought they were married. Another reported the woman was the receptionist for the business and that she'd worked for John Henderson, who'd once owned the business."

"Ahhh!" The Sergeant was ecstatic, turning immediately to the Inspector; "the perfect link between the two men!"

"Let's hear the rest, Sergeant. Is there any more, Constable?"

Christine Prowting slid her finger over some final notes before responding. "Her name appears on some restoration dockets as if she had carried out the work. The conclusion is that she had some hands on experience."

The Inspector wanted to reduce delay and let everyone get on. "Okay, everyone; thank you once again for a prompt turn out;" adding mainly for the benefit of his Sergeant, "It is beginning to appear that the Sergeant's instinct may be correct. But not all the facts fit. Let's all keep an open mind; these strong connections could still be co-incidences."

The Sergeant remained unable to recognise a polite put down. "I disagree, sir, I don't believe in these sorts of co-incidences and there has been a murder. The lack of previous just means they are very clever and have never been caught. It's clear to me that this was a falling out between thieves and one ended up getting shot. The perpetrators, afraid of punishment, simply ran away."

"As I said before, Sergeant, you have no direct evidence for holding that view. We must show a link between one or both of them and the dead man. Get me that evidence." The Inspector rose to leave, "first thing tomorrow, everyone; and unless otherwise notified - we had better make it the broom cupboard. I can't see me getting into my office for another week at least. He tousled his hair once more before sliding his cap smoothly onto his head and striding out.

The two Detectives prepared to follow, but were blocked by the Sergeant. "Let's not rush off just yet. I want to talk over a couple of things."

The two subordinates returned to their seats. The Sergeant sat in the chair recently vacated by the Inspector and went into lecture mode. "I know we are taught to collect evidence and let it do the talking, but sometimes you have to let your instinct do more of the work."

The two listeners frowned, wondering what was about to be unleashed. Forest was undeterred, "When you've a bit more experience you will learn to spot when something doesn't fit; just doesn't make sense. If you ignore it and scurry around collecting evidence you'll miss the opportunity to apprehend a villain before he gets away."

"Yes, but surely it makes sense to collect the evidence. You need it for court and you could be wrong about your instinct and miss the evidence anyway, Sergeant." Christine Prowting had her recent course guide lines still ringing in her ears. The Sergeant was aware of her course naivety and felt it his duty to temper it with his kind of common sense.

"Not in my experience! Once you've caught your man it's easier to tease out the evidence."

"You sound as if you're suggesting something improper." Brian Lucas was concerned.

"You mean like giving the suspect a good beating?"

"I suppose it depends on your view of teasing." Lucas felt the heat of the Sergeant's irritation.

"I'm not suggesting the use of illegal methods, Detective, but once you have your man you can work on his weaknesses."

"But all that is carried out under strict surveillance, with solicitors present."

"You can still get to that extra bit of information that speeds up everything. They need feeding during the day, you know."

"But that's strictly controlled and operated by the station uniformed, or the prison if on remand."

"That's correct; and I'm still not suggesting anything improper..." he thought for a moment, "...well not so improper. There are more opportunities when the suspect is in your possession, as it were, than when he's on the loose."

Brian Lucas and Christine Prowting found Derek Forest's lecture riddled with the sort of cant that had been publicly condemned. Each found solace in closer examination of the table's shiny surface as the Sergeant moved onto the main thrust of his lecture. "Inspector James is a good man, but he's a new man, straight out of university and clinging on too hard to the evidence trail. We can already see that Henderson and Morley are linked in some way; it's obvious. Henderson's pretending he doesn't remember anything and Morley has done a runner taking his woman with him; all very convenient."

"But the evidence, Sergeant?" Brian Lucas wanted to challenge his senior officer more robustly, but was cautious about the latter's influence on his future in plain clothes policing.

The implied criticism did not deter the Sergeant who held his views sincerely and accepted some of them lay nearer the margin of acceptability. His Constable's caution only made him more earnest. "I believe the two cases; Henderson and Morley will be shown to be linked and by tomorrow we will be working for a combined team lead by D.I. James, or the D.C.I. He leaned across the table conspiratorially, "We have to make progress today if we want to stay ahead of the game and maintain our own control by getting these two men."

The two detectives recognised Forest's passion, but were more resigned to carrying out their D.I.'s wishes. If that meant knocking on doors tomorrow then that is what they would do. Sergeant Forest failed to understand just how committed to a new philosophy recent converts can become. They were inclined to do everything by the book.

Sergeant Forest prepared to leave; on reaching the door he turned and addressed each of his pupils. "Lucas I want you to stay on top of forensics; we must have an identity for the victim today. It is going to prove the break point for the case. I believe it will link the two suspects and will create many more. In the mean time sit on top of the cctv results. We must find Morley. Prowting, Lassie; I need you to knock on doors. I know uniform have been there and done that, I appreciate you didn't join the service go knocking on doors, but I need someone with a little bit of insight and I think you have got that. Find out what happened to Jane Fisher. Where was she likely to go, someone will know: find them."

"Christine, would be nice, Sarge." She bristled with indignation that he thought of her as a Lassie and risked a less formal personal address to make her point.

Derek Forest fixed her with a deeply scrutinising stare. He reviewed his recent sentences before responding. "Hmmm, Lassie;" he said quietly adding, "Scottish, you see; it's quite normal." He enriched his scant apology with a broadened accent. "Well done both of you; now let's get out there and make a difference."

CHAPTER THIRTEEN

Jane Fisher was petrified. Sleep had been an elusive companion that night. Her mind was in turmoil as she played and replayed events. Now early in the morning she and Mike were forced to abandon their business and property for goodness knew how long. She hated the circumstances in which they did so.

Late the previous evening Jane Fisher had witnessed her partner kill an intruder. She was submerged in emotional confusion; struggling for the surface. She believed the intruder would have harmed them both, but could not reconcile his killing with that intent.

Jane searched for an alternative in which a reasoned debate would have prevailed and ended in hands shakes all-round. She knew that was a stupid notion; but her mind had stalled. Most of all she found it difficult to understand why they couldn't have phoned the police and let them sort everything out. Michael had explained that the intruder would have friends who would pursue them, but that seemed something set in a future that might never arrive. He'd said he had to get away to think. She loved Mike and trusted him. He must be right, but how was this going to end? At that moment she felt deserted; abandoned to find her own way through a treacherous swamp.

Jane had taken her bicycle as Mike suggested. A trolley suitcase holding a minimum of essentials had been secured on the rear rack and the cash from the safe and a few personal items had been stuffed into the small rucksack she'd carried on her back. She'd kept to the back roads to avoid cctv cameras. As she rode she tried to plan how she might conceal the bike before she got to Brockenhurst station. So many conflicting thoughts had invaded her mind that it was only possible to concentrate on one at a time. First, she had to get to the station.

It was nearing lunch time as Jane cycled down Rhinefield Ornamental Drive. The day had begun well; it was dry and the low early sun brightening behind lifted her spirits. Exercise was beginning to return her appetite. She planned to rest near the stream at the lower end of the Drive and attempt to eat some of her packed lunch.

As Jane neared Brockenhurst she suddenly caught the sound of sirens. In blind panic she bounced the cycle of the road and into the ditch. Jane flew sideways over the twisted handlebars and rolled across the damp grass. She lay for a moment recovering. They had discovered her! She had to get out of sight! Abandoning the bicycle, she hurried to the nearest tree and squeezed herself tightly behind its trunk and some adjacent shrubs. The sirens grew louder. The wailing seemed to loiter in the air as if waiting to pounce. Then suddenly it arrived as first a police car then an ambulance raced passed. The rapid Doppler fading failed to reassure her. Jane grabbed the cycle and resumed peddling with renewed energy. The resumed effort failed to reward as she quickly discovered that her hasty dismounting had left the cycle with a seriously buckled front wheel and one bent pedal. She persevered until it became clear that the decision about where to dump the cycle had already been made. She found a suitable hedge; removed her trolley suitcase from the rear rack; and rested the bike against the far side.

Jane Fisher wiped the inside of the window with a windscreen wiper action; leaned her forehead against the cool glass; and stared at the passing countryside. The whirl of metal wheels on metal track increased as the train accelerated. A slight swaying helped settle a confused mind. It was good time to plan the next phase of her escape. She would book into the George as soon as she arrived at Sway and then think about where she might buy a pay-as-you-go mobile. She hoped Mike had got away safely and felt a great pang of loss. She was desperate to speak to him. The phone was going to be essential. Mike had warned about using the hotel phone; any calls would be traceable. She wondered where the nearest phone shop might be and knew she must not make enquiries at the hotel. She would have to go to a local garage and ask there.

Jane glanced across the passing fields. The scene wasn't quite what she'd expected. Something was wrong! She had expected to pass under a bridge quite soon after leaving the station, but now the train was crossing a main road. In her haste she must have caught the wrong train! She panicked immediately. Where is this train taking me? She pressed against the window in an attempt to see ahead. "Where are we going?" She asked aloud. She looked around quickly in case anyone had overheard. She could only see three people and they seemed to be preoccupied. As Jane sank back she felt the seat back tighten. A passenger was sitting behind her! Someone was pulling the seat. A male's head appeared over the top. A middle aged man with a swarthy face and wearing dark glasses spoke in a deep rough voice; "Lymington and the Isle of Wight ferry." Before he'd finished his sentence he'd disappeared from sight.

She suffered a fearful frisson. Who was that!? She was being followed! How could they have got on to her so quickly? Mike had warned her several times about the dangers they faced. She had not given a thought to its possible immediacy. I must get off! She heard the train's horn sound a warning at the road crossing before Lymington station. She snatched up her rucksack, I must get off here!

Jane leaned against the door ready to leap onto the platform. The wheels had only just stopped when she was at once racing towards the road. She could hear rapid footsteps behind her! Other passengers? Jane could not look; she increased her speed. The footsteps increased to keep up. Suddenly a hand grabbed at her shoulder and spun her round. It was the swarthy faced man in dark glasses from the train. She screamed loudly and tore herself away. She had everyone's attention. A young man ahead of her ran back. As her potential rescuer reached her he slowed to walking pace and was looking over her shoulder. She turned to find the swarthy man holding her trolley suitcase.

"You were in such a hurry, you left this on the train." Seemingly unfazed by her bravura performance; he rested the case on the tarmac; and returned towards the station.

"Thank you." Jane uttered sheepishly.

Still shivering from her experience, Jane towed her trolley up Church Hill. Lymington would be a good place to buy a mobile phone. The compensation for her mistaken journey came at a cost. Her image would now be captured on many shop cctvs. She abandoned all thoughts of how she might leave her suitcase somewhere to avoid standing out from the local shoppers. It was inevitable she would be detected. The remaining solace was that she could go back to Brockenhurst and add a bit of confusion for anyone interested in her whereabouts.

Since her cover was already blown – she was already thinking like a criminal, she would treat herself to a hot meal. It would be late afternoon before she could get to the hotel.

Purchasing the mobile had hastened Jane's sense of loss. She would have to wait for the phone to register before she would be able to speak to Mike. She was desperate to hear his voice.

As she headed towards the station she thought about the Isle of Wight ferry. It was a short walk away. She could catch the Yarmouth ferry and be on the Island within an hour. A taxi could get her to the cottage within half that time. Deep in thought and subconsciously guided she found herself on the other side of the river heading for the ferry terminal.

"Single?" The man double checked.
"Yes, please."
The man accepted the note; gave her change; and presented Jane with a one-way ticket to Yarmouth. She felt elated. Within less than three hours she would be in Mike's arms. They would be at the cottage together. No-one in their wildest dreams would imagine they were there. They would be safe.

Jane stirred her coffee and waited for the ferry. She wondered how Mike would react. He had planned everything quickly, but carefully. He wanted her to be safe, away from those who would be pursuing him. She had agreed to follow the plan he had devised. If she deviated now she could not predict the consequences. Mike had probably thought of everything. Jane considered a cold hotel bed without him. She would not be able to sleep. If she missed him so much already, what would the future feel like?

Jane rose slowly from her seat and made for the exit. She wanted to watch the ferry arrive. As she neared the door she noticed somebody reading a newspaper. It was being held fully open with the black leather fingers of a glove visible at each side. The newspaper extended so far from the table Jane had to move to one side in order to pass. The paper swivelled as she passed preventing her from seeing its owner, but when she reached the exit she could see clearly his reflection in the window. It was the swarthy faced man from the train!

Jane Fisher began to hurry. She did not dare to look back. What could she do? If she chose to run all the way to the station towing her suitcase he would quickly catch her! Terrified and without thinking she ran towards the terminal exit.

A car horn blared instantly she stepped into the road and the bumper of a taxi that was just pulling out stopped against her leg.

The driver gestured an exaggerated shrug and grimaced. She rapidly mouthed sorry; and prepared to continue her escape. As she moved she noticed the car was empty. Holding out her left arm to prevent him driving off, she slid in contact along the nearside side and opened the front passenger door. "Please say you're free!" She shouted into the taxi.

The driver gawked, amazed. His initial reaction was to reject her immediately, but he saw something in her demeanour; a body language of fear he'd never seen before. She needed help. Without speaking he stretched across and dragged the case straight into the cab, pushing it between the front seats and into the rear. He held out a steadying hand and hauled her unceremoniously after it. Before she was settled he had launched the taxi towards the exit. "Seat belt!"

"Yes, sorry. I didn't mean to…"

"It's okay, love; you've got some sort of problem." The car reached the feeder road. "Can I slow down a bit, now? Are we alright?"

"Yes, I think so." Jane turned to look behind, but was unable to see.

"Someone's chasing you?"

"I think so."

"Husband; boy friend?"

"No. Someone I don't wish to meet."

"There's no one following at the moment." He adjusted the mirror. "It's okay, I don't need to know who it is, but I do need to know where you want me to take you."

"The station; the station." She repeated.

"Are you sure? It won't take him long to follow you there." He maintained his assumption that it was male trouble.

Now she was safe, Jane was tempted to ask to be driven directly to the hotel. But it would mean risking the driver remembering her when he saw the headlines in the paper or on television. He seemed safe enough. Jane felt secure and a bursting need to tell someone, but she remembered Mike. She could unwittingly expose him to danger. She had to remain courageous and hope that the train came before her pursuer.

The driver parked the car and opened the rear door to retrieve the trolley case. Jane got out and struggled to recover some money from the bottom of her bag. She turned to offer a folded note, but he'd gone and was already towing her trolley into the station. Jane hurried after him. The man declined her offer of money and sat beside her. "I'll wait with you until the train arrives."

"You're very kind, but please don't; you've done so much already."

"As a male I feel some responsibility when one of us goes awry. I will be making up for things."

"Things you've done wrong?"

"Ohhh, I'm not sure. You'd have to ask my wife about that!" The man laughed.

CHAPTER FOURTEEN

The D.I. perched on the edge of the table; one leg on the ground; the other hitched over a corner. He removed his baseball cap, twirling it on a finger before sliding it onto the table. Whilst waiting for the last of the group to enter he tousled his hair with his finger tips. As the last one entered he motioned Brian Lucas to shut out the noise coming from the passage.

"D.S. Forest has an update for us on Michael Morley." The Inspector moved away from the table allowing the sergeant to switch on an overhead projector propped up on a number of old magazines. The sergeant sorted some foils and placed the first on the glass plate.

"Before you start, Derek, where on earth did you obtain this fine piece of kit?" The Inspector gazed with mock admiration.

"The surplus equipment cupboard, sir; it was the best I could do at short notice." The sergeant began to adjust the distorted image displayed on a hastily erected paper screen.

"The surplus equipment cupboard?"

"Yes, sir, we do have one. There's not much there, so I have arranged to obtain a computer linked projector for this room. You can move it to your new office when it's ready."

"Should I ask how you've managed that?"

"Best not to, sir." The sergeant avoided the Inspector's inquiring look.

"Very well, Sergeant, take us through the new information."

The sergeant attempted to point at the underlined name on the foil on the glass plate with a ball pen. He misjudged the correct position several times before grabbing a rule from the table and approaching the screen. He tapped the rule against the name, Michael Morley. "We now have more background on this man." A glow of satisfaction lit his face. "I think we can place him fairly and squarely in the category of potential murderer." He used the word, potential, in deference to his senior officer's strongly held belief in accuracy.

The D.I. frowned. "That's still a bit strong, Derek."

Derek Forest felt challenged. "It certainly moves him from the ranks of Mr. Innocent, sir." He addressed his D.I. directly. "At first he seemed untouchable, possibly the victim of a burglary gone wrong, but now we have possible cause to believe he knew exactly what he was doing when he murdered the deceased."

"What do you have that links him?" The Inspector was determined to keep the sergeant to citing evidence.

Derek Forest turned to point at the screen before cursing under his breath then adjusting the foil on the plate. He pointed to the word, Iraq. "He was a soldier serving here. That's a lot different than posing as an intellectual antique art restorer."

"How long?"

"Eighteen months."

"Eighteen months? Hmm; what do you have on his service record?"

"Just a bit of the usual; not much, but we can assume he was fire arm trained and competent in unarmed combat."

"We can assume nothing: you have the admin summary record there: pay and provisions and a tax record, no doubt." The sergeant was about to argue when the D.I. raised his hand to stop him. "I can see that you have given us cause to re-evaluate this chap Morley: find out when he joined; in which units he served; in what capacity; and most importantly, why he left."

"We know some of that, sergeant." Christine Prowting suggested helpfully.

Her sergeant gave her a long hard look before shaking his head; "just bits."

"What bits?" the Inspector had noted the disapproving look.

"Unfinished investigation sir; give us a bit longer and we'll have the evidence."

"How long?" Kevin James was convinced he was being deceived in some way, but decided to let the matter rest for the moment.

"Just a matter of hours, sir."

"Okay; but I need you to fill in the blanks; too many unknowns at present."

"I think we've been over simplifying this man's tameness and innocence, sir. He would have been used to the sight of blood; would have known how to inflict the maximum damage to a human; and could handle a gun." There was a note of undisguised frustration in the Forest's voice.

"I appreciate your team's keenness, sergeant, and want to encourage it, but we have to maintain objectivity." The D.I. hoped that emphasising the word team would take any personal sting out of his criticism. "Let's develop what you know about this man's history and see if your theory will hold water."

The Inspector noted the quiet collective sigh from those assembled. He move back to stand at the table. "Look, all of you. I know that it's easy to form opinions early on. It's almost inevitable, but we must make sure that what we have will stand up in court and deliver us the guilty person. We must think as professionals." He moved away again to make room for his Sergeant. "Okay, Derek, let's have a look at what else you have."

The sergeant changed foils: "We can confirm Morley's relationship with John Henderson. There is a reliable witness who confirms John Henderson visited Morley on the day of Henderson's motoring incident."

The D.I. nodded approvingly and made some notes on his pad.

"Reported Movements;" the Sergeant started to read the list aloud. The Inspector waved a declining hand, "we can read, Sergeant, thank you."

The list detailed Henderson's visit as around 2pm and as lasting no more than 15 minutes. It showed that journey time trials carried out by the traffic division confirmed that John Henderson would have arrived at the incident location near Lymington about five minutes before the attendance time recorded by the traffic police on the day of the event.

The Sergeant waited expectantly as other officers copied notes and the Inspector added more to his pad. Finally the Inspector looked up and smiled.

"That's an excellent tie in, sergeant." He looked at the screen. "You said earlier that you had some local stuff?"

"I haven't had time to make any foils of it. I wasn't sure I could get this piece of kit."

"Just reading your notes will be fine."

The Sergeant peered at his notes for a few seconds. "Nothing on that day, but two uniformed officers interviewed one neighbour who saw Jane Fisher leaving the premises early the next day on her bicycle."

"Bicycle? Was that normal?"

"The neighbour said that it was unusual for that time of the morning, but that Fisher had been seen cycling at other times of day. When questioned further; the witness remembered that Jane Fisher had a suitcase fastened to the rack at the back."

"And she did not return?"

"No, the witness said something else was unusual: she went in the opposite direction; out of town."

"Are we looking at cctv?"

"Yes, sir. Nothing found yet. And surprisingly; nothing found at all on Michael Morley."

"No evidence of him leaving the house?"

"None at all. We know he was not there when we arrived; he seems to have disappeared without trace."

"Again, can we check all available cctv cameras for him?"

"There's no shortage of cameras. We are checking both council and civilian cameras."

"How do you think that he managed to avoid cameras?"

"Morley worked on infra-red surveillance in Iraq." The Sergeant sounded triumphal. "He would have known how to avoid detection. More evidence that he planned this all along."

"...evidence that he might have been able to do so if he had chosen, Sergeant."

The D.I. wished to avoid what would appear as constant correction of his Sergeant. He decided he would speak to Derek Forest privately and try to create a better working relationship. In front of the Constables he knew he ought to re-enforce his support for some good work. "Thank you, Sergeant, for improving our equipment and well done with the progress. I think we are beginning to understand this chap Michael Morley, but we need that last piece of evidence that will enable us to confidently charge him. In particular, let's keep on top of this cctv surveillance. However good he is, Morley is going to make a mistake; we just have to find it."

Kevin James looked at his Sergeant and assessed his response. Derek Forest seemed happy that he'd managed to convince the senior officer that Morley was the man to catch.

Satisfied he'd made a start, the D.I. asked if there were any other developments.

The Sergeant was happy to comply; "I've got Detective Prowting looking at family connections. We might find a clue or relationship that helps. So far members of the families seem to live at some distance, but we will check all links, just in case."

"When you were looking at the Henderson motoring incident, did you come across the Mercedes?"

"Still checking, sir; we could use more people."

"Okay, keep traffic involved. Now that it's murder enquiry I can probably persuade them to complete what they started. I'll follow that up."

"I've received initial p.m. results."

"You have?"

The Sergeant recognised the impropriety of him having received them first. "It's only the identity sir; I got nosy at the right time."

"What do we have?" The D.I. decided not to make it an issue; he would talk to forensics later.

"Klaas Oberlander; no known country of origin at present.

"Okay, I'll chase that as well; we really need to get everything we can. Discovering his background and, I suspect, his associates will speed up the whole process." The D.I. completed his notes. He stood giving his hair another good scrub with his finger tips before replacing his cap. "Thank you everyone. I think we still have a long way to go, but we've made a good start. Let's see if we can tie up these loose ends quickly."

He strode quickly out of the broom cupboard, "Let's get out of this paint smell."

As the others rose to follow, Derek Forest gave Christine Prowting a hard look.

"You did not mention what Morley did in Iraq." She understood why he was annoyed with her.

"…and you should not have spoken out of turn." Derek Forest scolded.

"I didn't."

"Only because I stopped you in time."

"But you were withholding essential information. Michael Morley was a Medic who eventually found the stress too much for him."

"It's not relevant." The Sergeant's temper began to fray.

"I think it changes everything and the D. I. should have been told."

"You listen to me, young lady, if we are going to get on then you'll have to let me decide who and when superiors get to know things." He tried to soften his tone to win obedience; "You do understand?"

She started to nod submissively, but was interrupted by Brian Lucas' arm around her shoulders guiding her out of the room.

CHAPTER FIFTEEN

Michael Morley awoke in pain. The bed had been cold and damp so he'd spent the night wrapped in the blanket he carried in his rucksack. As he tried to move he discovered his aching muscles of the day before had stiffened.

He sat up and took stock of his circumstances. He recalled he had a new companion with whom to share his misery; William Jonathon Parker. He smiled wryly at the thought of such a companion and wondered what Jane would say when he told her.

As Michael listened for sounds of his new cohort he heard a familiar sizzling. Sliding his feet out onto the cold floor and half dressed; he followed an equally familiar smell towards the kitchen.

Much of the mess of the day before had been swept to one side and on the worktop two large plates were ready to receive the contents of a frying pan. Bacon and eggs!

"This is a surprise!" He admired the view.

"'ello, matey; I thought you might like something in your belly. I guessed you'd been on the run for some time."

"I told you yesterday; I'm not on the run." He thought for a moment before adding; "it's more a kind of jog."

"You can call it what you wants, but I know you won't want no police around 'ere in a hurry."

Michael was going to argue, but there was a sudden realisation that Bill Parker was right; he was on the run!

"It's a bit nippy in here." Michael folded his arms tightly.

William Parker turned and looked at the tall shivering figure. "Don't worry; as soon as we've got this inside us I'll get us a fire goin' in the grate, matey."

"It's Mike," Morley informed him.

"Oh, okay Mikey. Mike it is." He levered out two eggs onto each plate followed by an ample littering of crispy bacon slices. He passed a plate to Mike; picked up the other; and headed for the living room.

"This is much better." Mike surveyed the improved tidiness from the doorway.

"It's all about contracts, Mikey."

Michael Morley furrowed his brow. "Contracts?"

"Like the one between us. You said if I kept the place tidy, I could stay here."

"Well, I'm sure…"

"No, you said quite clearly I could stay. If not, you can stop eating that bacon."

Michael decided not to point out that they'd probably come from his aunt's fridge. Then he wondered how old the food in the cottage might be.

"Do you buy food at the local shops?"

"Sort of, Mikey."

"Sort of? Well, if we are to have a contract I'd better give you some money with which to buy food."

William Parker said nothing for a while. He was remembering his past and felt ashamed that he now had to rely on someone else for support. He considered rejecting the whole idea and leaving. "It wasn't always like this." He said quietly.

"What did you do before this?

"Army from sixteen; learned a trade and started a plumbing business. In the end I had a business partner and about a dozen men working for me." His rough accent had disappeared and he sounded like a man who knew how to conduct himself. "Then I discovered how this partner of mine was improving trade. It wasn't long before we were both in the dock. I for my part was an associate in the crime. Did some time and from then on it was all down hill." He wiped the back of his hand across a damp cheek.

Michael finished his breakfast as he listened and placed the plate to one side. "I'm sorry to hear that, William. You mustn't give up. Try again."

"Are you going to help me?"

Michael remained silent.

"That's your answer, Mikey." The rough accent had returned.

"Trouble with the phone?" Parker leaned back in the deck chair and turned his head. Michael was testing house phone. He needed it to work or his plan for Jane to contact him would fail.

Still unable to see Michael Morley, Parker wriggled and attempted to sit up. As he turned his head the ubiquitous beach chair became unstable, tipping him onto the terrace. "Spilt my bloody beer!" He cried.

Mike came onto the terrace. "You're in a right state, already! What do you think you are playing at?"

"I'm as sober as you, Mikey boy." Parker deftly swept up the gurgling can of beer and assessed its remaining weight. "'bout half full," he estimated.

"Look, Bill..." Morley prepared to lecture him on drinking.

"William." The other corrected him.

"No, Bill is better. It's well known."

"William." Parker insisted; "anyway, why is Bill better?"

"It's the result of a well known piece of research that concluded the friendliest and popular names comprise four letters only. The second letter must be a vowel and the most popular vowel is "i" so Bill is better than William."

"But, my favourite name is William."

"Is that because you've heard it read out in court so often?" Mike bit his lip. He'd allowed his annoyance to override common decency. "Sorry, William, I was wrong to have said that."

"It's okay, I get used to it and I reckon you're having trouble with a lady friend."

"That obvious?"

"Yeah; can I help, if only with advice?"

Michael thought quickly. "Yes, you can. If you stop drinking before you become so confused you won't be able to help, you could get us some food and me a mobile phone."

"A pay-as-you-go, Mikey?"

Michael felt as if his mind was naked. "Exactly, can you do it?"

"You can trust me." William Parker put down the beer can. "They gets y' in the end, y' know. Murderer; train robber; it makes no difference."

"It's complicated, that's all." Morley avoided elaboration. He retrieved his wallet from his back pocket and removed a few notes placing them on the table in front of Parker.

"...and get us two ready meals; you know what I mean?"

"You mean chilled food we can pop in the oven and heat up?"

"Get us some fruit and pudding, if you like. If you see anything else that we might find useful, you may bring it. Oh, and don't forget; milk."

Michael Morley made his way back into the cottage only to reappear immediately. "...and don't say or do anything to draw particular attention to yourself." He added in pious hope.

"They'll be suspicious if I have any money." Parker knew from mature experience.

Morley nodded. He was right about this man. Parker was street wise. If this vagrant started flashing a lot of money, it would not be long before the police would be interested.

"Get a decent coat from the wardrobe. Why haven't you done so before?"

"Because they're not mine."

"I'm giving you permission to select a suitable coat. I'll leave it to your discretion how to spend the money, just as long as we do not starve as a consequence."

"Right 'o, Mikey boy; you leave it all to Bill."

Michael Morley watched as Bill Parker sauntered through the side gate. Dressed in a smart grey overcoat, he looked awkward carrying a green faux leather shopping bag. Michael had to persuade Bill to give up using a plastic supermarket bag. William Jonathan Parker closed the gate after him; waved a hearty farewell and disappeared up the slope.

Now that Parker was out of the cottage Michael could give the Panther some urgent attention. He retrieved it from the shrubbery and placed it on the kitchen worktop. Using the eyeglass he'd brought with him he re-examined the damaged body of the animal.

There was nothing new to be discovered. He pulled up a chair and sat with his eyes level with the Panther's head. Its eyes were narrow slits that widened slightly towards the middle. Each slit had been decorated with three evenly spaced jewels. Michael looked carefully and had little doubt they were diamonds. He estimated the largest of the three to be worth more than a thousand pounds, possibly a few hundred more. It was possible that Peter Langdon had been right to suggest that the carved animal would be worth much of what he owed John Henderson. Was that all? Was that the secret? He looked at the eye sockets through the glass. The surrounding was an exact circle; not the hand executed form he'd expected. A machine had cut the groove around the eye. Why?

Michael found a small screw driver; placed its blade into the eye socket outline; and carefully scraped it round the curve. He examined the result. His effort had removed the black paint from the contour. On closer examination Morley could see a distinct cut line. The socket appeared to have been inserted as a unit into the head. He scraped deeper exposing a deep circular join. Levering only threatened to split the hard wood. He wondered if the socket had been screwed into place.

After an hour of searching and experimentation Michael Morley had removed the two outer diamonds of one eye and deepened the holes to receive an improvised tool for rotating the socket. At the first attempt, the socket refused to budge and weakened the tool. But after Michael had scraped the join to remove some more residual paint, it turned freely. The cylindrical insert continued to extend until at two centimetres it fell loose into his hand. He looked at the insert. It was a solid piece of crudely threaded wood. He turned the head of the animal to catch more light and peered into the cavity. Nothing! He doubled checked and imagined he could see something. What at first looked like the back of the hole seemed to be something trapped there.

Morley poked with the screwdriver and saw that he was damaging a piece of paper. He changed to carefully teasing at its edges until he finally held a folded piece of notepaper.

Spurred on by his success Michael Morley had soon retrieved a similar piece of paper from the other eye. He unfolded both pieces and pressed them flat. He'd expected to find ancient yellowing maps revealing the hiding place of some immense treasure, but was surprised to find the sheets were bright white and looked brand new.

There were some hand written figures on each sheet. He compared the two and tried to decipher a meaning from the difference. He was unable to tell if they were meant to be read together, or gave complimentary information. He needed to get to the library and carry out some research.

CHAPTER SIXTEEN

Detective Sergeant Derek Forest was stressed. He thought the police had sufficient evidence to justify the interrogation and subsequent arrest of Michael Morley. Clearly, this man was the gangland assassin of Klaas Oberlander.

The Sergeant's chief tormenter was D.I. James. His Inspector seemed unable to acknowledge the essential part played by instinct. Forest felt the reliance on getting watertight evidence was responsible for delay and had prevented them finding their man. It had now become a problem of habeas corpus because Michael Morley remained free.

The Sergeant stood at the doorway and surveyed the open plan office. At the far side officers crouched in darkened alcoves poring over hours of cctv records. The remainder of his team except for one officer were out interviewing witnesses.

He crossed the room and stood behind Christine Prowting. "Haven't you finished that family tree yet, Lassie?" His Scottish accent broadened for effect. To her, he seemed to believe that using its full vigour would forgive him any chauvinistic familiarity. Christine Prowting bridled inwardly convinced his approach was born of poor parentage and perfunctory. However, she considered his seniority as a good enough reason not to embark on a lecture; for the moment.

She turned and raised her eyebrows expectantly. The Sergeant submitted a weak smile and tapped the file he carried under his arm. "I've got a lot more stuff for you to look at."

Christine Prowting ignored the comment; returned to her screen and referred to a particular entry. "This looks odd." She sat back so that he could see.

The Sergeant leaned forward uncomfortably close and peered over her shoulder. "What does? I hope this is part of your research and not your shopping at M&S." He joked.

"I don't shop on line; I like to feel the goods."

The Sergeant smiled as he managed to suppress an unworthy rejoinder. "So, what am I looking at?"

"It's Morley's family tree. I found nothing of interest in his direct line, so I began to widen the search."

"And?"

She tapped the screen with her ball pen; "Morley's Aunt Margaret; his father's brother's wife."

"She's got form?"

"None known; the interesting bit is that she married his father's brother, Sidney Morley in 1990; becoming Mrs. Margaret Morley."

"That's what happens in Scotland as well, lassie." The Sergeant mocked gently, "In fact I think it's considered quite popular the whole world over."

"Maybe;" Christine remained focused, "but then her husband died."

"Michael Morley's uncle, his father's brother died? Is this going to get much more convoluted before we get somewhere?"

"His aunt Margaret did not remarry."

"Good for her! Now, where's this going?"

"It looks as if she began a relationship with a Frank McCain."

"...and should I care?"

"She kept her maiden name, Brentwood."

"...and?" Derek Forest started drumming loudly with his fingers.

"...and I remembered from the census or the register of voters that there was a Frank McCain living in the same road."

The sergeant remained silent for some time whilst he juggled with the data. How could that get him to Morley? Realising he was wasting time he pressed on.

"How does this get me to Morley? How do you know they started a relationship? It's not yet a crime to live in the same street as someone else?"

"I didn't think anything of it at first. But I checked again when I thought I should be looking for the two names together. Then I found this: Margaret Brentwood and Frank McCain on each other's car insurance as other driver."

"Oh, wow!" The Sergeant could not contain his pleasure. He turned quickly to see heads bobbing up at the far end of the office.

"That is something else, Lassie. I mean Constable Prowting." He wanted to hug her, but managed to resist the temptation. "How did you come to think of that?"

"A kind of woman's logic, I suppose."

"So, does McCain have form?"

"No."

"So will this get me to Morley?"

"I think so."

"How? So far you have only been able to connect his uncle's widow with the bloke up the road? Is there a connection or not?"

"Yes. Frank McCain is listed as a boat builder on the Isle of Wight."

"A boat builder?"

"Well, he was a boat builder, he died recently."

"Recently died? So, most of the data has yet to be changed?"

"Yes, I might not have found them if it had been."

"The Isle of Wight sounds interesting. What else?"

"I've spent some time this morning going through any records I could find relating to his boat building business; also his associated activities."

"And you found what?"

"Nothing..." She heard the sergeant sigh. "..nothing that is," she added hastily; "...until I found a bill for repair work carried out on a cottage."

"He was fiddling the books, eh? Getting his house repairs charged to the business? How does that get us to Morley? For goodness sake, Lassie, get me there!"

"He may or may not have been fiddling the books, but what I found was evidence that he owned a cottage there."

"Owned?"

"Well, according to records, still owns a cottage on the south coast of the Island, west of Ventnor." The Detective Constable permitted herself a triumphal singing tone.

The sergeant retreated into silence: his mind raced through the equation: His aunt owns a cottage on the Isle of Wight; Morley needs to escape somewhere no one will trace him. Without thinking he placed a hand on each of Christine's shoulders and squeezed them firmly. "You've done it, Lassie!" He felt like skipping around the room. "You've got him! We've got him!"

Christine Prowting experienced a mixed choking emotion. The sergeant had recognised her effort; praised it even. She immediately forgave him his former indiscretions. "It doesn't mean he is there, does it?" She tried to offset any future disappointment.

"Yes it does, Lassie. I know it! I just bloody know it! And you're the one that's done it! Oh well bloody done, Lassie!" He rushed towards the door before quickly returning to her desk. "Make sure you capture everything you have told me. Get it all down. It's all evidence that's going to bring Michael Morley to book!"

"Shall I let the D.I. know?"

"No!" The D.S. said sharply. Then realising his fault spoke more calmly, "Not yet, Lassie; let's check with the others about the cctv evidence for the day Morley disappeared. Make sure they've checked the ferry terminals; that's going to be much more important now." He thought for a few more seconds, "check if anyone has looked for unexplained events along the coast line; missing boats, stolen, you know, the usual sort of thing a fugitive bound for the Island might do." He hesitated before adding, "I'm going to organise a car for you and Brain Lucas. You're going on holiday for a while."

"What today?"

"Yes. But keep quiet about it. If asked just say you are doing some special research for me."

"Am I supposed to track down this cottage?"

"Exactly, Lassie; I know you can do it; you're now my brightest spark."

"But shouldn't the others know?"

"The fewer people that know the better; it will reduce the risk of someone ruining the opportunity of capturing this murderer. But radio Brian Lucas let him know and get him back here."

"Do I have to go with Brian?"

"Why not?"

"He's too slow; we'll need to think on our feet."

"You'll find that under pressure and with raised adrenaline he'll be a different person."

"He'd better be." She picked up her bag, "I'll need to go home first, Sergeant."

"Okay, but make it quick. I will organise a pool car and get you booked onto the mid-day Lymington to Yarmouth ferry. Ventnor is less than an hour's drive from Yarmouth." His face broadened into an uncharacteristic smile. "You know; I think there is a good chance that by this evening you and Brian could be arresting our man."

The sergeant dangled a set of keys from his outstretched hand. "You're on the quarter past eleven. Better get a move on." He dropped the keys into Christine's hand before stepping away to reveal Brian Lucas. "It's up to you two which one drives, but its number five - with a full tank." He hesitated before adding, "Unfortunately D.S. Bourne overheard over your radio message to Lucas and did the usual thing with two plus two. I had to call in a favour to stop him repeating what he'd worked out from the call."

"Sorry, Sergeant; will it matter?"

"No, it's taken care of."

Christine Prowting looked at Brian. His face bore an innocent glow. She tried to tell if he looked like a man who had just been spoken to, but his face remained inscrutable.

"Shall we go?" Brian gestured towards the door and made no attempt to wrestle ownership of the keys.

The Sergeant caught Brian's arm as he passed, "I've had to work hard to justify this trip. I've had to cover it with another job, so don't let me down. Get this bastard."

"What about the local police?" Brian Lucas raised a previously unspoken concern.

"We don't want anyone fussing around with this before we have had a chance to look for ourselves. There'll be time for that later."

"But, if you think this desperado is armed, what about back-up?"

"Don't risk anything. Observe first. You're not in uniform and he should accept you as a nosy local if he spots you."

The sergeant guided his detectives into the corridor just as D.S. Bourne hurried towards the office. "Derek, I've been looking for you everywhere. You need to hear this." He brandished a piece of paper. "We need to talk now!"

"I've just got to get these two on their way, first."

"Read this first." He thrust a piece of paper at the Sergeant.

"Read? Just tell me, we don't have time."

"Nothing found on cctv, but we received a report about a rescue from a capsized yacht at Buckler's Hard."

"Buckler's Hard? I haven't been there in years...and?"

"Uniformed officers had to get a man in a kayak to move out of the way when the rescue launch tried to come ashore with the survivors."

Derek Forest's mind raced again. "Does Morley have a kayak?" His heart began to thump hard against his chest.

"I was told Michael Morley has an annual permit to launch at Buckler's Hard."

"That's how he did it!" Forest smashed a fist into the palm of his other hand. "He planned it! He'd planned it all along. Now tell me he's not a cold blooded killer! I knew it!" He turned to his two officers. "Go! Go get this bastard. We know exactly where he is."

"Are you ready?" Christine Prowting revealed her impatience. She was simultaneously apprehensive and excited; pleased to doing something serious, but concerned about the unknown danger.

Brian Lucas fastened his seat belt and smiled. "Yes, ma'am!" he mocked.

Detective Prowting drove the car cautiously towards the main road. At the junction a black off-road vehicle had half turned in the broad entrance to the station and stopped. She sounded the horn briefly, but the car remained stationary. Brian Lucas got out and moved along the side of the motionless obstacle. He could not see the occupants through the darkened side window, but could hear the engine running on tick over. As he prepared to reach up and tap the glass the engine was revved and the vehicle accelerated away. Lucas turned on his heels and ran back to the unmarked police car.

"Well?" He demanded belting himself in.

Christine Prowting sat impassively. "Well, what?"

"We ought to get after them!"

"Why?" Detective Prowting found her male colleague's sudden aggression surprising.

""Something's not right about it." He hastily recorded the first four characters of the vehicle's registration.

"It was just some Muppet doing a U turn."

"Did you see the aerials?"

"What aerials?"

"The two long whip aerials poking up from the rear of the vehicle?"

"No; what about them?"

"You didn't spot the smaller directional antenna in the centre of its roof either?"

"Brian, we haven't even left the station and you're already chasing ghosts. What will you be like when we find some real criminals?"

"That vehicle was a listening station."

"What utter rubbish!" She slammed her palms on the steering wheel. "It was probably one of ours."

"Well, I've not seen it before!"

"That's probably what covert means." Christine had the final word and turned the car towards Lymington.

CHAPTER SEVENTEEN

Michael Morley hurried towards the cottage. The phone had been ringing for some while, but had stopped by the time he reached the front door. He could now hear Bill Parker's beer laden voice speaking to someone. "Noo...oo; I don't think I know Morley. What? Mike?"

Michael snatched the phone from Parker's hand, pushing him to one side. "Jane?" he waited anxiously.

"Mike is that you?"

"Yes, sweetheart; thank goodness you were able to call. I was worried that all sorts of thing could have gone wrong. Have you booked in at the hotel?"

"Yes, but only after some trouble, are you alright? Who was that hideous man who answered?"

"That was William Jonathon Parker; he's taken up residence at the cottage."

"You mean he's..."

"A squatter? Yes; but we've sorted all that out. He's a sort of partner in crime now. What went wrong at the hotel?"

Jane explained about getting on the wrong train and all that had happened in Lymington before telling him about the hotel. "There was a problem booking in."

"How can you have a problem booking in? Were they full?"

"No, but it was seen as a bit suspicious if you pay in cash."

"That only happens in America."

"Well, no; it can also happen here apparently. You leave no identity if you pay by cash and, I suspect, they worry that you might run off with something."

"But you could pay up-front!"

"I know, but it took that and I showing them the Building Society pass book to convince them."

"So that's now settled and you are registered as Miss Brown?"

"No; Mrs. Brown. I said my husband would be joining me in a few days. I booked a double. It seemed less suspicious. In any case you said it might be useful if you had to leave the cottage."

"That's a bit expensive, but we'll cope. You must have enough money to last a couple of weeks at least."

"Yes, don't worry. What are you going to do now?"

"Examine the Panther and look for a few more clues, then do a bit of research in the local library."

"Take care. I miss you so much and wish you would come here. I'm sure we'd be safe here in the middle of the forest."

Michael and Jane swapped mobile phone numbers so that they would have complete security and said their goodbyes. Mike was relieved to know the plan was following its course. He had to make most of the opportunity and solve the riddle of the Panther.

"Sorry, Mikey." Parker recovered himself from the floor.

Michael helped him to the armchair. "Are you going to be alright now? I need to go to the library to do some research."

"I will have a nice dinner ready for us when you return."

Michael Morley hoped the Parker promise would hold true as he collected his note book and wet gear. The forecast was for rain later in the afternoon and some dark cumulus clouds could be seen in the west already.

"Use their computer, a search engine will be quicker." Parker called after him.

Once again Mike was surprised by this inebriated man's sharpness. "If they have one and I could get access, I would still not be able to use it without…" he stopped mid sentence.

"…givin' y'self away." Parker completed the sentence. "No good if you are on the run."

Michael Morley set out on foot. He followed the path from the cottage until it branched and passed through the Botanical Gardens. It was a pleasant experience and temporary distraction that kept him away from the main road.

He managed to confirm a few details he already knew, but still needed a wider view. John Henderson would be the right person with whom to discuss the problem.

As a mental relaxation and an opportunity to visit some of the places he knew in his youth he took the longer way back along part of the promenade and Ventnor beach before once again retracing his steps through the Botanical Gardens.

As he followed one of the higher paths nearer the road he caught a glimpse of something that made his blood run cold. He thought he saw a slow moving silver Mercedes. He resisted the temptation to duck; they were now ahead of him. If he had been spotted it would already be too late. He knew that John Henderson had been pursued by a silver Mercedes, but it was surely paranoid to fear every passing one! However, the sight of the prowling car continued to unsettle him for the remainder of his journey.

There was a distinct smell of cooking when he opened the front door. A definite steak and kidney pie aroma. Mike instantly began to salivate.

"Bill?" No response.

"William?" Mike modified his call in case there was umbrage in the air; still no reply.

Mike became uneasy. He could not identify what it was, but he felt a cold shiver. Was he simply extending the paranoia he'd felt in the park?

As a precaution, he returned to the front door and began searching for a suitable weapon. He pulled out the metal electricity earthing rod set in the soil next to the front door step. Suitably armed, he re-entered the passage and moved towards the living room. He peered through the crack at the hinges of the partially open door. No-one. He moved so that he could look into the exposed part of the room. Clear. As he eased the door open a loud noise burst in his ears. He rushed into the room metal rod swinging. A programme on the radio that had been left on had just reached a loud climax. He spun full circle and checked the room. He turned down the radio. Mike had to take several deep breaths to stabilise.

Moving back into the passage Mike checked towards the kitchen. The door was closed. Something was wrong! Bill always left the door open! He moved closer and listened. All he could hear was the creaking of the hot oven. He tried the handle, releasing it once the catch was free. He kicked the door open and rushed in with the metal rod in the defensive position. The room was empty. As he turned to leave he was aware of someone behind moving fast. Spinning on the spot, he was just in time to deflect the carving knife being swung by William Parker. He shouted. "Bill! It's me, Mike!"

Parker's knarled faced had hardened to that of an ancient oak. He looked terrified. Parker slid his back down the wall and rested his forehead on his folded knees.

Mike crouched beside Parker and consoled him. "What's the matter, William? What ever happened?

"Two men on the path," he stumbled over his words.

"But people come and go along that cliff path all the time, William."

"No, they came in!"

"Where?"

"To the door, the passage, the whole house."

"What did they want?"

"Don't know! They had guns; I went out the back door."

"What did they do? Did they stay long?"

"They searched the house then went."

"They didn't take anything, or break anything?"

"No. They just looked and went."

"Did you get a good look at them?

"Sort of; quick like. They were big men and spoke with foreign accents."

"Did you recognise the accent?"

"Dutch, maybe, or South African."

Discovered! This was bad. They were probably looking for him. How on earth did they know where to look? It did not matter how for the moment, he had to get away immediately.

"I've got to go, Billy." He retrieved the notes and the diamonds he'd removed from the Panther. "I must leave now. I'm sorry to go like this, but you will be safer if I do."

Mike felt the security of the cottage had been sufficiently compromised that secrecy was no longer relevant and flipped open his mobile. "Directory enquiries? I need a taxi."

CHAPTER EIGHTEEN

"What do we have on this Jane Fisher; Morley's live in lover?" D.I. Kevin James looked at Derek Forest.

The D.S. had turned on the computer and was projecting a data sheet containing parts of Michael Morley's family tree onto the wall. He slid a clean sheet of paper into the wall frame alongside the image and wrote the words Jane Fisher in dark blue with a felt tip pen. Adding a central vertical line his hand hovered at its end. "What do I write next, anyone?"

"Married John Fisher in June 2001." A female detective responded without hesitation.

He began to scrawl the information beneath the line. "Okay, previous name?" He continued without looking round.

"Needs verification, but preliminary evidence gives her as Jane Brown, born Winchester, July 1976."

"Verification? That's sounds like a legal disclaimer. What's the hold up?"

"Too much going on in parallel, Sergeant."

"I know it's busy, but this is a murder case and she is a vital suspect or witness. We must get on top of it and trace her. Let's think smart – should we be tracing Brown this early? All her documents; credit cards; driving licence etc will be in the name of Fisher. Although it's possible she may think of using Morley."

"We ought to check all – just in case."

"In case what?"

"She has run away. She could have resorted to any name, but more than likely her first choice of an alternative would be her maiden name."

"Okay, I'll see if I can get some extra help. Do we have sightings available on cctv?"

"Yes, a few."

"A few? Where?"

"She's just been caught on a domestic camera system. The image is not perfect, but it does look like her. Now we know where to look we have been searching other, nearby, cameras."

"What other images?"

"There's one in which she appears to be getting onto a train at Brockenhurst."

"On or off. Which?"

"I haven't seen the images and can only go by what has been read to me over the phone."

"Get a download of the image. What about a bicycle? A witness said she was seen leaving on a bike."

"D.C. Smith is checking cctv records at Winchester station in case she abandoned the cycle there."

"Do we know what happened after she got onto the train at Brockenhurst? Which train, by the way?"

"We think it's the Lymington train, but someone is checking with the station manager now."

The Inspector twirled his cap on the table. "Sergeant, have we anyone available to check at Lymington for cctv images?"

The Sergeant hesitated too long.

"Is there something the matter, Derek?"

"No, sir, I do have a couple of officers there at present. I will get them on to it." He turned to the officer beside him. "Can you get those two to check the cctv for around midday, please? You know who I mean?"

The officer nodded and moved to the door.

"They're in pool car five. You may have to use their personal radios." He called after her as quietly as possible.

"You had officers there, but not on this case?" The Inspector was concerned that the effort might not be ideally focussed. "Who have you got there?"

"Prowting and Lucas." He admitted reluctantly.

"I wondered why they were not here. What's going on, Sergeant?"

"They are on this case, sir, but at the time I sent them we did not know that Jane Fisher had caught a train to Lymington."

"On some mission? You were going to tell me about later, no doubt?"

"I always keep you informed about anything that affects operational matters, sir."

The D.I. noted the politician's answer, but decided to let it pass for the time being. "Why would Jane Fisher be going to Lymington? Do you think she means to contact John Henderson?"

"That's certainly a possibility, sir." The Sergeant avoided revealing his true thoughts on the matter.

"Maybe you should have an officer on standby at his house; discreetly, of course."

The Sergeant agreed, but took no immediate action. Once again the Inspector felt he was being misled, but thought it might just be a case of his Sergeant trying to assert his own authority and not appreciating interference from above.

The female officer returned to speak quietly to Derek Forest before leaving again. Inspector paused what he was saying to regard his Sergeant expectantly.

"Good news, sir." Derek Forest answered the unasked question. "Jane Fisher did go to Lymington. She was clearly caught on cctv buying a ticket for Yarmouth at the ferry terminal." Inwardly he cowered in expectation of Inspector James' next question.

"Why would she be going to the Island? What or who is there for her?"

The Sergeant wanted to manifest a broad Gallic shrug, but thought better of it. "We need to look at that, sir. I will get somebody on to it."

"Yes, and quickly, Sergeant. Contact the Island boys and get them to provide a reception committee."

"There was some additional information that needs checking first. Lucas and Prowting are on to it apparently. I expect to hear from them shortly." He played a delaying card.

"Additional? In what way?"

"There's a question about her catching the ferry. They're checking."

"Not catching it, you mean? You think it might have been a ruse?"

"Well, that would be expected if she and Morley had planned this all along; more evidence that he's guilty." The Sergeant could not resist the opportunity to remount his hobby horse. He returned to the wall sheet to add Lymington as a positive sighting.

The Inspector tried to stimulate participation in other thoughts about relations or friends Jane might have visited. He began to wonder why he felt as if he was trying to push a tractor through deep manure. He was about to become critical when the female officer returned. The Inspector didn't hesitate to take over. "Please tell us all what happened at Lymington?"

The officer looked sheepish at the sudden outburst from the Inspector.

"She got into a taxi. Brian...." She corrected herself, "Detective Lucas says they managed to recover its registration from the cctv and phoned the company."

"So, they haven't managed to contact the driver yet?" The Sergeant retrieved his control of the meeting.

"Oh. Oh, yes. The driver said she was being chased by a man. The driver took her to the station and stayed with her until she got on."

"She got back on the train after being chased by whom?" The Inspector puzzled. "That's a worrying development, Sergeant. She might be an innocent person pursued by those who went to Morley's house." He knew that would be a painful consideration for his Sergeant. "We need the cctv images for Brockenhurst again at around tea time that day."

Derek Forest had little choice but to comply. He ordered someone to go through the later cctv coverage for the station.

The quality of the images and the skill of those searching quickly brought results. It was apparent that Jane had returned to the station and caught a Bournemouth train. They now had the task of checking the cctv images at each station. The Inspector handed the meeting to Derek Forest and set a new time that day for a reassembly.

There was a buzz as the Inspector entered the room. He could tell by the uncontrolled smiling that there had been a major breakthrough. He waited as everyone settled down before speaking. "This has got to be so good – just give me the bottom line."

"Jane Brown got off the train at Sway." The Sergeant was pleased to puff out his chest.

"How on earth did you manage that, Sergeant?"

"Constable Grant, Sir." He pointed in her direction. "Brilliant piece of thinking."

"Well, Constable, how did you do it?"

The Constable was clearly pleased but had to be encouraged to speak. "I thought that it might be quicker to check the street cctv."

"Street cctv?"

"Yes, send a patrol car passed each station and look for houses that had private security cameras. Most people would be in at tea time and if we got them to check their own system whilst we went on to another we'd soon have lots of researchers all working at the same time."

"That's amazing. Presumably someone confirmed they had caught Jane on their system?"

"Yes." The Constable agreed quietly.

Inspector James touched Sergeant Forest's arm and said conspiratorially. "I hope you'll make an official note of that on the officer's record, Derek. That was an exceptional piece of work."

The Sergeant nodded.

"Okay; everyone. That's a decent piece of detective work. Now we have to get to Sway and talk to this lady Jane. We'd better get on to it, Derek." He tidied his cap before slipping it onto his head and breezing out the door.

CHAPTER NINETEEN

The taxi driver glanced in the mirror. "You said Gurnard?" Morley felt uncomfortable about being specific. He was tired and becoming careless. He thought he had a foolproof system for remaining undetected. But the arrival of the men at the cottage seemed to contradict that belief. Should he further risk his security, or had the incident at the cottage been co-incidental? He hesitated whilst he tried to think of a suitable answer, but quickly realised that delaying would mark him as the passenger who was behaving strangely if the driver was questioned later.

The driver glanced expectantly in the mirror again.

"Yes, Gurnard;" Michael Morley confirmed.

"And the address?" The driver maintained his earnest gaze; "I have to know the destination before I can accept a fare." He reached up and adjusted the mirror. "Health and safety," the man smiled. The man subconsciously touched a small sphere at one side of the mirror. Morley recognised it instantly as a camera. There would be a record of him; another breach of his golden rule.

"Sorry; I should have realised. The pub will be fine." He wished he'd had the time to think. There was the risk of capture if he'd remained at the cottage. The men who had scared Parker were certain to return.

On reflection, he wished he'd asked to be dropped off at the Cowes' ferry. It would have seemed more natural, but he would have wasted precious time walking round to Gurnard afterwards. The most important thing now was speed.

It was not an auspicious start. The threatened rain began to deliver its promise. The driver switched the wipers on to intermittent and selected dipped headlights. Despite the poor weather Morley had to press on; get to the kayak; and head for the mainland. He would decide on the destination as he paddled.

"Are you in any hurry?" The driver peered into the mirror again. "Only if you are, it's better to go through Chale Green; there are traffic lights just before Newport," he smiled; "you wouldn't believe it; massive water mains burst!" The driver studied him carefully. Morley's paranoia worked overtime as he tried to figure out a possible pre-planned trap. How could a randomly chosen taxi driver be involved in such intrigue? If he was, why didn't the gang simply pounce on him at the cottage? It didn't make sense.

"Or I can take a chance; we might get there as they go green. If it's red there can be quite long delays. The driver sensed the reluctance of his passenger to engage in conversation.

"Let's go through Chale; just to be sure." Michael tried to sound casual about his choice.

Thirty minutes; time to relax. He was spared conversation as the driver fiddled with his radio and scanned the text messages on his booking screen. Almost mesmerized by the black text scrolling across the orange screen, Morley was free to worry about Jane. He hoped she had not be followed and wondered how anyone could have tracked him to the cottage. He'd better check now. Morley fumbled in his pocket and retrieved his mobile.

"Jane?" She had responded immediately. "That was quick you must have had it in your hand."

"I was about to call you." Her voice was stress laden.

"Are you okay; you sound worried?"

"I'm not sure. There have been a couple of men behaving oddly."

"How do you mean?"

"They wander in and out of the hotel but don't appear to be staying here. I've not seen them eat or drink anything. It looks very suspicious to me."

"Have they seen you?"

"I don't think so; I've kept out of the way."

Michael reflected on how someone had discovered where he was staying. It could not have been by accident. He feared that the same thing might have happened to Jane.

"Do they look like policemen?" He thought that using their technology it was a real possibility.

"No; they look like evil personified to me."

"Where are you now?"

"In my room."

"Stay there!"

"Don't worry, but I do have to eat."

"Use room service!"

"How are you? Is the cottage comfortable and how are you getting on with your new friend?"

Michael Morley had a dilemma. Should he tell Jane about being discovered?

"I'm fine," he lied, "I've made progress with the mystery of the Panther and intend to go to the Henderson's and check a few things with John."

"That won't be safe; his home will be crawling with policemen and possibly the men who attacked him." She became concerned.

"Don't worry, I'm not intending to walk up to the front door and ring their bell."

"How will you contact him? Ought I to phone him?"

"No! We can't chance it. His phone will be bugged."

"I could call round, or catch Mary at the shops."

"No! They will have thought of that. I will find a way, trust me."

"I don't think I can last much longer hiding here and eating room service meals. It will look suspicious and I will get in the way of cleaning staff."

"What you must do discretely and without lingering, mention the two men to one of the junior staff and return to your room. Don't remain to see what happens." Michael had thought of a solution.

"How will that work?"

"The staff will report it to senior staff, maybe the manager and he or she will approach the men. That should scare them off for a bit. At worst you will be referred to as one of the residents and no-one will report it as odd behaviour on your part later."

"You really think that will work? Won't they simply find another way around it?"

"Probably, but it will restrict their freedom to come and go as they wish."

"I'm still worried, Mike. Should I leave and go to another hotel?"

"No! Definitely not! They have found you once. They will find you again." Michael was beginning to fear Jane was on the verge of doing something silly. "Wait until after I have spoken to John, I will use his help to meet you somewhere. I might even come to the hotel."

"How could you?"

"Look out for something special. I might come as the postman, you never know."

Jane laughed at the thought of Mike in fancy dress. "Will you come tomorrow?" Jane became hopeful.

"It might have to be the day after, but I can let you know."

Michael Morley was suddenly thrown violently to one side as the car swerved into the curb and rebounded to the centre of the road. The driver released a few strong expletives. "Bloody oveners!" He used the Islanders' expression for people from the main land. "They have no patience on these narrow roads."

"I've got to go now!" Michael closed the mobile; released his seat belt and twisted to check to the rear. Through the rain pebbled window he could clearly see what he feared. The unmistakably shape of a silver Mercedes was snaking across the road after its near miss. The taxi's left indicator began flashing as the driver yielded to allow the car behind to pass.

"No!" Michael was positive. "Don't let them pass!"

"It'll be safer to let them get out of the way."

"No! It will be easier for them to kill us both!"

The driver had some difficulty coping with the sudden rush of information. Such proposals were not in his vocabulary. "Kill? What on earth are you talking about? I'm telling you there will be mayhem if I do not let them through!"

The Mercedes' driver, encouraged by the taxi's signal began a fast passing move.

"Don't let them through! They have guns!" Michael hoped he was exaggerating.

The taxi driver released another string of expletives before centring the taxi on the road. "How do you know they have guns?" The driver half turned to face his passenger. "What have you got me into?"

"It's a long story; but you must believe me and do what I say, or we'll both die."

There was a loud groan from the front seat.

The driver of the Mercedes abandoned his attempt to pass and brought his vehicle close to the boot of the taxi. The car accelerated again nudging the taxi hard before swerving wide to the right and attempting a forced passage; its two offside wheels half way up the narrow sloping grassy verge. In the rain, the car started to lose traction and slip back into the taxi. Michael felt the taxi accelerate as its driver decked his right foot. The other driver was taken by surprise and swerved before yawing in a long skid as he braked to avoid overturning. The pursuing car came to rest before disappearing from sight as the taxi sped over the brow of a steep hill.

"Well done!" Michael encouraged from the rear seat.

"How do you know these people mean trouble?" The taxi driver was still having difficulty in accepting what he'd been told.

"How many drivers do you know who, after what you have just done to them, would not be leaning on their horns all the way after you?" There was a puzzled silence from the driver.

"The people in that car are not interested in shouting at us. They mean business." He elaborated. "Look out!" A sharp right hand bend lay immediately ahead. Too tight for this speed! Michael braced himself for a catastrophe; any intended exclamation frozen in his throat.

The taxi driver engaged his brain then his right foot; holding the brake pedal hard down and allowing the Automatic Breaking System to pump the brakes. The car leaned severely throwing the now unbelted Morley to collide with the left rear door before squeezing him into the foot well. The rear of the taxi broke away to scrape along the hedgerow before a final zigzag back to the centre of the road. The road ahead remained clear of traffic. Morley scrambled upright and looked back at the bend. He continued to watch until the taxi was round the next bend. "Well done again!" He gave a relieved sigh, "keep this up and we will soon lose them; only go a little slower on the bends."

You've wrecked my car! This is my business!" The driver wailed.

"I'm sorry; if we survive this I'll see that it is repaired." Morley promised. "Take the right turn after the hump-back bridge ahead." Morley knew the area well. "It comes up quickly, so be careful." The bridge lifted both men and taxi before dropping sharply driving the men's heads into the roof. The vehicle made the turn quickly and without incident and accelerated along a narrowing lane.

Michael Morley peered through the wiper swept area of the rear window. They had not been followed. The road ahead continued to narrow and an approaching junction could be seen. "You need a left at the junction. Make it as quick as you can to keep us out of sight in case anything is following." Michael urged. He wondered how familiar the driver was with these narrower lanes. The driver braked hard into the corner just as the Mercedes crossed in front of them. Michael shuddered. All their efforts could be wasted if they had been spotted.

"Which way?" The driver needed an update.

"We still need the left." Michael was rocking back and forth willing the car to get going.

"You're wrecking my business." The driver wailed again.

"The men in that car will wreck a lot more."

It was sufficient encouragement and the car accelerated. Michael looked to the right to check on their pursuers. The car had stopped about 500 yards along the road and was beginning a turn. The taxi had been spotted!

"After the left curve ahead there is a turning on the right. Take it!"

"But that's a farm track! It's blind!"

"Not if you drive past the front of the farm buildings at the side of the house. You can then drive along a path that leads to their other entrance."

"Other entrance?" The driver was unaware of Michael's cycling days during which he discovered all the local short cuts.

"Trust me; the farmer has two access roads."

The driver turned the taxi onto the heavily rutted farm track. "What about tractors?"

"Let's hope there are none parked where we need to go."

Both men could now see a five barred gate directly ahead. Mike was disappointed. "Bugger, I'd forgotten that gate. He felt the taxi slow. "Don't stop; keep going!" He shouted.

"But, the gate! I'm not ramming my taxi through that bloody gate!"

"No need; it's half open!"

"We can't get through that!"

A man wearing Wellington boots; a long raincoat; and waterproof hat could be seen standing at the gate. He saw them; and afraid of the damage the taxi now racing towards him might do, he rapidly pulled the gate fully open.

"We can now!" Michael exclaimed; urging his driver to have courage. The taxi roared past the astonished farmer and slowed a little to pass the farm buildings. A dog began barking as they neared the farm house and ran out into the vehicle's path. The driver had just begun to brake when the dog decided to run back inside.

"Keep going!" Morley sensed the driver's weariness with the chase and knew he had reached that point where the force for survival equals that for surrender. "We're almost there!" Morley hoped to sustain the effort for another few seconds. The man acquiesced and drove the taxi up the slope to the main road. He cautiously nosed the taxi out. The road was clear. "Take the right then pull over on the left by the field gate. Let me out there and I will be okay."

The driver heard the news with relief and obeyed. "My car, you've wrecked it!"

Michael got out and examined it. "I'm sorry, but it is only a few superficial scratches; you can claim on your insurance." Morley was surprised at his callousness and immorality. He reached into his pocket and pulled out the bundle of notes he had grabbed as he escaped from the cottage. He divided the roll and passed half through the open passenger window. "Take this for now and I will check back with you when all this is over."

The driver remained silent, staring at the loose roll of notes on his front passenger seat. He looked up just in time to see Michael Morley climb the gate and disappear into the raging night.

Morley kept to the edge of the field and headed down its muddy margin. Above the wind he thought he heard the taxi pull away. He turned to watch as its headlights flickered through the hedgerow. As the taxi became lost in the higher shrubs further along its lights were replaced by another set coming in the opposite direction. The new lights slowed and pulsed through the thinning hedgerow. Even in the absence of street lights Michael could now make out the vehicle's shape and colour. It was the silver Mercedes. It stopped and two occupants alighted and began searching the bushes eventually finding the gate. They climbed the rails to gain height and peered into the darkening gloom. Morley instinctively crouched in the wet grass. They must have seen him leave the taxi. He hoped that their interest in him would ensure the safety of the taxi driver.

It was some time before his pursuers decided on an alternative course of action. They abandoned any attempt to follow him on foot and he heard the car accelerate away. He had to move quickly. The men would surely be working out which road to take in order to head him off. Morley ran as fast as the slippery grass and obscure ground would permit. He estimated their best course and realised that it was going to be a close contest. They would probably mistakenly believe he would be heading for the Cowes' ferry. That would delay them. The kayak was his ace card, but he had to cross the coast road before they arrived. Once beyond that road there would be no alternative for them. It was impossible to drive down on to the beach at that point. It would take them some time to realise that they had to follow on foot. By that time he hoped to be away on the waves.

Suddenly a nearby dog began barking. Michael Morley was shaken. He thought farmers, anger, and guns. Not good thoughts at this time. Speed was what he needed most; he would concentrate on that and deal with the dogs; farmers and guns when they appeared.

It took him much longer than anticipated. He constantly found the boggiest of places in otherwise dry fields. Hedges were often reinforced with strands of barbed wire. These tugged at his clothes and held him until he untangled himself, or accepted the inevitable damage.

As he crossed the final field Morley could hear the sound of the occasional car passing on the road ahead; a road he must cross before his pursuers arrived. The last fence was climbed and he crouched on the grass verge. He heard a woman's voice calling. He pressed tightly into a hedge. A dog appeared trailing a long lead before he saw the woman. He held his breath. The dog, less than ten yards away did not even pause to sniff the air. It was as fed up with the wretched night as its owner.

Michael moved to the curb and looked both ways. Nothing! He had taken his first stride when he saw them. Lights approaching from the right! In his paranoid state he flung himself to the ground; the cold wet unforgiving ground. From that prone position he saw the wheels of the Mercedes pass a few feet from his face. The car immediately braked hard. Without hesitation Morley scrambled to his feet; raced across the road; and flung himself bodily over the hedge opposite.

Committed now and no option for turning back he slipped and tumbled down the long sloping ground that would take him to his kayak and the sea.

A clump of coarse gorse arrested his progress. He paused for breath. He could hear the screeching tyres of the Mercedes as it accelerated back to where he'd crossed the road. Would they follow? He didn't wait to find out, forcing his body through the undergrowth towards the kayak.

The kayak was still there; Morley could see the familiar green cover and the boat's outline through the undergrowth. There would be no time for the formalities of donning his wet suit. It was the most difficult of things to attempt even when dry, so impossible in his current soaked state. He abandoned the idea of stretching the elasticated edge of the spray deck over the cockpit. It could prove a slow job. He needed to gain time, even though it risked the boat being swamped by a large wave.

Above him Michael heard the screeching tyres of the Mercedes again. That was a good sign, it might take them some time to realise there was no way down other than walking. He had bought a little time in which to launch the craft. As he rolled it up right he felt the ballast rock force its way through the front cockpit spray deck and roll down the slope. Damn! Too late to recover it; he must launch now. The kayak slid easily down the remainder of the slope and soon its stern was in the water. Morley turned the craft to seaward; retrieved the paddle; and fastened its safety line. He slid into the rear cockpit; wriggled the kayak free; and pulled hard into the dark storm.

Apart from unknown hazards, his main fear was gunshots. He was still a sitting target. As he bent forward and thrust the paddle blades he could hear voices approaching along the beach. Men were shouting to overcome the wind and waves.

Michael Morley had only one clear objective: survival. He pointed the craft towards lights on the mainland and paddled.

CHAPTER TWENTY

Detective Inspector Kevin James lowered the blind to obscure the low winter sun. Returning to his desk, he eased his 75 kgs smoothly into its black leather chair. He swivelled the chair a few of times before stopping to arrange a green folder so that its edges were parallel to the sides of the desk. He looked up and motioned the two detectives to sit.
Detective Christine Prowting hesitated before following the example of Brain Lucas. Both were apprehensive.
The D.I. opened the green folder; removed a single sheet of paper and studied it for a moment. "So, you've both been to the Isle of Wight?"
The detectives looked at one another uncertain if the first to speak would be the one to receive an expected grilling.
"An easy enough question to answer." The Inspector spun his baseball cap on the polished desk with an index finger.
"Yes, we have," agreed Brain Lucas.
"It seems to have got a little bit exciting?" He ran a finger along a note on the file sheet.
"It could have been worse." Christine Prowting admitted.
"I'll say it could, constable." Kevin James leaned back. "An armed response team had to be called in."
"It was the safest thing to do. I think…"
The Inspector held up a restraining hand. "…it would have been a far quicker response, Constable Prowting, had the team been forewarned that you were investigating a possible armed murderer."
"We didn't know that's what had happened." Brian Lucas tried to justify their attendance at the cottage.
"We were there to observe and report back, sir." Christine supported her colleague.
"All I can say is why didn't you?" The Inspector raised his eyebrows.
"We thought the house was empty. We checked carefully all round the outside." Detective Lucas rallied an argument.
"Very good; then, believing you were pursuing an escaped murderer, you went straight in!"

"The man we found was dead." Lucas defended their position.

"Right again, detective, but possibly killed by the very murderer you thought you were looking for. You had no idea he wasn't hiding outside in the shrubbery ready to injure you as well." The Inspector checked the sheet in front of him.

"On whose orders did you embark on this trip to the holiday Island?"

The two officers hesitated before Brian Lucas replied. "Sergeant Forest, sir"

"Yes, and you both obeyed like well disciplined troopers."

Uncertain if it was a test question the two remained silent. Christine Prowting wanted to mention that she had warned against the secretive approach of her Sergeant, but, in favour of maintaining team loyalty, held her counsel.

"Okay you two. You behaved in good faith, but failed in you duty to each other by not calling in assistance when clearly there was a real risk of injury. As two newly appointed Detective Constables, I expect you to learn from experience and never repeat mistakes. Do you both understand?"

The two constables nodded and left their Detective Inspector's newly appointed office with a feeling of relief.

The departure of the junior officers was followed immediately by the arrival of Derek Forest.

"Hello, Derek, come in, have a seat. What do you think of the new office?" He swivelled a little in the chair and tousled his hair.

"It's certainly a lot better than the broom cupboard, Sir." The Sergeant thought he'd better start with formal responses until he knew how badly this interview was going to go.

"I've just had a chat with Lucas and Prowting, Derek."

"You mean about the Island?"

"Yes, I do, Sergeant."

"Well, we've certainly got all the evidence we need on Morley now!" Derek Forest sought to ameliorate any damage caused by what he knew to be a lost cause.

"What the hell, did you think you were playing at, Sergeant?"

"Going after Morley, Sir; we knew where he was and had to get him."

"But I didn't know where Morley was!" The normally steady speech of the Inspector had heated noticeably.

"Why wasn't I informed of this escapade to the Island? Why weren't our people on the Island told that Morley was there? Why wasn't armed back up available when two brand new detectives entered a cottage where only minutes earlier a murder had taken place?"

The Sergeant faced with what he knew would become a merciless tirade conceded defeat. "I'm sorry, Sir, but as the information came in I just had to grab it and run with it."

The Inspector reached forward lifted his phone from its cradle and offered it to his subordinate before replacing it.

"I know, Sir, I should have informed you. I guess I was focussed so hard on getting Morley that all else blinded me."

"I can believe some of that, Sergeant, but I also believe that you suspected that I might have exercised some restraint. You thought that as I believed Morley to be innocent, I would not agree to such precipitous action."

"Well...."

"...well nothing, Sergeant. You're damned right I would not have agreed. You could have sent those two inexperienced officers to their deaths."

The Sergeant fearing instant suspension gambled on confession being good for survival. "I agree, Sir, it was the most dangerous concept I could have devised. At the very least I should have contacted you and advised using more experienced officers backed up with an armed response team. I take full responsibility."

The response threw the Inspector sufficiently that whatever he'd been about to say was lost. He looked at the man before him and wondered if change could ever be brought about so quickly. "Sergeant, you must realise that you are heading for a disciplinary hearing...."

The sergeant lowered his head and prepared for the worst.

"...if you even think of such a thing again..." The Inspector pulled himself up to his full six feet in the leather chair.

"Have I your promise that you have not done and do not plan to do any thing like that again?"

"You have, Sir." The Sergeant replied instantly.

The response was too quick for the Inspector. "Derek, I mean it. If you have deceived me in any other way I want to hear about it now and not after any future debacle. Do you understand?"

The Sergeant knew he'd been picked up for the speed of the first response and considered for a moment before confirming his answer.

"Putting that behind us, what's the latest we have on Michael Morley, John Henderson and Jane Fisher?" The Inspector resumed his usual level tone.

"We know Morley was on the Island. We have confirmation from a terrified taxi driver. We are pretty certain he got there by using his Kayak. We believe he may have stored it somewhere near Gurnard; that's where he wanted the taxi driver to take him."

"And do we know exactly where he is now?"

"No, but I've alerted everyone along the coast around the Lepe area. He's got to be heading that way."

"Be careful, Derek. He's proved to be more than a match for us in the past."

"It's his army training; he's a trained killer."

Kevin James didn't pursue his Sergeant's strong bias. "What's the latest on John Henderson?"

"We've found a witness who can confirm that Henderson made threats to kill Peter Langdon.

"In what way, threatened?"

"He alleges that Henderson had Langdon by the throat and appeared to be wrestling him and shouting about wanting his money, or he would kill him."

"He's quite certain?"

"Yes, the witness alleges that Henderson added he would feed the man to his pigs afterwards."

"When did the witness report this event?"

"Yesterday, Sir."

"We are now a week in to this murder and he or she...which is it, by the way?"

"A male, Sir, a Mr.Nicoli Ludvic."

"And he has only just come forward?"

"He didn't come forward."

"Oh?"

"No, he was traced by us tracking down an object he had left in the shop. He's scared and not keen on co-operating."

"Scared of what Henderson might do to him?"

"That's what he said."

"O.K. We need to talk to him again. It might be necessary to make this official and get the Met boys to drag a statement out of him. For the moment I think we should just have him in again for a reassuring chat. But let's leave a final decision until after we've talked to the squad." The Inspector looked expectantly at Derek Forest.

"And that leaves us with Jane Fisher, Sir."

The Inspector indicated that his Sergeant should begin.

"We know she got off at Sway and as there are only a couple of places for her to stay we intend to make enquiries first thing tomorrow."

"First thing? I thought we were going to get on with this straight away."

"Yes, she has to sleep somewhere tonight."

"Why not keep right on top of it?"

"We would be if we could find her. She may be holding out until late to sign in."

"You've checked all the possible hotels and bed and breakfast places?"

"Yes, Sir. No-one registered as Jane Fisher. The only way is to search each residence doing a face check to make sure. We might have a bit of a break through though. We're checking the phone calls received on the phone in the cottage on the Isle of Wight."

"That sounds more like a winner to me. Searching hotels is not going to be easy if people are on holiday. They will be in and out like the proverbial."

"No; it's okay, Sir, not that many holiday makers at the moment, we've arranged to visit each hotel before breakfast."

"Expecting a meal whilst we wait, no doubt?"

"I expect that might feature in the arrangement, Sir."

"Okay, let's keep the priority on finding Morley for the present."

CHAPTER TWENTY ONE

Jane Fisher stared at the screen. Mike had abruptly switched off his phone. Was he in trouble? She had to know. Jane quickly pressed the redial. There was no tone; only the unable to connect message. He'd switched off the phone.

Jane sat clutching her mobile and worried. She imagined all the possible explanations for what had happened. Already feeling bewildered and conscious of Mike's advice, she never-the-less decided to go down for dinner.

It was early evening and the room was only just beginning to fill. She remained at the entrance until she had made certain the two men she'd seen before were not present. Jane sat at her table and was immediately attended by a waiter. She felt awkward about applying Mike's advice about telling the staff about the two men. It seemed too melodramatic. It only happened on television or on film. She decided against it, resolving to remain vigilant and finish her meal quickly.

She had almost convinced herself that nobody could possibly know who she was. However, understanding why she might be acting paranoid did not in itself cure the condition. Every person entering was a prime suspect as a potential pursuer or kidnapper; especially those who lingered or hesitated near the entrance. Couples and family groups she discounted as safe. Jane's real worry was the male of the species. Each male who entered appeared to be endowed with features that automatically attracted suspicion.

Her meal finished, Jane prepared to retreat to her room and make a coffee. Michael should phone around half past eight and she was still worried about his sudden interrupted call earlier.

As she prepared to leave she noticed two men lingering at the open door. Both men were in their late 30s. The taller was dressed in an expensive broad stripped dark suit with sharply creased trousers. The other wore a black leather jacket, dark trousers and sported a pair of dark Raybans on his nose. The two men were scanning the room. Just looking for a suitable table; was Jane's first attempt at impartiality. This assessment quickly upgraded to 'looking for me' within seconds as the latent paranoia kicked in. She felt a sinister chill and instantly developed flu head. Jane averted her eyes hoping to avoid attracting attention. She thought how much better it would be if her future strategy included the company of a friendly male at dinner. The very thing her mother would have advised against. It took no more than a few seconds hesitation to intensify her fears. She'd lost sight of them!

Jane slowly looked up and affected a casual glance around the room. She left looking towards the door until last. They had gone! But where! She began to panic and quickly re-searched the restaurant. Nowhere! She must leave now!

As Jane got up she sensed someone close behind her. She moved away from the table fast and instantly felt a blow from behind that sent her staggering forward. In her paranoid state she emitted a loud scream, and was saved from falling by the man wearing the leather jacket. The whole restaurant now granted Jane the attention she had desperately sought to avoid. The man in the Raybans removed his steadying hands from Jane's shoulders. "You need to be more careful." He spoke in a monotone, barely moving his lips. The man's companion with whom she had collided touched her shoulder from behind. Jane shivered with revulsion and snatched the shoulder out of reach. The man smiled a crooked grin, or was it a sneer? "As my friend said, you need to be more careful. You should always look before you leap." The words seemed full of innuendo. "It might save you a lot of trouble; people die just crossing the road, you know."

She slumped back into the chair, her legs refusing to support her. "What do you want?" Jane heard her pathetic breathy voice.

"Want?" The man seemed to sneer again. He turned and left Jane to join his friend at the bar. A few words were exchanged between the two men and the person serving and within seconds a waiter was asking her if he could be of assistance. Jane felt confused and threatened. She ignored the proffered sympathy and rushed from the room and ran up the stairs. She pushed vigorously at the room door before realising she needed the card key.

As Jane began to grapple with her handbag she heard the sound of running feet coming up the stairs. She fumbled and dropped the bag spraying its contents over the carpet. They were at the landing below and the feet were still coming. She thrust the card into the slot and tried the handle. Nothing! She tried again, harder. Still nothing! Trying to turn the card she dropped it. The sound of the feet told her their owners were on the same landing and still running towards her. She made one last failed attempt in which the card jammed in the slot. Her assailants were right behind her! Jane turned to greet them in a final act of defiance.

Two teenagers stopped in their tracks and stared wide eyed at the strange sight of the woman in front of them, arms in the air, adopting a defensive stance and at the beginning of a scream. Jane lowered her arms and smiled a heavy sigh of relief. The two youngsters slid cautiously past her then turning a corner recommenced running to the sound of laughter. Jane tried hard to calm herself, but her heart continued to pound in her breast.

As she returned her attention to the lock she did not hear the quiet swish of the lift door, or the tread of feet on the carpet behind her. The card would still not enter the slot completely. As she tried for a final time, a hand reached over her arm; retrieved the card from her grasp; and reversing it opened the door. She caught the familiar smell of leather as the man in Raybans stepped back. Without hesitation, Jane rushed into the room and slammed the door shut.

Jane had sobbed into the pillow for half an hour. What had Michael done? Why hadn't he gone to the police straight away? She knew the answer. He was pursued by both the criminals and the police alike. He hadn't chosen to have people break into their house. That was down to John Henderson and his dammed Panther. Now she, too, was in danger. These were serious people. They carried guns and had used them. She had seen how real the guns were when Michael had blown the back off one of the criminal's heads. She had to escape!

Jane sat up and swung her feet onto the floor. She rose cautiously and turned off the light. She waited a few minutes before slowly moving the curtain a little so that she could observe the car park below. A car passed on the main road and a couple were walking along the pavement opposite. In the car park there was no sign of movement. She watched for a while, but all she saw was the neat line of metal boxes their colours modified by the street lighting. After she'd released the curtains, Jane paused. Something was wrong! She looked again. At first she could not see it, but then it dawned on her. The colours were wrong. The vehicle at one end of the line gave her an uneasy feeling. It appeared orange in the glow of an old neon lamp that had yet to be replaced. That meant the car was probably a light colour in day light. Then Jane recognised the curves and the iconic badge on the bonnet. It was the silver Mercedes! The two men downstairs; it was them! She'd not been paranoid! She had to escape now; there was no time for packing. She just had to run!

Dressed in warm clothing, she opened the door and checked the corridor: all clear. At the top of the stairs she paused to listen. There was only a general hum coming from below. Down one landing and listened again: louder now, she could hear voices, but no sign of anybody climbing the stairs. Once on the ground floor she could see the dining room doors. It was still quite early and the restaurant was buzzing with the warm sound of people eating.

The atmosphere seemed so calm and friendly that she began to feel that her fears belonged to another world. Such dreams were dispelled immediately. The two men loitering at the open restaurant doors started to hurry towards her.

Jane panicked. She turned and ran to the main hotel entrance. Soon her feet were crunching hastily across the gravel drive. The sound of her pursuers' feet could be heard close behind. She now raced desperately towards the main road. As she reached the exit a woman emerged from a black off-road vehicle

"Help me, you must help me!" Jane cried and stopped running.

The woman extended a comforting left arm, "You're safe now, Jane, I will look after you." and as the woman's right arm embraced her the left one clamped a soft pad over Jane's mouth and nose. Jane detected the smell of chloroform before her conscious world dissolved.

CHAPTER TWENTY TWO

As soon as the first paddle stroke had been completed Michael Morley realised how much stability the missing rock had given. In the choppy sea, the boat started to slew from left to right with each successive stroke. It was like trying to steer a space hopper. He sorely regretted not taking the time to replace the rock before launching; but he had been under severe pressure to get under way. Morley remembered the rudder and slid the control lines to lower it. Stability was instantly improved, but not to the extent the rough weather demanded. He had to help correct the effect of each stroke by varying the force he applied to its blade. He knew he was attempting a tour de force and wondered if he would last more than an hour. He was constantly punished by the required strength and concentration

The wind and rain blinded relentlessly; Morley had to squint in order to see anything ahead. The lights on the mainland twinkled tantalisingly, but kept changing position. Michael had difficulty orientating himself. He began to think it might be sufficient just to survive and make landfall. Unexpected waves reminded him he had to concentrate on their direction. Each mass of water hit the craft from the port quarter. Most of it ran across the partially sealed front cockpit, but its residue managed to penetrate the exposed rear one. He knew this would eventually flood both cockpits.

Michael Morley abandoned his original plan of returning to the Beaulieu River. If he landed there with soaking wet clothing it would attract attention. Using public transport would also be out of the question. John Henderson's place would be a suitable alternative. He intended visiting John in any event to discuss what he'd found out about the Panther. Beaching to the west of Lymington would allow him the shelter offered by the Hurst spit. He could easily find a stowage place in the undergrowth. The Henderson's property almost backed onto the shore and he was familiar with the narrow back lanes to the house. One consolation was that on such an unsympathetic night he did not expect to see many dog walkers.

Morley hoped that the police had reduced their interest in John. He looked forward to being able to dry out and receive John's help in solving the mysterious legend contained in the Panther. The next day he would leave for the George Hotel. Michael's major objective was still getting to Jane before she fell apart.

Michael Morley was relying on the fact that Jane had organised a double room at the George. Staff there knew that she expected her husband in a few days. A serious problem would arise if the police or the gang were in residence awaiting his arrival. He would have to exercise great care. Perhaps John Henderson's thoughts on the matter might prove helpful. But, whatever the risks he had to protect Jane.

He steered the craft to keep the waves head on and aimed towards Lymington. The main current, caused by the tide forcing its way through the narrows created by the Hurst Castle Spit, was running with him and keeping the kayak moving forward; if a bit messily.

Distracted thinking about Jane, an unnoticed wind shift brought a large wave breaking from the port side. Crash! The kayak went onto its side. Michael barely managed to control it, but had instinctively thrust hard down on the paddle. He had just managed to right the craft when the wave's bigger brother hit it full port side on. The boat was lifted and rolled; capsizing it fully.

For a moment Morley hung upside down, but unrestrained by a sealed spray deck, he was quickly ejected from the open cockpit. He felt the foaming water swirling round his face. His initial gasp of surprise had filled his sinuses and the top of his bronchi. He struggled to expel the excess water and breathe. He immediately raised the upturned boat above his head to escape. A third wave lifted both swimmer and boat alike, but the lighter kayak was lifted out of reach before crashing down onto him. He briefly experienced unconsciousness.

As he returned to a sensible state he found himself flailing with both arms on the surface of the water like a novice swimmer. The next wave lifted the kayak away from him towards Lepe beach. He coughed hard to enable a fresh breath of air to be taken and struck out after the capsized vessel. The kayak had disappeared into the swollen Solent. Its orange and red colours were no longer visible. Michael had no choice; the kayak was his life boat! With his arms plunging deeply in the water; he pulled hard whilst still choking on the initial gasp of sea water. Will weakening; he had an increasing dread of heading in the wrong direction. He veered 45 degrees westward and renewed his stroking. His arm contacted the safety line of the floating paddle. Michael quickly entangled his arm in the cord before pulling it taut. His heart leapt when he saw the familiar colours of the kayak.

It took several minutes for Michael Morley to regain sufficient strength to right the capsized boat. He would have to bail it before he could re-enter.

The process needed strength. Treading water at the centre of its length he ducked under and grasping each side, lifted it clear of the water. The effect was to push the swimmer under, so the process had to be repeated quickly as the boat was rotated 180 degrees. After two attempts Morley had righted the kayak, but it still lay low in the water. More waves threatened to swamp it. He knew he had to get inside and begin operating the bailing pump to complete its rescue.

Turning the stern into the waves he cocked a leg over the end so that he was astride the rudder gear. The sea began to complete the flooding of the rear cockpit. When the next wave lifted the kayak Michael threw himself chest forward and grabbed the back of the rear seat flattening his body to protect the cockpit from the pernicious sea. On the next wave he raised his body; brought his knees under him and slid into the craft. Large strokes of the paddle brought the boat back to seaward. Without hesitation, Morley began operating the bailer as he had never done before. Realising it would take too long to be perfect; he stopped as soon as he knew he could make progress into the weather. He leaned forward and paddled with renewed endeavour. Whenever he had the opportunity, Michael operated the hand bailer for a few seconds.

It was difficult maintaining full control, but Morley was sufficiently encouraged by his survival and progress that he resolved to continue with his plan. He was heartened by glimpses of the southern shore of the New Forest. He felt the false satisfaction of almost being able to walk ashore if he got into any more trouble.

After passing the end of the Beaulieu River with its marshy outcrops, he continued his line towards Lymington. Without charts, he would have to rely on experience gained in broad daylight to navigate his way passed the River Lym and all its marshy outcrops in darkness on a stormy night.

The lights of the Wight Link ferry danced through the rain. They began to sparkle on wave tops as Morley's kayak closed the distance. He was relieved to see the ferry; it gave him a good aiming point as it slowed to negotiate a zigzag course at the entrance to the river. Approaching the exit towards the sea Morley saw the lights of a second ferry. Its presence required the incoming ship to stop until the channel was clear. It would be too dangerous for Michael to cross the channel until both vessels had passed. He needed to keep powering into the waves. It would help keep the boat stable. But, he knew he would soon have to ease up and wait for the ferries to pass each other.

Suddenly, the side of one ferry was illuminated with a bright light. It flashed across the ship then tracked away along the coast. Morley risked a dunking by half turning his kayak. In the distance he saw the source of the light out at sea. It was slowly scanning the southern shore of the forest. As he listened he could just make out the heavy throb of a marine engine. He knew instantly who they were looking for.

Michael had felt sure the taxi driver would report what had happened earlier. It must have been the most traumatic event in his life. He had hoped that with the weather so poor any search would have taken ages to organise. The swift response meant they were determined to catch him.

The taxi driver would have told the police where he had dropped Morley. It was a simple step for them to estimate where he was heading. But, did they know about his kayak? Perhaps they suspected a boat of some kind once they failed to find him on the beach. Whatever they had done they were currently breathing down his neck and he had to respond.

The outgoing ferry had passed and the incoming ship was beginning to move again. Morley could not wait. He plunged the paddles alternately into the dark sea and committed his final reserves of energy. His timing had to be spot on: too slow and he would perish under the ship's bow; too fast and his attempt would be seen and receive a massive blast on the ship's horn, giving him away. The kayak was lined up for a fast passage close to accelerating ferry when Morley felt the tug of a mud bank slow it. He could not stop now! The rudder! It was still lowered! He tugged on the rudder lines and raised it. Jerking his whole body upwards and wriggling he forced the craft free. As he thrust towards the ship once more he realised he had miscalculated its acceleration. It loomed above him! In one last effort he applied every ounce of his strength and heaved on the paddles. He thought he could feel the aluminium tubing of the paddles flexing with the stress. The wide flat car deck ramp now threatened him. Its lower edge was at head height above the water and could decapitate him! It was only feet away as he began to paddle across it. The ship's small bow wave lifted the kayak pushing it up into the ramp above. Michael Morley instinctively ducked as the ship caught the stern of the kayak taking off the raised rudder assembly. The craft tilted wildly and swung through 45 degrees, but Morley continued to power the craft out of danger. He was lucky! The new larger ships had reduced wake and permitted him a safe escape.

He stopped paddling and rested; completely exhausted. The slight wash of the ferry pushed the kayak gently to the edge of the river. Michael Morley looked back towards the Eastern Solent. The powerful search light was closer and was illuminating the Lymington River at one end of its broad sweeps. He had to keep going.

The sloping paved wall of the old salt pans came into view. Morley could tell there was too much mud exposed to enable him to paddle much further. He had hoped he might just mange it to the lock gate before he would have to extricate himself and the kayak. There was no choice. He had to wade across the mud dragging the kayak. The kayak had to be pulled an additional hundred yards or more before he would be able to stow it

Michael wondered if he might get away with stowing it among other small boats at the nearby dingy club. But it large orange and red shape was too likely to be noticed and arouse suspicion. He would have to try the thick under growth along the footpath.

It was an hour before Michael in his exhausted state was able to drag the craft up the slope and finally into the bushes. On several he had to resist the temptation to abandon it where it was and run. During that time he saw no-one. The poor weather had been a blessing as rain and wind had continued to rage.

Morley reached the tree lined lane that led to the back of the Henderson's home. He prepared himself for an unwelcome reception. He was covered from head to toe in thick smelly mud. He was not going to be the favourite guest of the evening. He considered the possibility of the police being present: a guard outside; a dog maybe. He would have to exercise great caution.

The way ahead appeared to be clear, but he paused to be certain. He thought he could hear a radio with music playing. The wind made certainty impossible. As he began to advance his eyes grew accustomed to the dark lane and he could make out a darker shape. Tucked well into the hedgerow about 50 yards ahead was the outline of a car. It was impossible to tell if it was a police car. He moved carefully towards it. As he grew closer, Morley observed that the car lacked any official identification. Music could clearly be heard coming from inside the car; the windows of which were completely steamed up. He ignored strong reservations; he was tired and needed to be successful. The weather for the first time that evening was assisting him.

The car's only occupant was clearly silhouetted against a distant light. Confidence and experienced gained in training for Iraq brazened him and, crouching low, he crept passed the vehicle.

Suddenly his sea sodden, rain soaked mobile burst into life. He'd been sure it was defunct! He plunged into nearest bushes behind the car and wrestled with his pocket to retrieve the offending instrument. He thought he'd managed to switch it off but, with slippery fingers and thumbs, he'd pressed the receive key by mistake. As he twisted the phone into his body to stifle the distant voice of the caller, he heard the car door open. He was about to be caught! He wanted to make a run for it, but knew he would not get far in his exhausted condition. Instead he crouched and waited. Above the howl of the wind he thought he heard the feet moving towards him. He dared not look! His dark wet clothing might provide sufficient cover. The driver who'd alighted from the vehicle must have wanted to avoid returning to sit in wet clothing, for almost immediately Michael Morley heard the car door slam.

Michael gave the driver sufficient time to settle before whispering an apology into the phone expecting Jane to be the caller. When he was sure it was safe he moved quickly along the road to a more secure position. "Jane? Is that you? I'm sorry I had a little bit of trouble."

"Michael, is that you?" A Dutch voice smiled from the phone.

Michael's heart leapt and began pounding in his chest. His worst fears had been confirmed. "What have you done with her?" He saw little need for social niceties. There was a long silence. "Well?" He demanded.

"Michael, you sound very tense. I have only good news for you: try taking things as they come; learn to relax a little."

"I want to know what you have done with Jane."

"All in good time, Michael," the voice continued in a calm flat tone. "I want to do you a little favour in return for another; it's as simple as that."

"Do me a favour? You can do that by releasing Jane right now!"

"Mr. Morley; I can see that you are not used to how these things are done, but you will learn." A sinister sarcasm lingered. "One has to agree a deal before one can put it into operation. Otherwise no-one will know what is expected of them. Surely you can understand that?"

Michael Morley tried desperately to second guess the game that was being prepared. He was wary of risk, but he also knew that if he didn't at least pretend to be interested then Jane would be in instant danger.

"O.K., what deal?" Michael twisted out of the wind as it became more difficult to hear over the constant gusts.

"Good. I am pleased to see how quickly you are learning. First, you have a small problem with the police?" The voice paused after the inflected question.

"Sorry?" Michael matched the questioner's style.

"Mr. Morley you must know that the police want to arrest you for murder?"

"I don't know that." Mike emphasised the word, know; "but if they are, they would quickly discover that it was an accident whilst defending myself against one of your thugs." He couldn't resist a note of triumph.

"Aaah, then might I suggest that you contact them as soon as possible and set the record straight?" The voice retaliated, losing a little of its calm.

"I might have to do just that; especially if it means getting Jane back." Touché! Mike thought.

"Yes, Jane, Mr. Mor….Michael, you must miss her very much, I think."

"You bloody know I do, you bastard; just let her go!"

"Wait, wait; calm down, Michael. It will do your blood pressure no good at all."

"You let me worry about my blood pressure and just release Jane!"

"Jane is fine. You may speak to her in a moment; once we have agreed our deal."

"What deal?"

"The one in which I do not provide the police with evidence that would lead to your conviction for two murders and one in which you provide me with the contents of a certain Panther."

"Two murders? What on earth are you on about?"

"So, you do not remember the second murder? How remiss, Michael."

"I've already told you, and you know very well. It was self defence against one of your thugs. There was no second murder."

"You deny killing the vagrant, William Jonathon Parker?"

That was literally a killer sentence for Morley. He was stunned. It took some time for it to sink in. "You bastard! The two thugs I escaped from on the Island. You had them kill Parker? He knew nothing!"

"So, I put it to you, Mr. Michael Morley, that to ensure the continued silence of a witness, you killed him!" The irritating smile imitated the voice of a barrister.

Morley realised that if Parker had been killed in the cottage not only would it provide a trail back to his aunt but, subsequently, to himself.

"You serpent of an evil bastard! If you had him killed then you have the Panther!"

"That is quite correct, Michael. But I was not interested in the animal only its contents."

"The Panther was empty!"

"That's what I thought you would tell me, Michael. Therefore I needed to have some guarantee that will make you change your mind."

"So you took Jane hostage. Let me talk to Jane right now!"

"Mr. Morley, you are getting ahead of yourself. As I explained earlier, we must strike a bargain before that can happen."

"There can be no bargain. The evidence will eventually prove me innocent. You have no bargaining position." He brazened out what he knew was a flawed argument.

"And, what about Jane; does she not feature in your part of any bargain?"

"No deal if I can't speak to her."

The Phone went dead. Mike examined the screen: good signal; good power; no connection. His one chance to hear Jane's voice and he'd let her down!

He had to overcome his frustration and think calmly. Clearly they expected the Panther to contain diamonds. Somebody had double crossed the gang. They now believed the person responsible to be himself and he'd just cut off communication with Jane!

But they had Jane's mobile. They could contact him at any time. They were playing with him: leaving him to sweat a bit. It would soften him up for a subsequent call. Perhaps this was the time to go to the police? He could tell his story and leave the police to find Jane. Too risky! The police would concentrate all their efforts on prosecuting a double murderer. There would be formal identification, finger prints, DNA the whole shooting match.

By the time they had appointed officers to the various issues to be investigated Jane would be dead and the criminals gone. He had to stay free! He still had the clues that those who'd double crossed the gang had left behind. The Panther was proving to be a dangerous toy.

Michael Morley stood on tip toe and peered over the fence. He checked the rear garden; no-one. He slowly turned the ring pull handle of the tall wooden gate; entered the garden; and made his way across the lawn to the conservatory door. It was unlocked! He puzzled at the Henderson's sudden disregard for their security. Police! They must have a Police guard inside the house! John would never leave a door unlocked, or the rear gate. He entered the conservatory quietly closing the door behind him. Feeling every bit the criminal, he listened. Silence. He was about to enter the house of a close friend as if he was going to burgle it. Morley felt a great compulsion to go round to the front door and ring the bell. He had to resist any such action. John and Mary would understand later. Now unsurprised to find the kitchen door unlocked, he entered.

Michael was familiar with the layout. He knew that beyond the closed door ahead was a large hallway. Immediately to the left beyond that lay a room in which small antique items were kept for cataloguing and examination. The room had seen less activity in recent years, because John Henderson increasingly relied upon the expertise of Michael Morley.

He opened the door to the hall. He could hear the sound of a television and possibly a voice. As he released the handle it slipped from his wet grasp creating a loud clonk. He had to act! He dived into the side room and closed the door. Michael Morley sank down beside the door on the hinge side. Anyone glancing in might not see him behind the door.

Loud voices approached from the living room at the other end of the hall. His heart was racing as he heard the footsteps enter the kitchen. A male voice called on a radio. "Charlie delta two; Charlie delta one, over?" After a short pause the call was repeated. After another pause came a response. "Charlie delta two; go ahead, over."

"Anything to report? Over."

"No, sarge, just more rain; no movement out here, over."

"Charlie delta one, out."

He'd been right about the Police!

John Henderson's voice could be heard asking what the policeman was doing. Before the police officer could answer Mary's voice asked the same question. Mike inferred from their tone that the Hendersons were not happy with the policeman.

"I'm just checking that the..." he paused mid sentence. "...what are these muddy prints doing here?" The officer bent to examine his find. Unseen by Mike who was now distraught that he overlooked such a simple precaution as wiping his feet, the officer swept up part of the print with a finger. "Fresh," he said holding up his finger for John Henderson to examine. John's mind raced in panic. There were frightening echoes of the fatal night when he'd shot the intruder.

"They're mine, I'm afraid..." it was John's voice.

"Yours?" John's wife was surprised.

"Yes, sorry love. When the officer went to the toilet earlier, I slipped outside to check the dustbins were still okay in this wind."

"But...." his wife was about to ask how he had managed that without her knowing when John interrupted her.

"I'm sorry; I meant to clean it up, but the officer returned and it didn't get chance."

Mary knew that to be a lie straight away, but thought it might not be the right time to query her husband. She hurriedly pushed the police officer to one side; retrieved the cleaning materials from under the sink and removed all the marks. The policeman was too astonished to prevent her. "Those were evidence," he proclaimed.

"Evidence of me going to the back door, officer;" Henderson extended both arms. "Guilty I'm afraid, you had better arrest me."

"Very funny, sir; but they might not been yours alone." The officer growled opening the door and peering into the gloom. The wind forced an entry and he had to quickly close it. Undeterred, he made his way for the hall where the prints stopped. The police officer bent and patted the carpet using the flat of his hand. "Hmmm..." He opened the study door and flicked the light switch. After a cursory glance into the room and an even more half hearted look behind the door, he turned out the light and closed it. John released an audible sigh.

"Something troubling you, sir?" The officer grew suspicious.

"Only your presence officer. I know you are an essential part of our protection, but it grates a bit."

"Bearing in mind what has happened so far, I believe protecting you is a very wise precaution."

Once the officer had locked the back door, the group returned to the living room. The policeman then radioed his colleague to inform him that he would have to use the front door if he wanted to get in for breakfast in the morning.

Michael Morley sank to the floor behind the study door and prepared for a long cold, wet soaked night.

CHAPTER TWENTY THREE

The D.I. went directly to the hotel reception desk. He had hoped he and his colleagues would appear like members of the public, but judging by the reaction of the receptionist they had failed. She looked behind as if expecting to be overheard before asking quietly if they were police officers. The D.I. nodded and discretely presented his card.

"The Mrs. Fisher you asked about is registered as Mrs. Brown. She is not in the hotel at the moment." She apologised.

"May we talk to the manager somewhere private?"

The receptionist picked up the telephone and informed the manager, Brian Baker, that the men had arrived. Whilst D.I. James waited, Sergeant Forest and Christine Prowting strolled into the dining room; casually observing those present before returning.

A smart suited man in his mid forties appeared at the foot of the stairs; introduced himself; and invited the three officers to follow him.

Once they were seated around a small polished table in an equally compact office; the D.I. removed two photographs from his pocket and slid them towards Brian Baker. The manager picked them up and studied them.

"Do you recognise those people?" The Inspector tousled his hair, "Either of them?"

"I believe I recognise the woman, but you should have asked my receptionist. I like to do the rounds during the evening, the personal touch, you know, but she and Margaret will have had much more contact with the guests during the day."

"Yes, I could have asked her downstairs, but I was trying not to draw attention. Would you invite her to join us please?"

The manager picked up the phone on a desk against a window.

"I assume Margaret is your receptionist's opposite number?" The D.I. began writing in his pocket book.

"Yes, she and Rose and sometimes other members of staff if there are other duties."

Rose looked at the photographs carefully and seemed hesitant to commit herself. She picked up one then the other, twisting each in the light as if trying to improve the image before exchanging it.

"Are you having difficulty recognising them?" The Sergeant asked, allowing his impatience to govern the pace. These had been the only photographs they had found in the Winchester workshop and the police had assumed they were of the couple. Neighbours had confirmed that the photographs were of the two, but had made no comment about how representative they were of their current appearance.

"Pick up one and stay with it until you have decided." Sergeant Forest suggested.

The D.I. shot his sergeant a disapproving look.

"I'm pretty certain this is Mrs. Brown." Rose laid the photo on the table as if it was a playing card, giving it a little snap as her finger slipped away. "But she's much older than this, now."

"That's very helpful." The D.I. encouraged, "but the other one; the man?"

A worried expression spread across her face as if fearful of answering an exam question incorrectly. The Inspector was sensitive to the possible creation of a false witness, obtained by bulling.

"Don't worry, if you cannot identify him – that, too, can be very helpful."

"I'm sorry, but I've never seen him before."

"You're absolutely sure?" insisted the sergeant.

The receptionist shook her head. The Inspector slowly moved his head side to side and held a warning finger up to his sergeant.

"Thank you, Rose, you have been very helpful. I wonder if you can tell us a little more about the woman, Mrs. Brown?"

"She registered a few days ago. She was very pleasant and polite, but kept herself to herself. I didn't see her go out into the gardens like other guests. She only appeared briefly at meal times."

The Inspector motioned to his sergeant and detective constable to go down and check the register. He smiled reassuringly at Rose. "Are you saying that she stayed in her room all day?"

"No. That's the strange thing. Whenever the maid went in to clean, the woman had gone."

"And neither you nor Margaret saw her leave?"

"I can't answer for Margaret, but when we discussed it she never said otherwise." She thought for a moment. "On the other hand, Margaret is only covering lunch time this week."

"But I thought you saw her come in for dinner?"

"Yes, split shifts this week. I do the morning after breakfast and then the evening meal time."

"So, it's possible she was able to slip in and out without you being aware?"

"Only at shift change, so-to-speak."

The Inspector made notes.

"Oh! I did she her the first day! She was sitting by the rear lawn enjoying the autumn sunshine." Rose had suddenly remembered.

"Only once?"

"Yes."

"Did she seem to you to be a reclusive type?"

The receptionist puzzled for a moment. "That's difficult. She tried to avoid public gaze. I mean you didn't see her like other guests who are travelling alone; sitting in the lounge hoping to share a chat with someone. But when you spoke to her she sounded like a person who was comfortable speaking to others."

"Okay. Now think for a moment about last night. Did you see her at all that evening? Think carefully." Rose was about to reply instantly in the negative, but stopped. "I think I may have done." She replied quietly.

"Sorry, did you say that you may have done?"

"I was busy printing off some bookings, but looked up because somebody had appeared at the entrance."

"And was that Jane Brown you saw?"

"I'm not certain. I just had time to say good evening before she turned and disappeared again." I did stand up to get a better view, out of curiosity, but there were others in the lobby and I couldn't see who she was, or where she went."

The D.I. beckoned Rose to follow him and went down to the reception desk.

Kevin James stood side by side with Rose at the counter. "Is this where you were standing when you tried to see who it had been?"

"Yes, but inside the reception area." Rose replied promptly.

The D.I. followed her gaze and imagined how the line of sight would have been blocked by others. "How many people would you say were in the lobby at that time?"

She considered for a few seconds. "I can't really say. It was near seven thirty. There were quite a number arriving together, so around half a dozen at any one time."

"Do you remember who blocked your view?" He was thinking of potential witnesses.

Rose looked astonished. "How would I remember…many would have been chancers…" she paused; "No; there were two men; a bit strange. They had been in and out for about an hour."

"Did you recognise them as guests?"

"Definitely not guests."

"Can you describe them?"

"One was a big brute; foreign looking; wouldn't want to meet him on a dark night."

The inspector smiled encouragingly, "and the other?"

"He was more normal in a weedy sort of way. Average height and build, but was always a step or two behind his master, if you know what I mean."

"What were they wearing?"

"Dark suits and, later, dark long over coats."

"Did you hear them speak?"

"No, they just came and went."

"Did you see them when they finally left?"

"The last time I saw them was after they pushed through the people in the lobby?"

"When was this?"

"After I had seen who I thought might have been Mrs. Brown."

The Inspector felt a surge of energy on receiving the latest information. "Do you have cctv cameras?"

"Yes, but you would have to ask Mr. Baker about those."

"She arrived here the day she left Winchester." The sergeant finished writing a note. "So, it's pretty clear, this could have been pre-planned."

"Not necessarily." The Inspector cautioned. The three officers were now sitting in the comfortable arm chairs in the lounge, sipping coffee. The sergeant had asked the female who had delivered the coffee if she recognised the people in the photographs. She only recognised Jane, but reported a strange event that is alleged to have occurred the last time she had seen Jane. She refused to be drawn on the details saying that she had not witnessed it personally, but that the bar staff had told her later.

"We had better try the bar staff." The Inspector forced himself to leave his comfortable seat.

"We could even get them to bring us a drink." The detective joked. The Inspector gave her a special withering look before softening it with a smile.

The barman confirmed he had been on duty both that week and the current week. The Inspector turned over the photo so the barman could see it. "Do you recognise this woman?"

"Yes," he replied without hesitation. "That's the lady in number twenty four."

"How can you be so sure?"

"Because I have to keep a tab record against the room number."

"You didn't get to know her name?"

"I think it was Brown; Jane." He winked.

"So, you got on that well?"

"No, not really – just a bit of banter."

"I understand you may have witnessed some sort of incident involving Jane?" He deliberately move to the using the familiar language in the hope of encouraging a more relaxed, fuller response from the man.

The man shrugged. "I don't know what happened. I might be right out of order in repeating what I saw."

"I would be grateful if you would just tell us what you saw, or believed you saw, and leave us to draw the appropriate conclusions."

The barman wiped the bar with a cloth and looked down as he spoke. "There were two men. They came into the bar about sevenish, looked around and left again."

"I take it there's more to it than that, but what did they look like?"

"A large chap; six and a few inches and weighing in the order of 15 stones or so; the other was pretty average, five ten and not much over twelve stones."

The detective sergeant busied himself noting the details. "Distinguishing features?" he prompted.

"No. Short hair; suits and I think I caught at least one Dutch or South African accent."

"Not sure about the accent?"

"No, it was just for a second; and there's the general hubbub in the background."

The Inspector swung an arm in a wide arc. "Right, so how was this related to Mrs. Brown, Jane?"

"Well, the two men returned later and hung about here." He indicated the end of the bar. She should have been at her table by sevenish. At that time the two men who had continually kept going to the dining room doors and looking into the passage, left suddenly."

"Then what happened?"

"I went to the door."

"Why?"

"Because of the way they'd been behaving."

"What did you see when you reached the door?"

"They were leaving by the main entrance and going towards the car park."

"Did you see Jane?"

"No. But I think they were following somebody. I could tell just by their actions, they were pushing roughly through those trying to enter, but I did not see Mrs. Brown."

"But this was the time you had been expecting her to arrive for dinner?" The D.I. observed. "Is there anything else you can add that you have not already covered?"

"I don't think so."

"If you do remember something, contact us immediately; it's very important. I would ask that you do not discuss what you have told us with any body else."

"But I have ..."

"I know you have already; I'm asking that you stop from now on, okay?" The man nodded.

"I'd also like my sergeant to get down what you have just told us and have you sign it as an official statement?"

"You want me to go to the police station?"

"I would prefer it, but if it is inconvenient, I'll have him do it here." He turned to his two colleagues and asked them to help the barman prepare a statement for signing at his convenience.

"I think we now have a time and date for Jane Brown's disappearance." The D.I. finished writing with a sense of satisfaction. Not one born of success, but more with a feeling that perhaps she, at least, might be innocent; a feeling tempered with a sense of foreboding. He now feared she may have become a hostage.

The D.I. and the sergeant strolled out into the car park and surveyed the building for cctv cameras. There appeared to be two: one covering the car park at the entrance area; and another covering the far end of the car park.
When they returned to the lobby they found Brian Baker waiting for them; beside him stood a lanky youth whom he introduced as Jeremy. He explained that Jeremy was their cctv expert who would be able to find any sections of recording the D.I. might wish to view.

Jeremy guided the D.I. to a small windowless room that had the distinct feel of having once served as a broom cupboard; something with which he'd become familiar.
    Once inside, each man squeezed into the green patio chairs provided. Within seconds a 30 inch lcd screen was scrolling thumb nail images showing a date and time. Jeremy explained that each image could be activated to reveal its video once the D.I. had chosen a time and date.
Jeremy selected a split screen to display both cameras side by side. The images were of excellent quality and full colour. He demonstrated how he could switch to a full screen image if required. "What exactly would you like to look at?"
    The D.I. requested starting at 18.50 on the day Jane had disappeared. "I might want to look at images before that, but I will let you know. I only need a quick look now before I seize the computer so that our forensics team can give it a thorough look at."
    "Seize it? You can do that?"
    "Absolutely: I should do it right now, but I need see if there is anything my officers can attend to straight away. Lives may be at risk."
    "Right." Jeremy began the scan at 18.50. "If it's urgent I can speed up the feed rate."
    "Okay; give me times two. Any faster and we might miss something."
    "Early evening, there won't be a lot happening."
    The D.I. leaned forward; rested his chin on his extended fingers; and watched intently. On the right hand screen there were five cars present; a mix of new and older cars.
        On the other screen nearer to the entrance were two vehicles; an older model silver Mercedes with the classic icon mounted above bonnet and a

new four by four off-road vehicle sporting long whip aerials. The D.I. had just begun to turning over in his mind thoughts about the John Henderson incident and the alleged role played by a lightly coloured Mercedes when two men appeared from the direction of the lobby. "Hold it!" The police Inspector cried.

Jeremy stopped the frame.

"Go back and let's see it at normal speed." The Inspector flipped open his note book and recorded the time shown on the image.

The video ran at normal speed showing two men fitting the many descriptions that had by then emerged, making their way towards the Mercedes. They checked their watches and looked around the car park as if expecting someone before returning to the lobby.

The larger man re-appeared at 19.15. He went straight to an off-road vehicle with large whip aerials and stood beside the nearside door. The passenger window lowered and a female face appeared.

"Stop!" exclaimed the D.I.

"I can only give times two on the magnification." Jeremy had anticipated the next request.

The D.I. leaned forward. He did not recognise the face, but it was so clear that he knew one of his colleagues would quickly be able to identify her. "Well done. Please carry on."

At the 19.30 point the inspector was intending to close down the search and leave the rest to his colleagues. But, just as he moved a woman appeared, leaving the lobby in a hurry. It was Jane, he recognised her from the one photo he had seen. As Jane ran towards the car park exit the female occupant of the black off-road car opened the passenger door and intercepted her. She placed a comforting arm around Jane's shoulders before smothering her face with a cloth pad. Jane collapsed to the ground. The two men caught up with her and lifted Jane and stuffed her unceremoniously into the back of the car. The men then climbed into the Mercedes and it sped off at high speed quickly followed by the off-road vehicle with its whip aerials swaying on its roof.

CHAPTER TWENTY FOUR

John Henderson stepped quietly down the stairs. The rain outside was still pelting the windows and the wind occasionally rose to gusts that made the house shake.

At four a.m. he felt he had the best disguise for his movements. Babies arrived and old men died at this hour of day. It was the universal time of low ebb and he hoped his police protector would be suffering his own particular nadir.

He checked the sitting room to ensure his uninvited guest was snoozing peacefully, then entered the hall and made for the study door. He paused and listened before quietly opening the door and slipping inside. "Michael?" He called softly. He heard an instant rustle as his surprised visitor struggled to his feet.

"John? Is that you?" Michael was nervous about discovery.

"Yes," confirmed the voice from the darkness, "I thought it could only be you." He crossed to the window and parted the curtains a few inches admitting a dull glow; sufficient for two men to recognise each other. "I was alarmed when I saw you had left your foot prints."

"I'm sorry, I was so exhausted; I wasn't thinking straight." He shook John's hand firmly. "I was impressed by your quick thinking."

"I feared for a moment it wouldn't work, but Mary's timely action removed the evidence before he realised."

"Please thank her for me."

"I certainly will; when it's safe to do so."

"I'm afraid I've brought you new problems. I'm sorry. I did hesitate; unsure whether or not to come to you."

"Why?"

"I was worried that I might not be welcome."

"Not welcome?" A note of pain crept into the voice. "I can't imagine a time when Mary and I would not make you welcome, my dear boy."

"I knew I would make things worse for you."

"I can't think how you might do that, but it will certainly be worse for you if one of my guardians arrest you."

157

"I know, but I had to risk it. I have to ask you about Jane."

"Jane? I thought she was with you."

"No, we arranged that she would go to the George hotel – only the police don't know – they must not know."

"Your secret is safe with me. You must believe that."

"Sorry, John; I apologise if it sounded otherwise." Michael patted his friend's arm. "But, I fear Jane has been taken hostage by the same people who were after you."

"You're joking! That's awful. Are you absolutely sure?"

"I need to get to the George and check for myself."

"How on earth do you know she's been taken hostage?

"I received a call from Jane's pay-as-you-go mobile. It means that she's either lost it, or, as I suspect, is now held hostage."

"It's probably some clown who's found the phone."

"I don't think so. The voice at the other end sounded pretty certain and knows about the Panther."

"My dear boy, we must tell the police right now!" Henderson grabbed the door handle.

"Wait! No you must not do that!" Michael seized his hand firmly.

"But this is serious. You need all the help you can get!"

"You can't; they would simply arrest me and put Jane on the back burner."

"I could go to the hotel for you." Henderson listened at the door. "It would be a pleasure to get away from my guardian."

"It's a kind offer, but it would be too risky. If the gang were there you could become the next victim."

"I can phone from a phone box and enquire after Mrs Morley?" Henderson was unsure of the pre-arranged name

"It's Mrs. Brown; Jane's maiden name."

"Well, I could do that."

"No. You might be followed or worse." Michael Morley then realised that Henderson kept referring to the police as protectors. "What is your true status with the police, by the way? Are you still accused of Peter Langdon's murder?"

"Status undecided, my boy; but bait in a trap best fits the bill at present." Henderson stepped back from the door.

"I guess we are both suspects and victims at the same time." Michael noted the irony. "We both have to prove our own innocence by finding evidence against ruthless murders."

"That's the way I see it. If only I had rejected Langdon's offer of the Panther." Henderson sighed.

"We can't rewind. We have to move on and keep ahead of both sides."

"By the way, what's happened to the Panther? Have you made any discoveries?"

"I had to leave the Panther. It's along story, but what I have found are these." He removed the soaked remains of the three notes and the diamonds he'd retrieved from the Panther.

"From the Panther? I assume hidden in some way?"

"Yes; three notes one inside and one in each eye socket. They were not meant to be read by any casual observer. The diamonds were those you might have seen adorning the eyes."

John Henderson set the diamonds to one side and handled the pieces of paper carefully. He began to tease them open. "We'll need to dry these cautiously, Michael."

"I was hoping you would be able to do that and make a start on interpreting them."

"I'd be glad to, but first we must attend to the problem with Jane."

"I will leave before the police start moving about in the morning."

"Yes, but you can't go anywhere until you have dry clothes." Henderson returned to listen at the door. "I will fetch some of mine from the airing cupboard and bring a couple of towels." John Henderson turned as he left the room. "My clothes will only fit where they touch, but it's the best I can do." He patted his rounded stomach.

"No chance of a bath then?" Morley joked.

"'fraid not; that would be sure to wake the whole house." He whispered. "But I can bring a bowl of water;" adding; "you must prepare to leave quickly. These boys will be about early enough."

"See what you can do with these." Henderson reappeared in the doorway. He passed his friend a fresh change of clothing; a pair of black brogues and two towels before placing a bowl of water near the window. He returned to the door. "I've been thinking. I really believe I ought to insist on going to the George myself. I'm sure that Mary would agree. No-one would suspect a thing. If I drew a blank it would give nothing away." He raised a hand against the anticipated protest. "This is something I owe both you and Jane."

"I can't let you do it." Morley hissed from the dark as he wrestled to remove his sodden clothing. A long silence followed whilst John Henderson tried to think of a way of convincing his friend. Suddenly he brightened. "I've got it!" he exclaimed at normal volume.

"Shhhhh!!" Michael hissed in condemnation.

"I've got it!" His friend repeated in a quieter voice. "I will invite the police there for lunch. Both of them shall come with me!" He declared proudly.

"Nice thought; but bribery?" Morley was cautious, "and you wouldn't be inviting the two you have now. Their replacements will be along as soon as it becomes light."

"Tricky that, my dear boy." Replied a disappointed Henderson, "but maybe the new chaps will be even more susceptible – they'll think it's how their colleagues had been treated; the jealousy thing!" The speaker had renewed confidence.

Michael Morley was touched by the enthusiasm with which his friend was trying to help him. He was really throwing heart and soul into solving the problem. But Morley had another plan; a far riskier one. He remained silent until he had completed his transformation. It felt good after all the suffering at the hands of the unsympathetic elements. He was comfortable and dry at last.

The light outside was beginning to send yellow hues to form ghostly shadows of the furniture across the floral carpet. Michael watched as they began to move through a widening arc. "This has to be something I do myself, John. I appreciate what you are offering to do, and under other circumstances I would be proud to accept your help."

"What do you plan instead?" Henderson was mystified and felt slighted.

"I plan to go there and make myself known. I will take up the room reserved by Jane and stay in residence."

"That would be suicide! The police would pick you up straight away."

"They might if they knew I was there. That would depend on the hotel staff."

"If you confirm that Jane has been kidnapped, you will need all the help you can get. You must surely then go to the police!"

"They would only think I was trying to create a diversion. They would believe they had their man; their double murderer. They would assign a low priority to looking for Jane. This way will be the quickest way to find her."

"And share her fate!" Henderson cautioned him.

"That's exactly what I plan to do; for better or worse." He was resolute.

"What do you mean, double murderer?" Henderson caught up with Michael's previous statement.

"Oh! Just to add to my joy, the bastards have killed Bill Parker on the Island."

"Bill Parker?"

"Sorry, that's more of the long story, no time now. But if true, then I'll be wanted for two murders now."

John Henderson sighed again. "Will this never end?"

Michael Morley fabricated a smile. "We have to keep going. I must for Jane's sake."

As he turned to go there was a quiet tapping on the door. Michael pressed himself instinctively into the corner behind the door's hinge. Henderson grasped the handle and slowly opened the door.

"Was that you shouting just now?" Mary's voice hissed. "What were you thinking of? You'd wake the devil himself!" She pushed past John and entered the room. When she saw Michael crouching ready to spring; she softened her tone. "Michael! How are you? How is Jane?" Without hesitation she gave him a huge hug.

"Mary! Michael has to get away. We mustn't delay him; Jane is in trouble and he will be if our two guardians find him!" Her husband closed the door.

"If you stop raising your voice, it would help."

"I was only sur…"

"Shhh!" Mary interrupted her husband. She opened the door a few inches in time to see the crumple suited detective entering the kitchen. "We must leave! Quickly John, come on!" Only Mary had time to vacate the room before the officer retraced his steps, intercepting her in the hallway.

"Ah, I was awok…" The detective looked embarrassed, "I thought I heard a noise," he corrected himself. His mistake had cost him authority. That had now passed to Mary.

"I expect you heard me coming down the stairs. My foot often slips on the last step." She smiled beguilingly, "I must get John to retread the step." She made her way to the kitchen. "Would you like a coffee?" She called over her shoulder.

The officer did not answer or follow, but remained lingering in the hall. Suddenly he turned and headed for the study.

"John!" Mary almost screamed. "John! Will you join us for coffee?"

John Henderson's high intellect kicked in. He flicked on the study light and snatched up a vase from the inspection table raising it towards the light. The door flew open and a wide eyed detective stared in disbelief.

"Hello, detective;" John appeared unfazed. "Take a look at this vase, would you? Hasn't it been restored wonderfully?" Henderson offered for inspection the brand new flower vase his wife had bought only a week earlier. "One of Michael Morley's best efforts yet, I think."

The detective, who was concerned not to drop a valuable object, took a step back.

"What are you doing here at this time of the morning?" The man tried to recover his authority.

"The same as you, I expect." Henderson exaggerated the careful return of the vase to the table; "hoping for a coffee." He indicated the door, "Shall we make our way to the kitchen?" The detective remained suspicious. He sensed manipulation, but was unable to identify its specific nature.

"Do you normally get up at this time of the morning?" Suspicion was part of the detective's breeding. It was an instinct that had little room for doubt; especially for evidence pointing at guilt.

"Only since the accident," Henderson clutched his coffee mug tightly. "You get stuck in a time warp: at night the mind usually dwells on the new experiences of the day. When the day remains sterile, the mind holds on to some previous trauma, there is no scope for new learning. Ergo: no learning; no sleep."

The detective had no room for what he considered to be esoteric waffling and held a much simpler view. He believed an innocent man was one who slept peacefully through the night. Only the guilty suffered tortured dreams. He saw the climax of his role as curing the suspect by proving him guilty and releasing him from that torture. "Do you know where Michael Morley is at this moment?" The detective's instinct kicked in.

"How could I know where he is when I am held a prisoner in my own home and you are here to supervise me?"

"I believe that it is possible through means of which I remain, as yet, unaware; or through some earlier contact during which he made known to you his plans."

"That's a remarkably convolute argument."

"Convolute or not, I have a gut instinct that I am right."

"Then I hope the instinct in your gut will not keep you awake at night."

The detective, without further comment, carried his coffee back to the sitting room.

"Unlock the door." John winked at Mary. She followed the detective to make sure he had settled in a chair and placed her mug on the small table. Excusing herself for a moment she returned to the hall and quickly retrieved a key.

The Hendersons and the detective were in earnest conversation in the sitting room. Michael Morley left the study and went to the side door at the end of the hall. He tried the door and found it unlocked; Michael smiled. As he stepped into the porch and opened the outer door he was aware of John Henderson standing only feet behind him. Without looking round he said, "Thank Mary," and made his way down the drive. Henderson picked up the uncollected mail from the day before.

"Who was that!" exclaimed a harsh voice from behind Henderson.

John turned and revealed the mail in his hand, "Only the postman," he smiled.

The detective raced to the double pillared entrance to the drive and out into the middle of the road. A passing car screeched to a standstill with its horn blaring. An angry detective exchanged furious words with the driver.

John Henderson re-entered the porch and closed the door.

CHAPTER TWENTY FIVE

Michael Morley pedalled steadily towards the George Hotel. Riding Mary Markham's cycle felt strange. Suddenly, he had been taken back to a bygone age with its ubiquitous planetary gear three speed hub. There was a marked difference on even slight inclines. He had to concentrate on keeping up momentum, changing gear in plenty of time. His own 21 speed gear drive would have eaten the steepest hills. Fortunately, the terrain was mostly flat and he had time to enjoy the freedom cycling brought.

From his superior height, he was able to see over hedges and peer into an otherwise unseen world. The brightness of the day cast an unrealistic glow on life. He temporarily forgot the struggle in which he was engaged until the harsh blast of a car horn brought him crashing back to reality.

His mind ached to know where Jane was. He tried to imagine where she might be and who might be with her. Was she simply a prisoner or was she in real danger, tortured even? He had grown mentally tired and physically weaker as he dwelt on her well being. He had to force himself to concentrate on a logical strategy.

Morley tried to anticipate the negative side of his current plan: he wondered if the police or the mob had worked out where Jane was staying. The warning he had received from Jane's mobile had initially given him a great scare. He was afraid for her safety. But, supposing they had only stolen her phone? The idea seemed improbable, but after the passage of time the harshness of facts blurred; he even speculated that the police had used it to scare him into surrendering. The great unknown was whether or not the hotel was staked out. It seemed bizarre that he, an antique furniture restorer, was even contemplating such thoughts; but caution had to come first.

The George appeared a welcome and familiar sight. It rose with a historic splendour from its gravelled frontage and extensive rear lawns. It held only the forecast of a pleasant welcome and a warm interior. However, in his current quest, Morley knew its innocence was a manifestation of some euphoric deception.

He cycled passed and carefully examined the parked cars and people adjacent. All seemed normal. He continued a hundred yards or so before returning to pass again. On the second occasion he looked for anyone who seemed to be lingering suspiciously, or sitting in parked cars. Soon, he realised the futility of such guesswork; and knew he had to go inside.

Morley walked confidently past the reception desk and approached the restaurant. One door was locked open, so he was able to linger near it and observe those inside without becoming obvious. An elderly couple at the bar were booking lunch; a younger couple were walking away from it carrying drinks. The latter pair settled in the red leather armchairs at a table near the far windows; close to them, sat a lone goon like figure reading a newspaper. He estimated the man's height as a good six feet and as someone worked out. The man wore smart black jeans and a dark heavy top coat large enough to conceal several weapons.

Morley instinctively withdrew deeper into the shadow of the passageway. Of all those present, it was the goon like character who had the greatest impact. Conscious that he was probably developing an eccentric paranoia, He decided there was no immediate threat to him and concentrated on checking where Jane was.

Again adopting a confident style, Morley walked assertively past reception and immediately climbed the stairs. Room 24 Jane had told him. He listened as he ascended in case he was being followed. The hotel was very quiet. He found the room on the third floor. He walked passed and turned a corner before retracing his steps to ensure he was alone. He stopped at the door and listened. Not a sound. He knocked quietly on the door. Receiving no reply, he knocked a gain, much louder. Morley tried the handle, but the door was securely locked. As he stepped back he collided with a man in a dark suit. He apologised and stepped away.

The man was in his late thirties and of average height but solidly built. He looked at Michael as if assessing an opponent before nodding and continuing towards the stairs. Morley waited until he had disappeared and reflected on the inappropriateness of such formal clothing in a holiday environment. This was clearly a second suspect for his growing collection. Michael decided his best move was not to lose sight of a potential enemy and hurried back to the lobby.

He arrived just in time to see the man in the suit disappearing into a room at the rear of reception. The man seemed to be staff. The door closed leaving the reception desk unattended. Morley seized his chance and stretched across the counter in an attempt to retrieve the key. He had just managed to wriggle sufficiently to touch the key when the rear door reopened and the receptionist emerged. Her bright red hair added fire to the mixture of shock and amazement scrawled across her open mouthed face. "Can I help you?" She asked with a tone that suggested quite the opposite.

Michael groaned inwardly. "I'm sorry, there was no-one around and I just wanted to retrieve my key; number 24."

The woman stared at the large bell next to a sign that read, please ring for assistance. Without speaking she flexed her fingers and stroked the pad on her computer. She looked up and scrutinised his face. "You'll be Mrs Brown, then?" Michael felt his face blush. This was not one of the potential problems on his list of things to avoid. He remembered that Jane was using her maiden name.

"It's a bit complicated…" he reached for his wallet. "…Mrs Brown, Jane Brown, is my secretary," he hesitated before further qualifying, "my partner."

The receptionist waited for him to open his wallet and retrieve his credit card as identification. He paused. This would expose his real name and visit. The police or the mob would be able to place him there. He agonised for what felt like minutes, but he needed to know what had happened to Jane; there was going to be risk what ever he did. He handed the card to the red haired woman. She read the name, frowned, but continued to search some notes the computer revealed against the booking. Michael waited for the anticipated rebuff. The woman ran her finger across the screen. Michael panicked; the police must have left a note; he prepared to run. The red haired red haired face smiled and confirmed that there was a note, reading aloud that Mrs. Brown had said that her husband would be arriving sometime during her stay. The receptionist emphasized the word husband as she spoke and looked carefully at his face for reaction.

"Something that needs future attention," he smiled in relief.

"Hmmm." The receptionist removed the key from its hook and handed it to Michael. "Dinner is from seven o'clock," she added helpfully.

Morley thanked her and turned to retrace his steps.

The receptionist began entering Inspector James' number.

As Michael made for the stairs he noticed the goon like character leaving the restaurant and heading for reception. The man looked directly at him.

Morley raced up the stairs two at a time. He entered Jane's room and closed the door. He stood with his back against it and took stock of the room. Everything was neat and tidy, but the daily cleaning by the hotel staff would have seen to that. He tried to imagine Jane in the room. How would know she had been there. He drew a deep breath, but there was only the faint lingering scent of cleaning fluid. There were no personal items on display.

Morley turned to place an ear against the door. Not a sound from outside. He wondered if the goon had heard the conversation. Was the man following or worse, summonsing help from his criminal associates?

He went to the window and peered down. There were only a few cars and no suspicious movement of people. He turned his attention to the wardrobe and drawers. Everything was as he expected. Jane was a very neat person and everything was tidily arranged. It was difficult to tell if any item was missing or what she had worn on the last occasion. He was a man and, like his fellow genre, a complete novice at that sort of thing.

He was about to enter the bathroom in the hope of better clues when he thought he heard a bump against the door. He stood mesmerised as the door slider moved slowly. He had just adopted a protective crouch when the door was thrust open and the shorter goon appeared. His right hand was fully extended and held a hand gun pointing directly at Michael's head. This was not the first time he had faced a gun like this. His mind flashed images of the previous occasion when his reaction had led to all the problems he was now facing. The thoughts were debilitating. He had simply frozen. The goon was saying something, but Morley could only hear a kind of growling sound. Michael realised he stood a chance of taking on this smaller man, but he couldn't turn the thought into action.

The man became more agitated at Morley's lack of response and he grasped the gun double handed and steadied the weapon as if about to fire. Morley tried to move his legs, but he was a prisoner locked in the memory of his previous encounter. He waited for the explosion that would discharge him into oblivion.

Suddenly, the suit appeared behind the gunman. Michael smiled involuntarily. The goon read the look and began to turn. Two rapidly moving arms engaged the gunman removing his weapon as it discharged a single shot into the floor. In seconds the man was firmly clamped head down into the floor, his arms locked behind his back. The explosion had awoken Michael. Suddenly, he was completely alert and running; down the stairs out into the car park. He retrieved Mary's cycle and pedalled like fury away from the George and out of immediate danger.

Michael Morley's next moves were not part of any plan. Where could he go? John Markham would be closely watched now and his own house and workshop would be a crime scene. He knew that a gun discharged in a hotel was bound to bring the police immediately. The hotel staff could confirm his name; he imagined how the police would simply conclude that yet again this dangerous now double murderer had to be caught.

The man in the suit, who ever he was, would be able to swear that it was the goon who was holding the gun. What on earth possessed a member of staff to tackle a gunman without hesitation?

Now that he had more time to think, Morley realised the action had been smooth, professional. Who ever he was, he was not a civilian.

The most important thing was to avoid detection. Michael needed to find shelter; to maintain his anonymity. In the distance he could already hear approaching sirens. He had to get off the road. The forest nearby was open heath land, he needed better cover. He stopped at the next gate on the left and saw a gravel path leading to a large group of oak trees. As he closed the gate behind him a police car whined its way past in the direction of the George hotel.

The woods offered good temporary cover; he would be free from detection by infra-red cameras above as the trees were still in full leaf and remained wet from the previous night's rain. He had to find a permanent residence. Staying at a hotel was not an option. He would have to use his credit card and that evening's television news bulletins were bound to carry his photograph. Living rough did not hold a particular appeal and he needed to be able to keep clean and dress above suspicion so that he could still move freely whilst he tried to locate Jane.

He pushed his cycle out of sight into a group of rhododendron bushes and sank to the ground, his body and arms convulsed in a fit of shaking. The re-enactment of his first encounter with a gunman had brought back not only a vivid memory, but also a sense of futility. Would there ever be an end to his nightmare? Would he ever be able to recover normality? An introverted despondency grew.

The sharp crack of a braking branch wrenched Morley from a shallow sleep. He had dozed off. The sun had moved some way towards the horizon. His watch showed that he had slept for more than two hours. Adrenaline started to accelerate his heart and he scanned the immediate area for signs of activity. Restricted to a narrow field of view, Morley stirred his body through the pain barrier of stiffness to crouch so that he could peer behind to the left. Another sharp snap sent him sprawling on the ground. He feared discovery and cursed his inability to stay awake. He readied himself for action and turned to the right. The two forelegs of a New Forest pony stood on fallen branches only feet from his face. His sudden surprise was equalled by the horse. It twitched and reared back two large strides before turning and trotting deeper into the wood.

Morley stood and leaned against the tree. His mouth was dry; he needed water to drink and something to eat. He had to sort himself out before nightfall.

Exploring revealed a wood of uniform density with no sign of human habitation. Reaching a fence at the far side of the wooded area he saw a large meadow beyond. As he prepared to return to the road a flash of white on the far side caught his attention. Moving to gain a better view; he could see the white side of a caravan.

As he approached, Morley could see more than half a dozen holiday caravans. He paused to check for signs of inhabitants. The site appeared to be deserted. Perhaps these were just holiday lets now out of season? There was the possibility these were caravans used by migrant workers. Farmers often made such provision to attract foreign workers during busy periods.

Michael Morley checked that the site was free of security devices before testing the door of the nearest van. It had been locked using a simple key. Checking a few more confirmed a similar arrangement. He tried to look inside one, but the windows were misted inside. It looked as if they had not been used for a week or more, but he wondered if some sort of routine maintenance was used to keep the inside dry and avoid fungal growth. How often would the owner check?

Michael Morley decided that a caravan would meet his immediate needs and set out to collect his cycle and retrieve its tyre levers. They would adequately deal with the lock. Knowing John Henderson, he was sure that he would not have permitted his wife the embarrassment of a puncture without the means to repair it.

CHAPTER TWENTY SIX

D.I. Kevin James gazed at the rain dancing on the pavement below. He watched Chief Inspector Julia Monroe cross the road springing over imaginary puddles. He wondered why she hadn't driven to work.

The Inspector moved away from the window in his new office and returned to the problem of his five year old son's birthday. The planned party activities included finding presents hidden in the garden. The sudden change in the weather called for a major revision.

"Okay to come in, sir?" The Inspector had not heard his Sergeant's knock.

"Yes, yes; come in. I'm sorry Derek; I was re-planning an important event."

The Sergeant glanced at the rain racing down the window. "That will be Peter's birthday I take it?"

"Yes, I'm hoping my wife will be able to organise a plan B."

"Yes, a useful asset in organising a party – a wife." He heaved a resigned sigh.

"Sorry, Derek, I had forgotten." The Inspector reflected for a moment. "You've never thought of re-marrying?"

"No. Anne's premature death just closed a whole book somehow. I had to concentrate on our two boys."

"Of course; grown now and doing well?" The Inspector queried.

Any further discussion was interrupted by the appearance of Brian Lucas and Christine Prowting. Each made an apology for lateness, citing problems with rain soaked clothing.

"Okay this time, but study the subject of planning contingencies."

"I wish my boss had been that understanding when I was your age." The Sergeant growled, "I would have been given the worst duties for such an offence."

"They'll learn." The Inspector smiled. "You have some important progress to report, Sergeant."

"Yes. And I hope it's the important information I want to hear." Julia Monroe stood in the open doorway. She closed the door and leaned against the adjacent wall, folding her arms. It was clear from her lank dripping hair that she had come directly to Kevin James' office after entering the building. "Sorry, to gate crash your meeting, D.I. James, but I have a number of appointments today and I like to hear the progress on this one before I have to leave."

Kevin James indicated a chair, but the D.C.I. declined the offer. "I really can't stop and I don't want to wreck the rest of your meeting."

The D.I. twirled his baseball cap on the table then sat at the head of the table. D.C.I. Monroe watched, mesmerised.

The D.I. caught her look: "my son insisted," he twirled the cap again and smiled.

"Now, Sergeant, what have you got for us?"

The Sergeant flicked on the over head projector. "First, we were faced with the murder of a man who visited Michael Morley at his premises in Winchester." He indicated a name with a laser pointer. "The victim had been shot at point blank range; a very deliberate killing; more like an assassination. It had all the hallmarks of a gangland settlement. The chief suspect is Michael Morley who is well connected in the antique business." He clicked to a new image. We now know the victim was Klaas Oberlander, a Dutch National. He is not on any of our domestic data bases, but is known to the police in Holland. He has, or had connections on the African continent; South Africa in particular, and is thought to have spent most of his time commuting between there and Europe. He was suspected of visiting the UK, Germany and Holland in connection with smuggling, but has never been caught. Oberlander is subject of an international arrest warrant for murder and has a record of gangland violence."

"Sergeant; I've got to stop you in full flow. You still have no evidence that links Morley positively to Oberlander and certainly not to his death. As I have said before, the death could have been the result of an attempted robbery that ended in an unplanned tragedy."

Derek Forest breathed a heavy sigh. "Bearing in mind the international warrant and the man's record there has to be a criminal connection here! In cases of attempted or successful robberies the victims usually contact us, or are at least present when we arrive. The murderer, for that's how it appears, had fled the scene."

Julia Monroe looked at Kevin James and shook her head. She pointed to her watch and gave a delicate shrug.

"Okay, Sergeant, we can go over specific details later, please continue." The D.I. had accepted the hint.

The Sergeant refreshed the screen and used the laser again. "We've contacted the South African authorities and they confirm a positive link between Oberlander and a man known only as Baas Buurman. It's not believed to be his real name. They are convinced that Buurman is the main organiser of an extensive diamond, possibly blood diamond, smuggling ring and that Oberlander was his international runner. Buurman is a secretive individual who has others carry out his orders. This has made it difficult to catch him out. Nothing of Buurman has been seen or known since Oberlander's death. It's possible that he has been forced to come to England to organise a replacement."

The Sergeant moved down the screen. "We now have an identity for the murdered man's accomplice. It was a Wayne Turner, a UK citizen and a nasty piece of work. He's a dim witted junior enforcer and has a well established record for violence. There's more than enough evidence to show him at the Winchester premises and Oberlander even had Turner's telephone number in his wallet.

"Klaas Oberlander, a Dutch National; and an international arrest warrant. We need to identify any other contacts of this man. There must be some we can watch. It will be the only way we are going to catch him if he has entered the country. We need to get on to this asap Inspector!" Julia Monroe's voice betrayed frustration.

"What have you done so far, about this Wayne Turner, Sergeant? He may be the weak link in this international chain. " The D.I. was impatient.

"Nothing yet, I was going to discuss it with you this morning. We've only just made the connection."

"Oberlander left his body. We need to have another look; just in case. Check everywhere he has stayed." The D.I. twirled his cap, thoughtfully.

"That will probably prove difficult. He's not likely to have advertised."

"No, but if you do get lucky, Sergeant, you will find other gang members. We might even solve a few crimes."

"We do have a possible connection with another already." Derek Forest flicked to another display. "We can connect Wayne Turner to Otto Visser, another Dutch National."

"Two Dutch Nationals? That sounds like a trend. What do we have on this Otto Visser?" The D.I. frowned.

"He's dead."

"Dead? How does that help us, Sergeant?"

"He was murdered in London a day before Langdon and we think we may be able to link both men."

"That's a major piece of information, Derek, why are we not already pursuing it?"

"I thought that would be the purpose of this meeting!"

"I would have preferred it if you had consulted me straight away."

"I was busy trying to confirm another connection so that I could give you the whole story."

"Another connection? That would begin to look like progress, Sergeant. What's the new connection?"

"There is a man, given as BS, appearing in some of Peter Langdon's paperwork; lots of references connected with unspecified purchases and sales. It looks like a clear attempt at disguising something illegal. However, Langdon had slipped up. In the back of his diary he had recorded the man's full name, Buster Schmitt, before rubbing it out and replacing it with the initials. He had not been careful enough and we were able to recover the full name."

"That would be real progress if we can quickly; and I mean quickly, locate and question these people..." Julia Monroe gave the Sergeant a hard look. "...and you think Morley also had a gun, Sergeant?" She was wary of the unjustified speculation.

"If Morley was a member of this organisation, almost certainly. I think he was probably a central element in fencing stolen antiques at least." The Sergeant was resolute.

"So, can you connect the gun left on the premises with Morley?" The D.C.I. challenged.

"Not yet; number ground off, but the forensic lads are looking at ballistics and for anything else we can use."

D.I. James retrieved his cap from the table and stood. "I think we'd better bring in this Wayne Turner before he disappears into the woodwork." He looked at the Chief Inspector anticipating counter input, but she nodded a quiet agreement and prepared to leave. "I'm tied up all today, but can we have a meeting in my office at nine tomorrow, Kevin?"

Kevin James looked uncomfortable but agreed.

The D.C.I. turned at the door. "Before I go, where are we with this Henderson man?"

The D.I. looked at Sergeant Forest; "Sergeant?"

Derek Forest quickly advanced the images on the screen. "Here we have the eyewitness account given by Nicoli Ludevic, a local man who was in the shop on that day. This is going to put Henderson behind bars quite quickly."

The Detective Chief Inspector glanced at Kevin James and raised her eyebrows expectantly.

"It's not quite that straight forward, I'm afraid."

"I'm sure it's not, Inspector." She turned on her heels and left.

"The D.I. dismissed the two junior constables and asked the Sergeant to remain. He closed the door and sat down again at the table.

"Sergeant; Derek," he personalised his address. "I appreciate your unstinting enthusiasm; your keenness to get to the end game, but I still worry that it can become unbridled enthusiasm."

"I don't understand, sir. We both want to get the bad guys off the street and the sooner we can do so the better it is."

"I know, but you need to consider alternative possibilities before rushing in."

"I do, sir, but with my nose. I have had years of experience catching these people and I can tell who we need to bring in straight away." He tapped the side of his nose. "You would spot them, too if…"

"…if I had worked the streets as you did all those years ago?" The Inspector finished the sentence for his Sergeant. "I hope there's no tension between us as a result of our different routes into policing."

"None at all, sir; I only meant that I'm good at the ground work because of my street experience and that you are good at bringing it all together, because of your education."

"I'd rather think of us as working together as a team, Derek. We are on the same side."

"Aye, me, too; I don't want any conflict."

"Good. Let's look for a moment at some of the evidence." He read some notes he had made earlier. "You referred to the dead man as the victim, and his death as a gangland killing. We now know that he was a serious criminal with a record of violence."

"It still could be a gangland killing if Morley is the gang's fence or enforcer."

"Maybe, but we do not have the evidence. What prevents you from seeing the possibility of Morley being the victim of a failed robbery attempt?"

"The fact," he emphasised the word, "that Morley is nowhere to be found."

"There may be a perfectly good but worrying explanation for that: We know his assistant, Jane Fisher has been taken hostage. We saw the cctv with our own eyes."

"I'm sorry; sir, but that could have been gangland retribution because Morley killed one of their own whilst refusing to pay up."

"I also remind you that Morley was about to be shot according to one of our undercover officers who managed to save him."

"It's a pity he didn't manage to arrest Morley."

"That is unforgivable, Derek. Thanks to our undercover officer, we now have one of the gang in custody."

"Yes, he will be able to confirm Morley's role in the murders."

By the way, why you didn't mention the abduction of Jane Fisher and the attempted killing of Morley in front of the D.C.I., Derek?

"It's still un-assessed evidence and she was clearly in a hurry. I didn't have time to mention that Morley was a soldier; a trained killer either."

"There are thousands of soldiers trained each year, Sergeant, and only a tiny minority ever use their training to harm others."

"Fair enough, sir, but I believe Morley is among the rare ones."

"We had a conversation the other day, Derek, in which I asked you if there was anything, anything at all that you were not telling me. I simply seek a reassurance that remains the case today."

"I have told you everything you need, other than day to day administration, in order to run this case."

"I hope so Sergeant, I really do." He prepared to leave, "I'd like us to get after Wayne Turner straight away."

"I'll organise some armed cover."

"Sergeant Forest; make sure you keep those two out of harms way."

"Yes, Sir."

CHAPTER TWENTY SEVEN

Michael Morley awoke with a headache. He was hungry and in need of a good breakfast. Michael knew he could not stay where he was; someone had already been moving around during the early hours. Morley had to get back to John Henderson. It was not an ideal choice because the police would probably still be around, but he'd have to risk it.

The police had probably discovered by now that Jane had been kidnapped. They would have someone trying to piece together what had happened.

Although worried about Jane's safety, he thought she would remain secure if she could not be used to intimidate him. Once they knew where he was the stakes would change. At present, no-one could contact him using Jane's phone, because the water had finally done its worst.

Michael pulled Mary Henderson's cycle from under the caravan. He'd managed to spring the caravan frame and door sufficiently with the tyre levers to enable the lock tenon to reassemble in its mortise. The caravan would be as secure as it had been before his arrival.

He used the sun to locate south and tried to imagine where the path behind the woods might lead him. It was in the general direction he needed and would temporarily at least keep him off the main road.

Michael Morley had just prepared to press down on a pedal when a young boy appeared in front of him. The youngster, clothed in what might at best be described as well used country attire, looked about seven or eight years old. Michael stopped and smiled at the child hoping he would stand aside. Instead the boy moved closer.

"Hello." Michael Morley adopted a cheerful approach.

The child then smiled broadly as Morley was simultaneously hit by a massive lightening strike from behind. He rolled off the cycle onto the ground with his head on fire and bells ringing in his ears. He turned to look behind in time to receive another blow from a man of about thirty wielding a wooden stick.

Rolling away from the attack, Michael struggled to his feet and prepared to defend himself. Another man joined the first and drew a knife. Unsure whether or not a simple apology for simply living might work, Morley turned to take on the biggest threat.

The man waved the weapon in a competent way and manoeuvred to permit his accomplice to circle behind Michael. This wasn't going to work out well!

Michael Morley decided that attack really was the best form of defence and launched himself at the man with the knife. The man managed to avoid his grasp before running off and disappearing into the woods. Michael spun on his heels prepared for the other man, but found that he, too, had disappeared together with the boy.

Puzzled by his experience and with his head throbbing, Michael stooped to pick up the fallen cycle. As he did so he heard the distinctive click of a shotgun being closed. He turned slowly. A middle aged man dressed like the archetypal gamekeeper stood, feet comfortably apart, porting a shotgun underarm pointing towards the ground. His face was stern.

He looked Michael up and down and noted first the cycle then the blood seeping from Morley's head wound.

"You're not one of them." He spoke crisply, nodding towards the trees.

"One of them?" Michael was glad he was not.

"What are you doing here?" The man pressed.

"Being rescued from further harm, I hope."

The man broke the shotgun and approached. "You were attacked by them, then?"

"Yes, I was just leaving."

"Leaving? Where did you come from?"

"I got lost." Michael lied. "I was looking for a short cut through to the road."

The man looked at the bike. "Wife's cycle is it then?"

"No, it belongs to the wife of a friend. I'm on holiday and they thought I might enjoy an early cycle to explore."

"This is a private path on a private estate. You could be mistaken for those people;" he nodded once more towards the trees.

"Sorry, I'll just go back to the road then."

"Where are you heading?"

"Lymington; I was hoping for quiet back roads or bridleways."

"Straight on would be best for you, then." The man's voice softened. "I'll accompany you to the gate on the far side. That way you'll avoid those people, or getting shot by accident."

He thanked the man and walked with him in general conversation.

Michael moved along the service road behind the Henderson's house watchfully. There was no sign of the unmarked police car that had stood there the evening before. He cycled slowly passed the front of the house before returning to the rear. There was no sign of any police officers; it seemed incredible.

He looked over the rear fence. Mary was in the garden! He cautiously tried the rear gate. It was now locked. He called softly. "Mary, Mary, it's Michael."

There was no immediate response. He was about to call again when he heard someone on the other side. There was the sound of a bolt being drawn and the gate opened.

"Michael! Where have you been? We were so worried about you!" She stepped aside so that he could enter. Mary made a final check of the lane before closing the gate. "It was on the news. A murderer had tried to murder someone in a hotel. They didn't say which one, but we thought it must be a reference to you."

Michael looked astonished. "You thought a reference to a murderer must have been to me?"

Mary held his hand. "You know I didn't, but we thought that would be exactly how they would want to portray the news. What happened?"

"Can we get inside first, Mary? I feel a bit naked out here."

"I went to the hotel. Jane had disappeared. The mobile phone message I received was valid, this mob have her."

"But, what about the murder at the hotel?" John Henderson wanted to understand.

"There was no murder. There could have been, but I had a rescuer."

"Rescuer, who?"

"I think he was meant to be my captor, but had to intervene to save me first."

"Goodness, my boy! But what about Jane? Have the gang contacted you again?"

"They can't, my phone is duff."

"So, what d'you think will happen now?"

"I'm sorry, but I think they will come for me here."

"Here?" Mary looked worried.

"It's the only place they know for certain."

"Oh, dear. What will happen to us?"

John Henderson comforted his wife, saying it was their duty to stand by Michael and Jane.

"I will go out to meet them if they come, of course." Michael sought to reassure his friends. "This is my problem and I need to solve it."

"Nonsense, Michael. But I still recommend you report to the police. It would be best in the end." John sounded very firm.

"I'll think about it, John, I promise." Michael remembered why he'd visited John the day before. "What did you discover about the Panther's notes?"

John led the way to his study. On the table he'd carefully dried and pressed the three pieces of paper. "They are reasonably intact as you may observe." John slid the largest towards the edge so that Michael might read its legend.

Michael pored over it. "It still looks like a shopping list to me." He turned to judge John's reaction.

"Exactly, my dear boy." He indicated the upper part of the list; "you see all these? They have all been ticked, crossed through."

"The list's purpose is incomplete. Other items remain to be crossed out." Michael was puzzled that the list contained nothing recognisable. "What is it that has been completed?"

"I think they are initials, a few look like nicknames, but I'm sure they all refer to people."

"Those who have received diamonds!" That made sense to Michael Morley. "…and the figures alongside them?

"Carats or grams, I'm willing to bet." John nodded his head sagely.

"The figures are different for every initial and there are two figures used; one much larger than the other. " Michael noted.

"One for the master and one for the courier." John was certain he knew the list's purpose.

"The ticks stop at Ot Vis, so he or she did not receive their cut." Michael pointed to the initials. "Or ran off with the Panther."

"Why do you think that was the one who ran off?"

180

"Because he hasn't bothered to tick it!" Michael was beginning to understand what had happened. "Did Langdon know anyone with these initials?"

"You think he was the last one to touch the Panther after this fellow? That ties up with what Peter Langdon told me. He said the person who gave it to him had waited for someone to collect the Panther."

"Or he knew exactly what had happened and lied."

"So the rest of the people on the lower half of the list are feeling pretty miffed!" John Henderson could see the scale of anger that was following the Panther. "A lot of people still want their share of these diamonds."

"What about the smaller notes, John?"

"Now, these are a puzzle." John stroked his chin.

"I marked them with a pencil; with L for the left eye and R for the right. In case it would be helpful later." Michael pointed where each faint letter was just visible.

"Good thinking, my boy."

"Does that help?"

"It might. What we have then is this;" John Henderson selected a pencil and wrote on a clean sheet of paper. "If we imagine we are looking face on to the Panther then its right eye comes first with 0,2 something; it's a bit smeared – then there are these hieroglyphics which I do not understand. The left eye gives us 52,2 something – again the accompanying legend does not help. The commas are the continental form of decimals."

"Some kind of bearings? Presumably the thief had to hide the diamonds if only to have a bargaining chip if he was caught by the gang." Michael stretched his imagination. "In which case you would have Eastings and Northings as a boy scout might say."

"The 52 seems a familiar figure for a Northing and using the Easting similarly would put us somewhere in Cambridge." John Henderson remained cautious.

Additional discussion was curtailed by Mary's appearance at the door. She looked worried. "John, there's a large black car in the lane."

The men needed no further prompting; both rushed to the rear of the lounge and keeping low raised their heads until they could see the black roof of an off-road vehicle. The whip aerials were unmistakable. The car was stationary. John motioned Michael to return to the passage. "Upstairs!" John pointed. Morley followed without question.

A rear bedroom window permitted the men to peer down on the vehicle without being observed. The four by four had parked so that it prevented escape from the rear gate.

"The front, quickly!" Henderson realised the significance immediately. They arrived at a front window just in time to see a heavily built man wearing a pinstriped suit reach the drive. The man stopped and began surveying the house. He spent some time observing each aspect before walking slowly towards the house.

"What are we going to do?" Mary had arrived at the bedroom door.

"Hide the notes!" Michael Morley pushed roughly passed Mary and raced down to the study, "Sorry, Mary," he called belatedly.

John took a final look as the man below reached the front porch; "Quickly Mary!" He guided his wife to the bathroom. "Bolt it and stay in there until we've dealt with the problem."

John hurried after his friend only to find him, lingering near the study door.

"There's a problem, my boy?"

"Yes. If they believe we have the clues or the diamonds they will ransack your house. If I can get away they might not. The best way is for them to see me escape. They will have to come after me."

"The other way would be to give them the clues and let them work it out." John suggested astutely; "then we might see the last of them."

"We aren't entirely sure they know what we have got from the Panther. In any case we would have to act out our reluctance to hand them over convincingly; if they suspected we were fobbing them off it might turn out worse."

"You're probably right, Michael. These people don't easily accept no for an answer." Henderson remembered his last encounter with the gang. They had been perfectly willing to kill. "What should we do?"

"Take these and hide them." Michael passed John Henderson the slips of paper.

The front door bell sounded. They could make out the shadowy outline of a head and shoulders beyond the glass fan light. Michael braced himself for a fight. It wasn't something he wanted, but if it was required of him he did have fitness on his side. He moved towards the door.

"No, Michael!" John Henderson restrained him, "there's another way!" He pushed his friend down the passage leading to the laundry. "Use the side door!"

"But if they get in here it will prove bad for you and Mary!" Michael protested.

"I will tell them you were here, but you made off some time ago."

"That's a dangerous policy; they might kill you for your silence."

"I'll take my chances and I still have that old samurai sword!"

"John, please don't try to provoke them."

"Just go! We can't let the bad guys win!" Henderson sounded unconvincing.

Michael Morley felt his friend was very much afraid for Mary. If he failed then she would become the next victim. Michael's conscience could no longer bear the strain; he pushed his friend to one side and strode determinedly to the front door. He paused for a final second before wrenching the door wide open.

CHAPTER TWENTY EIGHT

The Sergeant tightened his belt as the car took a sharp left hander. "Bloody hell! I didn't ask for warp factor two!"

The detective smiled. For a moment it felt good to scare his Sergeant. Then his professional training took over and he eased back on his right foot. "How good do you think this information is, Sergeant?"

"The best."

"Is it Morley we're after? D'ya think we'll get him this time?"

"The message was about the suspected return of the gang." The Sergeant could not disguise the note of disappointment in his voice.

"But we are on our way to Henderson's house."

"I thought we had that staked out, but somebody called off the hounds for some reason."

"Perhaps it was to draw out the gang." The driver was optimistic.

"Bloody budget cuts, more like."

"Who was the informant?"

"I don't know for certain, but I think I heard the D.I. telling the Chief it was Mrs. Henderson."

"Wow! That must make the information reliable."

"That's why we've been tasked as urgent. Other units will be competing to be first."

"Fancy they're paying him another visit. That poor bloke must be gutted; especially after what they did to him last time before they ransacked his house." The driver sympathised.

"There'll be no end to this until we've put them away."

The driver fell silent and concentrated on keeping his speed as high as safety would permit.

"Delta two; delta one, over." The Sergeant checked on the position of the second car.

"Delta two, receiving, over."

"Position, over."

"Just climbing the hill now; is that your lights I can see ahead, over?"

"Probably, we've just passed the church at the top. We'd better kill the twos now, silent approach, over."
"You take the back lane; we'll cover the front, over."
"Understood, out."

The car slowed at the junction. At the end of the road and parked a hundred metres from John Henderson's house the Sergeant could see a Police ARV waiting for them. He instructed his driver to slow and radioed the Armed Response Vehicle team for a report.
"Unidentified male; six feet, suited; approached front door and rang bell."
"Who came to the door?"
"No-one yet…hang on; standby!"
The man at the door had turned, hurried out of the drive and was running away from them towards the lane that passed down the side of the house and then crossed behind it. The Sergeant grabbed the radio. "Delta two: one male running your way!"
"Received; we've disturbed an off-road vehicle matching a wanted description; it's taken off and is heading in your direction; we're pursuing."

As the fleeing man reached the beginning of the lane the 4x4 emerged. It stopped to pick up the fugitive then accelerated towards the waiting Police vehicles. At the same moment the figure of Michael Morley could be seen rushing out of the front door apparently chasing the first man.
The Sergeant punched his driver in the hip. "That's Morley, get him!" The command was so robust that the driver swung the car around the ARV in contravention of any protocol and raced after the vanishing shape of Morley. As the Police car straightened up it was deliberately rammed by the 4x4; send it spinning across the road to collide with the second Police vehicle emerging from the lane.

"What the hell!" The Sergeant struggled to deflate his airbag. His face felt raw from the force of the bag. He turned to his driver. "You okay, Detective?"
The driver began to reply when his expression became aghast. The Sergeant was bleeding profusely from a head wound and started uttering some incoherent foreign language before he collapsed against the door. His driver immediately radioed for help. He looked at the other Police car. Its

occupants were alive, but too dazed to offer assistance. The ARV made multipoint turns in an attempt to get after the escaping 4x4. As it passed on the verge two of the four man crew got out to assist. The remaining officers set off after the gang calling for back up. The wail of their siren soon combined with those of approaching paramedics and other Police vehicles.

The ARV crew managed to release all of those trapped inside vehicles except for the Sergeant who was left in situe for the Paramedics.

"Morley! We must get Morley!" The driver stumbled onto the verge. A female paramedic urged him to forget what ever he had intended to do and coaxed him to lean back against a wall.

"Bring them into the house." John Henderson and his wife had arrived at the end of their drive. The Paramedics were more concerned with identifying the most seriously injured and getting them to hospital.

"Let's bring out chairs." Mary suggested.

"Good thinking, my dear." John Henderson hurried in to assist his wife.

The D.I. waited patiently until all of the officers were seated comfortably. None had spoken. Most sat shame faced. He looked from one to another with an inscrutable gaze as he slowly spun his cap on the polished table. Finally he resorted to a prayer like pose with his finger tips under his chin. "Right everyone. Let's do a health check first." He turned his attention to his Sergeant, "How's the head, Derek?"

The Sergeant found it difficult to cope with official concern. It seemed to him to always be punctuated with insincerity. He looked down and spoke to the table. "I'm fine. I'm told that head wounds tend to bleed profusely and that it's only superficial damage."

The D.I. smiled weakly.

Kevin James consulted each officer to ensure they were fit to be present and resolved to send a couple home after the meeting. He returned his attention to Derek Forest. "You know you are entitled to sick leave, Sergeant?" He inflected. "I really should be imploring you to go home now."

"As I said earlier, sir, it's my intention to bring in this murderer Morley. He is one trained killer we need to lock up."

Christine Prowting wriggled uncomfortably. She was becoming increasingly embarrassed by the Sergeant's insistence on Morley's army experience in Iraq being a key indicator of his guilt. He made it seem as if the antique restorer had been a member of the SAS.

"Do we need to share something, Detective?" It was not for the first time that the D.I. had caught the flicker of disapproval on Christine's face.

The Sergeant gave her a quick challenging look.

"Is there something you would like to say, Sergeant?" The D.I. had looked for a telling reaction. He'd seen it. He was now convinced something was seriously amiss.

The Sergeant answered simply. "No, sir, I just want to finish this enquiry and get on with the task."

"That task being to catch this murderer Morley?" Kevin James emphasised murderer and this time watched Christine Prowting's reaction. She tried to suppress any, but the Inspector saw briefly that she was unable to.

"Do we know what Morley did in Iraq? You were going to let me know a few days ago, Derek."

The Sergeant shuffled uneasily and shot another look at Christine Prowting. "Haven't got around to it yet, sir."

"I know that, Sergeant."

The D.I. addressed the meeting in general. "Does anyone know what horrific things that Morley got up to in Iraq?" He looked at each in turn, "somebody must know, or have we been so incompetent that we didn't bother to check the background of our chief suspect?" The D.I. felt immune from criticism; because he had never thought Morley was anything other than an innocent man.

"I heard a few grumbles then." The Inspector exaggerated. "Come on, what did he do?" He looked directly at Christine Prowting. She noticed the exacting stare and knew that he understood already and only need to be told officially. Could she publicly contradict a senior officer? Her colleagues would condemn her, but an innocent man's life was at stake. She knew the Sergeant was fully aware that Morley had been in the Medical Corps and had left early on health grounds after the trauma he'd experienced.

"Christine?" The D.I. waited.

"I think he was wounded, or looked after wounded, something like that." She hoped that her apparent vagueness might be sufficient.

"You think his job was being wounded!" The Inspector mocked in the hope it would trigger an outburst from someone. Christine felt a growing anger. It wasn't her fault that the Sergeant wouldn't confess!

"Do you agree with that statement, Sergeant?" The D.I. knew he had to break this impasse.

"He might have been wounded, I suppose."

"Sergeant it is not your job to suppose anything, you are expected to know!" The inspector closed the meeting immediately and sent everyone away, detaining the Sergeant.

"Okay, Derek, we're alone now. No witnesses, no one to repeat anything. I've asked you several times if there was anything driving this case that I didn't know about. You have repeated a mantra of innocence each time. I believe there is something I need to know and need to know quickly. I want you to tell me everything right now!"

The Sergeant began to stutter. It appeared he was trying to confess, but was unable to do so. The D.I. decided to make it easier for him. "Let me ask you a question at a time. I want the truth as an answer. In which Corps; Brigade or Company did Morley serve in Iraq?"

"The …Medical…Corps." The Sergeant replied.

"So he was never in a combat role. Yet you persisted in letting me believe he was!"

"Not that I'm aware…but he would have…"

"Stop Sergeant! I no longer wish to hear your continued speculation."

Detective Inspector James continued to interview Derek Forest until he fully understood the extent of the Sergeant's prejudice. As he digested the implications it dawned on him that, driven by it, the Sergeant had been misdirecting the investigation and that Michael Morley and Jane Fisher were not only two innocent people, but they were now in imminent danger.

The D.I. sent his Sergeant home on sick leave and set about the urgent task of undoing the harm.

The D.I. called Christine Prowting and Brian Lucas to his office. Christine came with some trepidation, believing she was in trouble for hinting that something might be wrong and informing on a colleague.

"I believe that Sergeant Forest needs some rest, but we need to continue this investigation. I think we can now regard Michael Morley and Jane Fisher as innocent and in danger." He tousled his hair vigorously. "Are you happy with that conclusion Detective Constable Prowting?"

"Yes, Sir. Thank you, Sir."

Right, let's understand where we are." He stared up at the ceiling. "The gang always seem to be one step ahead of us. It's as if we have a leak in this station. Do either of you know who or how that might have come about?" He looked at Christine in case she would give away another signal, but she looked surprised at the suggestion. The Inspector turned his attention to Brian Lucas. "And you, Constable?"

Brian Lucas suddenly looked elated. "I knew it; I knew." He bounced with excitement. "I told you it was suspicious!" He said triumphantly. Christine Prowting seemed puzzled.

"The black van! It was outside when we left. I said it looked like a listening station. It had all the right aerials. They've been stuffed with scanners listening to us. They know everything we know."

The Inspector looked at Christine for confirmation. She nodded thoughtfully.

"That is a serious mistake for us. We need to use this knowledge to mislead the enemy; we have to in order to rescue two innocent people."

"The first thing you two can do is search the cctv footage covering the outside of this building. Get that van's registration."

CHAPTER TWENTY NINE

Michael Morley recovered consciousness. It was dark and his head was throbbing mercilessly. Something prevented him from sitting up. He tugged and listened. A metallic sound! Morley was handcuffed and chained to a wall. The concrete floor had forced a penetrating cold through his entire body. His arms ached as much as his head. Michael listened for the sound of another human; their breathing; movement; curiosity about his presence; nothing. He forced a cough that reverberated through his head. There was no response. He was alone.

It added an unwelcome dimension. To be tortured and abused with others was one thing, but to suffer alone seemed to amplify sensitivities.
Michael tried to remember the sequence of events that had brought him there. His memory was as fractured as his head, but he managed to assemble a few incongruent glimpses. He could recollect chasing someone; a black vehicle; people jumping on him.
Jane must have been high on his agenda for he could remember that she was missing. He tried to think why he knew she was in danger. The harder he tried the more transient such glimpses became.

Someone was coming! Michael Morley could hear the footsteps above the constant grinding in his ears. There was the sound of a key being inserted in a lock. He closed his eyes anticipating an explosion of light.
A voice greeted him from the continued blackness as the door grated on its hinges. "So, Michael Morley; you are awake. That is good." The South African accent was as dark as the room and the word, good, hung like a threat. He felt sure it wasn't going to be good for him.
"You really have given us a fine chase, Michael." The speaker created the ambience of a favourite uncle administering a mild rebuke. "But now, I think we need to have a little chat. Are you ready to talk?"
"Who are you?" Michael heard himself say during an out-of-body experience.

"Can you hear me, Michael?" The South African voice repeated. "We need to talk about what you have done with my diamonds."

"Diamonds ...yours?"

"Yes, you must remember; and I have something equally precious of yours."

Michael Morley struggled against the cerebral cacophony and pain. "What do you have of mine?"

"Why, Jane, of course!" The room echoed with the attempted mild humour. "You must remember Jane."

"If she's mine, then you must give her back." Morley sagged.

"It's no use; he's still out of it." A second voice echoed; the newcomer spoke with the softer tones of a Dutch accent. "You'll have to wait until he comes round properly."

"Nonsense; he's beginning to understand." The speaker struck a match that flared brightly in the pitch darkness. "It won't be long before he'll be begging me to allow him to give back what he has of mine." A cigar smoky breath extinguished the light.

In the darkness the speaker's swinging foot connected with Morley's ribs. Morley yelped and tried to twist away, but was prevented by the chains.

"What do I have of yours?" Morley coughed.

"That's better! You see, Franz, he understands much more clearly now." He lashed out with his foot again. "I think this will improve his memory quite quickly. Where are my diamonds?" The questioner inserted a tone of impatience into the demand.

"I left the Panther at the cottage." Michael remembered Parker's cold blooded murder.

"Ah! But the Panther was empty, Michael." Another remedial kick caught Michael nearer to his shoulder where he had been tortured earlier. The excruciating pain it produced raced across his shoulders and down his spine.

He winced and let out a long sigh of exasperation. "The Panther always was empty."

"Liar! Liar!" The voice screamed full volume at him; then immediately resorted to the softer approach. "Michael, Michael; this is not going to get us anywhere if you just resort to denial."

A subsequent blow took its victim completely by surprise; the full force of the questioner's foot glanced off the side of Morley's head, stunning him.

Whilst Michael Morley was unconscious, Franz, the interrogator's companion, argued that handing out that sort of violence risked damaging its victim beyond benefit. The black cavern resonated with the sound of a violent corrective strike connecting with a face. The interrogator's companion remained silent.

When Michael Morley came round he checked if his captors were still lingering in the blackness. "You said you would release Jane if I gave you the Panther."

"No Michael, I said if you gave me my diamonds; and you must not believe all that people tell you; that would be very naive."

"I had no choice; you had Jane."

"Exactly; that's much better now you are thinking properly." In the darkness, the voice crossed to the other side of him. "You have no choice. You must give me my diamonds and I will release Jane and you two lovers can go off into the sunset, or wherever else you may choose to go." Michael could hear the scuffing of his captor's feet as they meandered on the concrete. "Deny me my diamonds and it will certainly not improve your health." He could hear the smile in the speaker's voice, "or your loved one's." He added emphasis to his remarks with an aimed kick. It was so hard that Michael heard his ribs break. Michael struggled for painful breath after painful breath.

"There were no…diamonds in the …Panther."

"Liar!" Another kick found the same spot causing an involuntary scream from its recipient.

"Liar!" His tormentor repeated the action striking Morley's hip.

"Wait, wait!" Michael Morley appealed, realising the torture would continue until he was dead. He had to say something other than he didn't know.

After a short silence the South African accent returned in its tolerant form. "I am a patient man, Michael, I will wait and listen attentively as you tell me where I can find my diamonds. My impatience will only grow with your denial and deviation. Do you understand?"

"I was given the Panther so that I could estimate its market value." He spoke with broken words against the pain of breathing.

"Are you denying that you opened it?" The voice menaced.

"No. I did open it; there was a cover that could be removed."

"Good, that's better. So, you opened it and removed my diamonds." The voice had moved closer and its breathy articulation came from near his left ear.

"I opened it, but the space inside was empty." Michael did not mention the pieces of paper he had discovered.

"Not good enough!" the voice spat into the captive's face. Michael felt the hot moist breath on his skin.

"It's the truth whether you…choose to like it…or not." Morley's painful chest was worsening. He felt a pair of hands groping for his leg.

"Shall I break this leg?" The second voice asked in a clinical tone.

"Ah, Franz; you have a leg. Good; perhaps you could break it if Mr. Morley continues to deny having my diamonds after the next question." Michael could feel the man's hands shaking as he nodded with enthusiasm.

"Right, Mr. Morley. This is going to be my final time of asking."

"You can ask that question as many times as you like, but it cannot change my answer for it is the truth." Morley shouted through the pain. "Do you think I would let you or your goon torture me to death and not tell you what you wanted? Why would I do that? I don't care whose diamonds they are – they wouldn't do me any good dead would they?" In the darkness, he twisted towards the voice. "Think about it, you brainless dolt. Why wouldn't I tell you?"

His torturer remained silent contemplating what had been said before uttering his next command. "Break his leg, Franz."

"With pleasure," Franz seemed to smile as Michael's left leg was lifted in preparation. Morley knew that the man would have to bend forward in order to hammer down on his left knee with sufficient force to break it. His right leg, trapped beneath the left, came free. He moved it to one side. It was so numb that he had to imagine its position. He wriggled his toes to encourage blood flow and felt the sharp stinging pain as the flesh re-inflated in his leg and foot.

Franz's weight shifted as he raised his arm to deliver the breaking blow. Morley had to act now! With every muscle tense and protesting its pain he swung the fully extended right leg at his estimated position of Franz's head. There was the satisfying sound of a good connection and Michael guessed he had struck Franz around the cheek. He needed to capitalise on his success. Michael heaved his right leg half way back and repeated the blow a little lower. A second, weaker connection, hit Franz somewhere near the jaw. Michael felt the sharp pain of broken metatarsals. His left leg was released followed by loud groan and the sound of a body crumpling to the concrete floor.

"Franz, Franz?" The first voice called and Michael Morley heard the rustle of clothing as someone near him rose and began groping along a wall. A sharp click broke the silence. The bright white beam of an industrial lamp flashed across the ceiling then down the wall and along the floor until it stopped, wavering, at the prone figure of Franz. Morley's aim had been good and the light revealed a man with a disfigured face and a steady flow of blood.

Michael Morley guessed his respite would be short lived. There would be a lot of anger to follow and he was still vulnerably chained to a wall. He tried to see passed the lamp and gain a glimpse of his captor, but he needed more time for his eyes to adjust.

"Franz!" The voice called; its South African accent echoing in the confined space. Franz managed a plaintive groan and rolled onto his side.

The lamp was turned sharply onto Michael's face, blinding him. "You bastard, Morley; you will pay for this!"

"I already have. It was you who ran me down with your van then tied me to this bloody wall before kicking the stuffing out of me."

The light was placed on the floor with its beam still directly in the captive's face. Morley could hear the South African moving towards him. Then the voice with its strong smell of cigars was close to his face. "You are going to talk before long, Michael." The voice had resumed its unemotional tone.

Michael could see Franz at the edge of the beam. The man struggled to the kneeling position, dabbed one hand on his face and examined it. Blood stained, he muttered something incomprehensible as he stood, steadying himself against the wall. He spat a bloody dribble onto the floor before suddenly lashing out a foot at Michael's head. Morley managed to twist away and partly deflect the blow, but the strain sent a fiery pain shooting through his body.

Franz repeated what he'd said as he aimed a second blow, missing completely, launching himself backward onto the concrete floor. He remained there, curling himself into a foetal position and groaning in waves of agony.

The South African spoke softly into Michael's ear, "I think Franz will want to speak to you about this, later." He allowed himself a quiet snigger, "that is, if I leave him anything." He raised his voice so that Franz might hear, "isn't that right, my little friend, Franz?" Franz simply groaned a response.

Michael Morley realised that unless he could come up with something pretty fast he would be a dead man. He thought of Jane and hoped that she was okay and would escape the trauma he was suffering. She had only been used by the gang as the honey trap. Once he was dead, she would be of no use to them. Then the cruel truth dawned. She would be a witness risk and a danger to them. If they still had her, she would surely die too. He had to stay alive!

"Look, who ever you are, I have given you what you wanted. You have the bloody Panther; what more can I do?"

"My diamonds, Mr. Morley; must I repeat myself? Give me back my diamonds and you and your lady friend may leave. I'll want nothing more."

"I've told you; there were no diamonds, the Panther was empty."

I've already heard these words, Michael. I'm afraid I will have to find another way of persuading you."

Franz rolled onto his back and sat up. "I…will…bloody well…kill you." He managed to splutter through more blood and phlegm. "Bloody well…kill…you." He crawled across the floor until he was within range of Morley's head. He crouched low and spat blood laden words into the prisoner's face. "I can still get you to talk; when you see what I can do to your bloody bitch, you bastard!"

"Jane! You have Jane here?" The danger was nearer than he had thought. "Don't worry, Michael; Jane is in our care and will come to no harm." The South African released a long soft sigh. "As long as you tell me what I want to know and give me back my diamonds."

"There were no diamonds. You can torture me as long as you like, but there is nothing I can say – nothing! What must I do to persuade you?"

"I think we will let Franz get your young lady to tell us. You would like that, wouldn't you Franz?"

Franz grunted; "I'll show you things you will not have imagined possible!" The thought of such freedom to practise some carefully honed skill seemed to revive him.

"Franz, my stupid little colleague, do you think you could go and bring Jane for me?"

Franz made no reply; pushed passed the man holding the light; and staggered away into the darkness.
"If you harm a single hair of her head..." Michael moved into bravado.
"You will do what, Michael? The voice laughed coldly.
"I will kill you." The reply was heartfelt and gritty.
"But...clearly...my silly stubborn antique restorer, thief; you are in no position to do anything." The voice enjoyed its own joke and laughed again.

The confrontation was interrupted by the sound of Jane's voice raised in protest. Franz's craggy urging came closer. The light flashed through 180 degrees to reveal Jane's tearful but determined face; then back to blind Michael.
"You see, Michael, what great care we have taken of Jane." After a short pause he added, "until now, that is."
"Michael is that you? Are you alright?" Jane's voice was etched with concern.
"I'm fine, don't worry about me." Her partner lied, "What about you, what have they done to you?"
"Nothing; I'm alright and much better now that I know you are okay."
The South African voice laughed. "Did you hear that, Franz? That was the sound of true love. Doesn't it make you wish you were in love, Franz?"
"Maybe I will be in a moment." Franz dribbled feigned joy through his painful mouth.

Michael Morley felt a sickening helplessness in his stomach. He was physically damaged and still chained to the wall. He knew there was little he could do to help Jane and faced the probability of having to witness himself and Jane dying in a hopelessly messy end.
"You bastards – can't you see that you will gain nothing by torturing us. Just release us. Release Jane at least; she knows nothing about the Panther or your bloody diamonds!"
"Unlike you, eh?"
"I've told you: there are no diamonds!" He punched out the words slowly.

"Ah, that's where you are wrong, Michael. Franz will now reveal just what you do know." The beam raced along the wall until it lit first Jane's face and then eventually found Franz. "Franz?"

The beam broadened to show both Jane and Franz who had grasped her by the shoulders and was attempting to force her to the ground. Jane twisted away revealing that her hands were tied behind her back and began screaming.

"It's no use screaming or shouting for help no-one can hear; we are deep underground." The voice laughed again. "And it's not as if the police will come to the rescue at any moment."

"They would probably only come to arrest me." Michael lamented ironically

"Oh, exciting news. You must tell us; have you been fiddling your tax returns as well as stealing my diamonds?"

"It was just a question of who would get to me first; you, or the police."

"Well, it's your lucky day. I found you first, so the police won't be bothering you."

"Stop!" Michael shouted, "I will tell you what you want to know." He was hoping for an inspirational and convincing lie, but it had yet to arrive.

"I'm sorry, Michael; that did not persuade me. I need to feel that you are really going to see this thing through. Sincerity is what I want to hear. Carry on, Franz."

"Yes Baas." Franz rolled Jane onto her back and began tearing at her blouse as she wriggled and twisted to frustrate his effort.

"Stop you evil little bastard, I will tell you where the diamonds are and anything else you want to know!" Morley's voice echoed its final plea around the brick walled room.

"Okay, Franz. I think our friend has seen the sense of co-operating."
Just before the light beam was extinguished, Michael saw Franz reluctantly move away from Jane. He noted that Franz had referred to the bigger man as Baas. It had to be a nick name, or possibly just Boss.

There was a click and the light was back in the prisoner's face. "Right, Michael, I am as they say; all ears. You may begin."

Morley had no idea at all about the whereabouts of the diamonds. He needed to be more resourceful. He began by risking a stall. "First, release Jane then I will tell you."

"I don't think you have a negotiating position; and Franz is standing by to continue what he began if I think you are in any way stalling. The sort of sentence I am expecting to hear will begin with the words, your diamonds are…" He flashed the light at Franz. "When you have finished that sentence Franz will go and collect them. When he returns and I can see that I have all of my diamonds, Franz and I will leave and you will be free to do what ever you wish."

"No deal!" Morley sounded resolute. "You could just kill us; you must let Jane go first."

"You try my patience. Franz, oblige me, please."

Franz responded so quickly that Jane was taken by surprise. He tore at her so roughly that both the blouse and her bra came away in one attempt.

"Get off me; you slimy bastard!" Jane made a late attempt at recovery, but with her hands tied she knew she would not succeed for long.

"Leave her alone! I will tell you where they are!"

"Don't stop, Franz. You had better be quick and convincing, Michael." He flashed the light back to illuminate Jane and Franz. His colleague was now pulling at Jane's skirt.

"Alright; they are in London!" Michael heard himself say in another out-of-body experience.

"In London? And where precisely?"

Morley hardly heard the question above Jane's screaming.

"Stop him, please!"

"You need to hurry along with you story, Michael."

"In an antique shop!" Michael lied.

"Do you mean the antique shop owned by Mr. Peter Langdon? The Peter Langdon murdered by your friend, Henderson?"

"He'd never do anything like that!" Michael thought it better not to confirm what he knew.

"Ah, you are not aware of that? Does that mean you are lying to me?" He turned the light back to Jane and Franz. The man was holding his abdomen and rolling on the floor. Jane's feet had proven as effective as Michael's in defence.

"Franz, can't you do anything properly?" He turned the beam back onto his subject's face. "I'm increasingly disappointed in you, I though we had brought you to your senses."

"No! It changes nothing!" Morley pleaded.

"Really? Perhaps you could explain?"

"The diamonds were removed without Langdon's knowledge."

"And how would you know that?"

"John Henderson told me." He realised he was causing trouble for his friend later, but faced with the immediate danger to Jane, hoped he might still survive to put that right.

"So, John Henderson told you he had removed the diamonds from my Panther whilst Mr. Langdon was otherwise engaged?"

"Yes."

"And Mr. Langdon, who knew the Panther contained the diamonds, was prepared to leave Peter Langdon alone with them?"

"Yes, they were business partners." He lied again.

"Not what I heard. Acquaintances at the most, Michael, but I do not believe Partners." He sighed loudly. "I feel that you are still stalling for time; wasting both our lives, Michael. Stop this now, or I will order Franz, whatever condition he is in, to finish what he began."

"It's the truth!" Morley became desperate. His story had to be believed.

"The Panther and its diamonds were to be part payment of a debt."

"Langdon was using the diamonds, my diamonds, to which he had no entitlement, to pay a debt?"

"Yes." Michael was relieved to note a growing acceptance by his interrogator. "John Henderson suspected that others might know about the pay off, or the presence of the diamonds, and took the precaution of removing them."

"He removed the diamonds? How was that going to work?" The tone of the voice had changed and revealed genuine interest.

"He hid them without Langdon knowing. John intended to recover them later when it was safe to do so."

"And where did he decide it was safe to hide them?"

"There was an old cracked vase that Langdon kept as a display item. It was quite large and of little value. John Henderson felt it was unlikely ever to be sold and therefore would provide a safe place." Morley's confidence began to grow. This story was a runner.

"And Henderson never returned to recover the diamonds?"

"No, somebody put him in hospital before he had a chance to; probably someone working for you."

The voice remained silent. Its owner was remembering how his men had searched Henderson's car after they had run it off the road. John Henderson's anxiety that the diamonds might be intercepted had been shared by the voice's owner. The story had some credibility.

"I will send Franz to collect them."

Morley panicked. "If what you say is correct and Langdon has been murdered it will be a crime scene. The police might even have discovered the diamonds and be waiting for them to be collected." Michael desperately tried to gain time; to what end he was uncertain; but it might prolong his and Jane's lives. Even as he thought his mind passed into a terminal phase where the only thing left to be hoped for was a tidy or quick end.

He shuddered at his own despondency and made a last attempt at thinking positively: The police would be looking for him, but only to apprehend him; Jane might by now be missed and someone may have contacted the police. There was a remote chance that they would consider her plight more urgently.

The man referred to as Baas by Franz had moved away and could be heard shuffling about on the far side of the room.

"Hmmm." The man said several times as if considering a series of alternatives. The process took several minutes during which Michael Morley was grateful for the respite from the constant kicking he had been receiving. Finally, the man returned to stand near him.

"You may be right, Mr. Morley, or you might just be wasting my time and trying my patience." He moved closer adding; "for which you will be severely punished." The man made another tour of his victim before confiding a decision. "I'm going to assume that what you have told me about the diamonds is correct." He coughed to clear his throat. "Also, I accept your reasoning that the shop may very likely be a crime scene."

"That doesn't seem to leave you many successful options." Michael Morley managed to utter despite the increasing pain in his chest.

"Ah, that is where you are wrong, Michael Morley." The man's heavy clothes rustled as he made a rapid turn in the dark. "You see, I have many friends and associates. There is one in particular whom I can contact right now and from whom I can call in a favour; one that will require him to go to the shop; enter it; and recover my diamonds." He laughed quietly. "You see, Mr. Morley, there is a solution to every problem."

Michael heard Jane give a gasp of fear. He realised that she would have known the story was false and that the consequences, once discovered, were going to be dire. She began to cry.

"Jane, it'll be all right." He tried to comfort her.

"Ah, yes, listen to your man, Jane, he knows that it is almost over," adding, "what ever happens."

Morley felt the man step over him and, he imagined, walk towards Jane. He braced himself for what he expected next. The sudden yelp that exploded near him came as a surprise and sent a memory shock wave through his body.

"Get up, Franz! You useless individual, you fell asleep!"

The deep groaning of a man in severe pain followed. "I was only waiting for your instructions, Baas;" whimpered the injured individual.

"Well Franz here are my instructions." The sound of a foot connecting with a body could be heard. "Take your mobile phone and go outside. When you are there call, Buster Schmitt, give him my regards; and tell him I'm calling in a favour. Then tell him where my diamonds are to be found."

"In the vase?" Franz checked nervously.

"Exactly, Franz, so you have been paying attention; when he has them tell him to phone you back with confirmation."

Franz could be heard hobbling his way to the door. There was a brief flash of light as he checked where the handle or lock was before the door closed with a resounding slam. Michael Morley wished he had been prepared for the light. He could have checked on Jane and the layout of the room.

"Going to be some time?" Michael tried to keep his question short.

"Not at all, Michael; the good news is that Franz should be back within a few minutes. You see, Schmitt lives very close to the shop."

Morley felt his spirit sag. The truth would be known and he and Jane would soon be no more. He wondered if they would be taken from the room. It might give them a chance – more so if he wasn't so badly injured. Perhaps he could be instrumental in helping Jane escape.

Franz returned quicker than Michael had imagined. Perhaps this Buster chap had been out! Morley could hear Franz shuffling back to his boss. The subordinate uttered something that Morley could not catch. Then there was a long unsettling silence.

"Michael Morley, I have misjudged you. I have to thank you for being so co-operative and returning my diamonds to me. I am told that every single one has been found."

Michael could not believe his ears. He was immensely happy to hear that the diamonds had been found, but was aware that his had been a completely made up tale chosen at random. Had it been a good guess; the sort of thing John Henderson would have done? Or was it a trap of some sort that he'd yet to understand?

A second, more terrifying, thought occurred to him. This was simply gross sarcasm on the part of his captor just before killing them in a fit of unbridled rage?

CHAPTER THIRTY

Michael was pulled forward. Renewed pain took him towards unconsciousness. He wondered if this was to be his final minute and thought about Jane. Hands roughly tugged at his back and he heard the metallic snap of a pad lock being opened. Sharp pain cut through his chest cavity as his body was twisted. Broken ribs pierced internal muscle and threatened organs as Baas grasped his chained wrists and attempted to pull him to his feet. He and Jane yelled in pain simultaneously. Michael guessed that Franz was attempting to get Jane to her feet. Each protested their injury and begged that their partner should be treated with more care.

"My friends, I must apologise for our apparent brutality, but it is only to enable you to experience freedom a little quicker." Their chief torturer explained through strained breathing.

The two captives were half carried half dragged to a door that, once open, forced them to close their eyes against the strong light. Quickly adjusting, they knew that to accustomed eyes there was barely sufficient illumination to see the steps leading upwards.

The continued severe pain once more drove Michael Morley to unconsciousness and, unable to protest, he was dragged rapidly to an upper door. Once open, Morley was pulled through it by the large man and dumped onto damp grass. The man returned to assist his colleague in bringing the sharply protesting and kicking Jane up into the daylight. She was released to crumple onto the grass alongside Michael.

"Michael, can you hear me?" Jane was pleased at being able to look at her partner for the first time in days. Simultaneously, she felt the relief of seeing that he was still alive and the devastation of his appearance. "Look what you've done to him, you ruthless bastards?" She screamed at her captors.

Franz, who was bent double recovering from the effort of dealing with Jane, straightened. He walked slowly the ten yards to stand beside her and cocked one leg in preparation to land a punishing kick.

"Franz!" snapped his boss. "Leave her; I need to talk to you." He grasped Franz's arm and pulled. "Now!"

The junior partner in this affair lowered his leg, but continued to stare at Jane.

"You useless, cunning, evil little bastard!" she yelled at him and began to lash out with her legs. She caught him cleanly on one shin making him cry out in pain. "See how you like it, bastard!" Jane had been driven beyond the point at which one considers consequences.

This was too much for a junior partner who was always forced to cower. Franz raised his leg and, as originally intended, drove a hard blow into Jane's thigh.

"Agggh!" Jane groaned. She rolled away from the man and quickly tried to stand. As she turned to face him his superior struck Franz with his closed fist. The blow landed hard and Franz immediately fell to the ground.

"Why must I always tell you twice, Franz?"

Franz sat up holding his side. His face was covered in blood emanating from a large wound at the hair line.

At that moment Jane saw the gun and trembled. The erudite, polite man, who always apologised for his criminal behaviour as if it was an unfortunate hobby, had revealed what he was; a ruthless individual likely to kill if it suited his ends. Jane wondered how she had been so foolishly distracted by this outward persona. As a prisoner she'd imagined a better side of him as if it would free her. Now, she could only imagine death.

The big man bent to his colleague; mopped his blood with a large white handkerchief; and whispered something. Jane strained hard, but could not hear what had been said. The leader helped his junior partner to his feet. This time Jane did hear.

"Are you ready Franz? You must deal with the girl, I will deal with Morley. But first I need you to confirm that you did speak to Buster Schmitt. How do you know it was him?"

Franz held the handkerchief to his head and groaned.

"Come now, Franz, pull yourself together. How do you know you spoke to Schmitt?"

"He said it was him." Franz sobbed.

"That is not good enough."

"It was his phone and it sounded like him."

"Yes, you called his mobile." The leader thought for a little longer. "And he did go and check at the shop?" He emphasised the word, go.

"Yes, he said the police had left it all taped up, but no one was there."

"And he counted the diamonds?"

"He said weighed. He knew the expected weight – he was the next one on the list after Visser."

"Good. That makes sense."

"What did he do with them?"

"I already told you; he said that knowing you he'd better make sure by removing them. The police might find them?"

The big man put a comforting arm around his colleague. "You see, Franz, it's good to make certain, because what we are about to do is rather final. We won't be able to come back later and ask more questions."

"Are you really going to?"

"Yes, my silly little friend. We have to get away quickly; the police may be getting closer. These two are assets that have turned into liabilities." He pointed to the distance. "Over there will be a good place. Let's just make sure before we have to struggle again."

The senior partner looked towards their two prisoners lying on the ground. "I don't think they will be going anywhere in the meantime."

The two men crossed a rough gravel path and disappeared beyond some tall gorse bushes.

Jane crouched against Morley's side. "Michael?" She touched his shoulder and rocked him gently. He winced and tried to turn.

"Uh?" Michael Morley rocked himself into a more comfortable position and looked at Jane.

"Hi Jane; is it all over?" He looked up at the blue sky.

"No, Michael, we have to get away quickly. We are going to be shot."

He didn't need elaboration; he could tell from the fear in Jane's voice. "I need to get up, first." He tried to sit up. Jane supported his back, but in pushing him forward the sharp needles of his ribs punctured him. He cried out in protest.

"Shhhh!" Jane warned him. "They are not far away."

"Just the two of them?"

"Yes, but with at least one gun."

"Good odds then." He smiled through the pain.

Jane stood facing and astride Michael who was sitting upright. She bent and reached under his arms and attempted a straight lift. Her own injuries tormented her as slowly Michael's body lifted to the upright position. He winced with pain, but his ribs seemed less troublesome.

"Let's try a few steps." Jane braced herself.

"Yes let us all try a few steps, Jane." The two men emerged from the bushes and crossed the path.

"If you would be so kind, Jane, perhaps you might guide Michael this way." He indicated the direction from which he had just emerged.

"I'm sorry, Michael, we can't even run for it. I've let you down."

"Nonsense; it's these people who are to blame. But I'm the one who got us into this."

The tall man turned to his colleague. "Did you hear that, Franz? I still like the sound of true love. It is truly touching, do you not think, Franz?"

Franz did not reply. He appeared terrified by something else.

"What's the matter, Franz, losing your nerve?" The man waved his gun at Franz in a menacing manner.

Franz still did not react but stared over the man's shoulder.

"Drop your weapon! Armed police! Stand still!" The cry was repeated as, rising from ground cover, appeared the black uniforms of an armed response team.

"Michael, Jane, get down! Down on the ground!" ordered a cry from behind them.

"Jane, do it!" Michael shouted, but Jane had frozen, her mind in overload. Michael tightened their hug and they fell like a freshly cut tree. Before he hit the ground he felt a sharp pain on one side of his head and then blackness consumed him. Simultaneously, there was the sound of several weapons being discharged.

EPILOGUE

A bright light had penetrated the closed blinds. Michael Morley squinted. He could just make out two figures standing near the foot of the bed and felt the presence of one sitting either side.

"Doctor; doctor!" A familiar voice called from one side. It was Jane!

"Jane." He tried to move his arm.

"Don't try to move, Mr. Morley." A white shape had appeared and bent over him and he could see a nurse checking the box above his head. Wires and tubes trailed down into the bed.

"Do you know where you are, Michael?" It was the doctor.

"Hospital?" Michael was sufficiently conscious to know it would be a good guess.

"We need to do a few checks, first." The doctor wanted to guide the visitors away.

"No!" Michael responded immediately. "Let them stay!"

"Doctor?" Jane appealed.

"Okay; just for a moment, but you must not task him." He targeted his comments at the two suited man standing near the foot of the bed. Two men who'd devoted their time to Michael's capture. Men he'd never seen or known; Detective Inspector Kevin James and Detective Sergeant Derek Forest.

"Jane, are you alright?" Michael's first concern was for her health.

She lightly held his hand. "I'm fine, it's you we all been worried about."

"I know I got knocked about a bit; probably a few parts missing by now."

"No, you're all in one piece, my dear boy." John Henderson reassured his friend from the other side of the bed.

"John! They haven't arrested you yet?"

"No, and we have no intention of arresting anyone here." The Inspector moved closer. He removed his baseball cap before seeking permission from Jane to continue. "We realise that both yourself and Mr. Henderson have been victims of a serious gangland diamond smuggling operation. We are satisfied that you played no part in any of their associated activities."

"We are embarrassed that we left you vulnerable to intimidation and danger." He looked towards his Sergeant who stepped forward and managed a carefully worded apology for his part in doubting the two men's innocence.

"I still don't understand how you found us." Michael, if grateful, was more than a little curious.

"Once we had connected all the names of this gang, it was clear that you were not only innocent, but in danger. We arrested all of those members still alive and in particular the man after Otto Visser on a list, a man known as Buster Schmitt. We planted an officer at Langdon's place equipped with Schmitt's mobile. That way we'd know if he had any continued part in the story. What ever happened we'd know if anyone tried to contact him."

"So when our captors phoned you were able to confirm Schmitt had the diamonds?"

"Only just; our man didn't know what on earth they were on about, but was sufficiently quick thinking to answer positively. We knew then we had to act quickly. Fortunately it coincided with us extracting evidence from one of the men our undercover officer managed to capture at the hotel. He gave us the location of the hide out."

"The man who tried to kill me at the hotel?"

"Yes, you were very lucky."

"Please thank your officer for me," Inspector.

"I will need to speak to you both later and get a few things into perspective, but we will leave you to recuperate for now. I look forward to your earliest complete recovery, Mr. Morley."

"Wait!" Michael prevented them leaving. "What happened to the two men who held us hostage?"

"A South African man known as Baas Buurman and a Dutch National named Franz von Zeist were shot resisting arrest during an attempt to ……"

"…kill us." Michael completed the sentence; "they were killed?"

"Yes." The two officers left immediately without further comment.

"Can somebody please tilt me?" Michael began to feel alive once more.

The nurse raised the head end without inflicting any pain on its grateful occupant.

"That's better, thank you." He turned to Jane. "You're crying. Please don't, I'll soon be out of here." He moved his head from side to side. "Why have I got some sort of padding on the top of my head?"

"They shot you!" Jane was distraught. "They could have killed you!"

"Well, they had been having a good go at that already." Michael tried to lighten the mood.

"Oh, Mike." Jane wrapped her arm around his.

John Henderson rose to leave the two young people to their privacy.

"No wait, John. Don't leave yet, I need to catch up on the Panther."

Jane flinched. "No, that damn animal has been more than enough trouble. I never want to hear about it again."

"But there remains an unsolved puzzled....or does there John?"

John Henderson looked at Jane; he appreciated her concern and was not about to cause problems between two dear friends.

Jane acquiesced with a resigned shrug and smile

"Well, I've spent ages looking at the two dimensions. They definitely look like map references and at first sight references to somewhere in Cambridge."

"What's the problem?" Michael was warming to the original challenge.

"I can't imagine any connection with the gang or diamonds in Cambridge."

"That might have made sense to Ott Vis the last man to have the diamonds; somewhere no-one would think of looking."

"Possibly, but I don't think this Otto Visser; that's his full name by the way, was bright enough for that."

"What alternative do we have?"

"Well the Northing, the latitude, seems okay; it's the Easting, the Longitude, that doesn't seem right."

Jane tugged gently on Mike's sleeve. John Henderson remembered he was taking up their time together and stood the leave. "Goodness look at the time, I must be going." He froze and remained staring at the clock.

"John?" Michael was concerned. "What's wrong?"

John Henderson mused aloud. "Easting; Longitude; time! That's it; it's in hours! The Easting is the number of hours to the east. At fifteen degrees to the hour the location is somewhere on the continent!" Without turning he addressed Michael. "Have you and Jane got current passports, Michael? I've just thought of a wonderful holiday for us all!"